MW00880186

The Vigilante and Other Stories

Marshal

Myers

Copyright © 2016 by Marshal Myers.

ALL RIGHTS RESERVED

Cover Art © J.S. Barger

Find out more about Marshal Myers and his other books at
www.marshalmyers.com.

No part of this publication may be reproduced or transmitted in
any form or by any means, electronic or mechanical, including
photocopying, recording, or any information storage and retrieval
systems, without written permission from the publisher.

This is a work of Fiction. Any similarities to any persons, whether
living or dead is purely coincidental. All places, names, etc. are the
product of the author's imagination or used fictitiously.

A Word from the Author

*note: Some of the stories contained in this book are incomplete and are presented, unedited, as a study of how I have developed as an author over the last ten years of honing my craft. Bon Appetit, though in all seriousness, there could be riches to be found in this Grendel's cave of a hodgepodge.

All my life I have known that I am different. I am in a wheelchair and couldn't run and play with the other kids, but it wasn't until I was twelve that I discovered what an impact my physical situation would have on my life. Up until that age, I had never felt that my physical limitations would keep me from doing all that I wanted to do and being all that I wanted to be. I grew up wanting to be a fireman, a secret agent, a football player; I even had the quixotic dream of being a chivalrous knight. As I grew older, I could identify more and more with Helen Keller: "I seldom think about my limitations, and they never make me sad. Perhaps there is just a touch of yearning at times; but it is vague, like a breeze among flowers."

I remember one night when I saw the movie *What's Eating Gilbert Grape?* I was filled with a sense of uneasiness as I watched Leonardo DiCaprio play the part of a developmentally delayed teenager. The next day, I was with my mother at the grocery, thinking how I was like Arnie, the character portrayed in the movie. I would always be a burden to my family and a step below the "regular" kids. I finally broke down in the car and began sobbing. I poured out my heart to my mother, and she, in her loving wisdom, told me that although I was physically disabled, I could still do great things. She told me that she knew when I was born that, one day, I would have to come to the realization that I was different and would lead a different life. It remained to me to decide how to handle it. I could choose to spend the rest of my life feeling sorry for myself, or I could focus on the things that I could do.

Since then, I have decided that what I want to do is bring joy to people through my cheerful demeanor. I wake up each day with a positive, can-do attitude. I smile in the face of challenges, and I determine to do the best that I can with what I have been given.

Helen Keller spent years learning how to communicate and speak with the help of Annie Sullivan. Although she felt frustrated many times, she persevered and became one of the greatest inspirational figures of her day. She chose not to dwell on her limitations, but to work hard and find joy in everyday life.

Even though I have felt discouraged by many unfortunate circumstances, I do what my mother and Miss Keller encouraged me to do. I do not dwell on my limitations, but focus on what I have been blessed with, and what I can do to help others. I never let my fountain of joy run dry, and because of that, it overflows and spills into the hearts of others.

"My Master and King, the Creator of all worlds, has entrusted me, Lamathrath of the Nexus, with a duty that is mine and mine alone. I am to observe and record the stories and histories of all the Other Worlds, wherein the Name of the Lord is praised by all faithful races, be they elf, dwarf or any other. Here in the halls of my library do I write the tales of all worlds. Welcome, gentle readers!"

Book I: The Gunslinger and the Prioress

1. The Age of Innocence

Normally, gentle readers, I write unto you and unto my God of great men and warriors, such as Rothgaric of Irminsul or his son Leofric. But today, or rather today in heaven's time, I write to you of a simple man. A warrior, you ask? Undoubtedly. A Paladin? Perhaps, later in life at any rate. A man of blasphemies, but he would grow into the loveliest creature to come from the world of Wesdon Varld. Many settlers of this area often chided their sons when they went to the outpost or the cart road or that of the stagecoach or even the newfangled iron horse, not to take their guns to town, but this man would grow up to never be parted from them though that was never his mother's wish. Who is this man who seems now but a villain? Why, my friend, Egil Shee, God's own vigilante. -Lamathrath of the Nexus

The boomtown of Pawtuckry could barely even be called a town. It had been established by Harald Shugston, a priest of the church of Yah, as a missionary town to the barbarians. He himself had built a small clapboard church and placed on it a steeple, but then a lone prospector who had once been a sailor on the Kalten Sea, had struck gold. Once he did, he had filled his mariner's coat with as much dust and nuggets as he could carry and gambled it all away at Haul Away Joe's saloon in Varpeton. The itchy ears of these reprobates had easily picked up on the tune of "There's gold in them there dunes."

Pretty soon the entire area for a countywide was swarming with a litter of buggers so that if the dirigible had been invented at this time, an aeronaut would have had the impression of a thousand tiny ants swarming over a peanut butter pie. With the coming of boomtowns comes the unavoidable consequence of the building of bars and saloons. And with the coming of bars and saloons comes violence. I have never thought of it before but seeing as this is the environment in which however piously on his mother's part, our erstwhile hero came of age, no wonder he became bloodthirsty.

Father Shugston, being a pious brogued man of the islands of the Kalten Sea, did his best to guide the populace of drunkards back to God, or should I say Yah, but his efforts were fruitless, as the only fruit they knew was not of the spirit but rather of brandy, and they continued every night to fathom the bowl. Yet with alcohol comes the sickness of alcohol, and they found themselves in need of a doctor, so it was that there came Dr. Thomas Shee, who always wanted to be more of an alchemist, as you will soon see as the story unveils.

Dr. Shee came to seek a practice and to make his fortune and thought that the country air away from the city would be good for his wife Nora. She was a muscular robust woman with long blonde hair and eyes that shown like the mist upon the Kalten Sea. She came from the northern islands of that Sea and still spoke their rhythmic, lilting tongue. But above all she loved the name and the word of Yah and would listen to the Reverend's sermons and benedictions with rapt intensity. However, she was a bit of a powder keg herself, for like someone who I do not yet know in the primary universe, she hated the love of liquor. She would storm into the public houses of Pawtuckry armed with holy book and woodsman's axe and leave broken bottles in her wake and the barstools fair in shambles. And she had a voice that could soften the most devilish murderer's heart. Often late at night many hours after the service, a drunkard would be drawn to the chapel by her heavenly voice extolling,

As I went down in the River to pray

Studying about that good old way

And who shall wear the starry crown

Sweet Yah! Show me the way.

Come on, fathers, let's go down,

Let's go down, don't you wanna come down

Come on, fathers, let's go down,

Down in the River to pray.

The man would begin to weep. He would fall down on his knees in front of the pew, and Nora Shee, who came to be called the Songbird in that area and even into the desert her reputation grew so, she would lead him to repentance and to follow his God.

There was a prayer however that the Almighty had not granted to beautiful Nora. Every Sunday, she would hear the priest delivered exhortation to mothers to train up a child in the way that they should go so that in their old age they would not depart from it. She beseeched the Lord Yah Almighty to grant her a descendent that she might pass down the wisdom given to her. But for years it seemed that this was not to be.

But one morning several years later, Nora Shee began to feel very strange. One morning as she was making the biscuits and eggs for breakfast and for the poor and destitute of the area, she felt a great tightening and churning in her stomach. Young Nora felt so sick to her stomach that she felt as if she might drop the pan. She ran out to where her husband was preparing his mule for a house call.

"Thomas! Thomas! Praise the Lord Creator, I doubt him no longer. I am with child. Your child. My child. Our child. I shall deliver him unto the Lord to nurture his soul."

And it seemed that for the months she carried him, she sang louder with great spiritual gusto and joy. The priest came often to visit her and they prayed for the welfare of the child. Laying his hand upon her belly the good father would say, "I sense by the Spirit of Yah that he will be a strong lad and someday he will speak the words of Yah, though maybe in a different tone. He shall wander the creation of the creator and step into a world all his own for the glory of our God. A sword may pierce your heart one day, for the son that causes his father pain shall remedy it. On the day of the feast of the Son of Yah, the man child, ruddy and strong, was born and christened Egil, "the holy warrior".

"You shall be strong, my son," Young Nora crooned to her baby as she rocked him. "You shall be strong in the name of Yah, and though you may kick against the goads at times, I know surely that one day you shall serve him with your whole heart and may even be a prophet. I declare this over my son by the name of the Offspring of Yah."
Nora of the Kalten Isles kenned little the power of her prophecy, or of how much her son would rebel against it in the coming years. But now was the time for merriment and peace. Not as man reckons speed, yet still with swiftness, trouble would descend upon the house of Shee, and the wheel of destiny would begin its inevitable revolution.

2. Boyhood

"Good morning my boy

Good morning my love

You are a gift from the heavens above

You are your father's

Your Master's and mine

We're all sons and daughters of the divine."

So sang Nora Shee as she came to wake up her three-year-old son who had had a little cold for the past week. It was fortunate for the little man that his father was an apothecary, though in truth it was his mother's tender loving care and angelic singing that always helped most in his healing from the fallen angels of sickness. Young Egil despite his early age had grown a fiery mop of almost cherry red curls and mossy green eyes, both in inheritance from his deeply Kalten maternal grandfather, the firebrand lay preacher Angus O'Callaghan, and even at a young age, the fiery haired lad was beginning to speak with his grandfather's frenzied broguish passion. Both his father and maternal grandfather had red beards both bushy in the curly, and dancing Doc Tommy was sure his son would have that, shall we say, hirsute trait.

Joyous Nora led her small son out with her to do the daily chores on their farm. This included feeding the chickens, milking the cow, and hanging out the laundry.

And for each of these she had a song:

"Tick tock tick tock

Tick tock tock pockery.

There is a little ship

That lies moored upon the dockery

Tick tock tick tock

My little tasty pullet.

There for you to eat are these little yellow bullets."

And the favorites of hers and of little Egil's were the laundry shanties that she sang from the old country.

> "In Kalten Toone there lived a maid,
> Mark well what I do say!
> In Kalten toone there lived a maid,
> Who was always pinchin' the sailor's trade.
> I'll go no more a roving with you fair maid!
>
> *A rovin', a rovin',*
> *Since rovin's been my ru-i-in,*
> *I'll go no more a roving,*
> *With you fair maid!*
>
> I took this maiden for a walk,
> Mark well what I do say!
> I took this maiden for a walk,
> She wanted some gin and didn't she talk.
> I'll go no more a roving with you fair maid!
>
> *A rovin', a rovin',*
> *Since rovin's been my ru-i-in,*
> *I'll go no more a roving,*
> *With you fair maid!*
>
> She said, "You sailors I love you so,"
> Mark well what I do say!

"All you sailors, I love you so,"
And the reason why I soon did know.
I'll go no more a roving with you fair maid!

A rovin', a rovin',
Since rovin's been my ru-i-in,
I'll go no more a roving,
With you fair maid!

She placed her hand upon my knee,
Mark well what I do say!
She placed her hand upon my knee,
I said "Young miss, you're rather free."
I'll go no more a roving with you fair maid!

A rovin', a rovin',
Since rovin's been my ru-i-in,
I'll go no more a roving,
With you fair maid!
I gave this miss a parting kiss,
Mark well what I do say!
I gave this miss a parting kiss,
When I got aboard my money I missed.
I'll go no more a roving with you fair maid!

A rovin', a rovin',
Since rovin's been my ru-i-in,
I'll go no more a roving,
With you fair maid!"

After she was done with the chores she would always sing a little more and she and little giggling Egil would dance. (How much have I missed his Yankee Kalten laughter of late. For it was another woman of music and healing that would bring it back from the dark prison recesses of his mind in years to come, but nothing was akin to the dancing that would take place on summer nights when his father would rossen up his bow and tune his fiddle. Mother, father and son would dance in circles while singing to his lovingly insane playing, such as:

"The Fox, he went out on a chilly night
And he prayed for the moon to give him light
For he had many a mile to go that night
Before he reached the town-o, town-o, town-o
He had many a mile to go that night
Before he reached the town-o

He ran till he came to the farmers pen
The ducks and the geese were kept therein
He said a couple of you are gonna grease my chin
Before I leave this town-o, town-o, town-o
A couple of you are gonna grease my chin
Before I leave this town-o

He grabbed the great goose by the neck
He threw a duck across his back
And he didn't mind the quack, quack
And the legs all danglin' down-o, down-o, down-o
He didn't mind the quack, quack
And the legs all danglin' down-o

Well the old gray Woman jumped out of bed
Out of the window she popped her head
Cryin' John, John the great goose is gone
The Fox is on the town-o, town-o, town-o
John, John the great goose is gone
And the Fox is on the town-o

He ran till he came to his nice warm den
And there were the little ones eight, nine, ten
Sayin' Daddy, Daddy better go back again
It must be a mighty fine town-o, town-o, town-o

Daddy, Daddy better go back again
For it must be a mighty fine town-o

The Fox and his Wife, without any strife
They cut up the goose with a fork and a knife
And they never had such a supper in their life
And the little ones chewed on the bones-o, bones-o, bones-o
They never had such a supper in their life
And the little ones chewed on the bones."

But this day was a gala day that would change the rest of his life. When little Egil's father had gone down to the mercantile to see about Mr. Federman, Dr. Shee had come back with the most wonderful thing imaginable, at least to the mischievous rascal his son was becoming.

He came back with a small slingshot made of lacquered wood, and with the tightest drawstring you ever did see.

"Mercy, Tommy! Do you want him to become a mercenary?" Young Egil's mother said.

"But, mother…!" Egil began to whine.

"Now, dearie. I'm just preparing his natural talents. It is of little consequence. See? He loves it." Indeed, for the little wee man had already scooped up a handful of gravel and was beginning to rain down fiery judgment upon the chicken coop. The pullets were not laying for many days after, but old Tom Shee smiled, that little Kalten twinkle returning to his eye.

As Egil began to grow, Thomas and Nora began to worry that he did not have very many friends in the village. He was cordial enough, particularly to his elders, yet he continued to take long walks alone, not returning until after dusk. He seldom spoke to boys his age, and only seemed to be interested in perfecting the art of what his mother deemed "…That godforsaken weapon toy you gave him." Whenever law men would come into town from their fights with the barbarians of the plaIns, the ever-growing young

Egil Shee would sit and listen to their war stories for hours with rapt intensity. And afterwards he would always be able to repeat to his parents word for word what they had said.

"I do you wish you had the same memory for the Scriptures, my boy," his mother would often tell him, a wistful look in her eye. Even Thomas, his father, who had always encouraged his son's boyish endeavors, began to worry.

Somewhat of a relief to his parents was that he did not become taken with girls in that stretch of the Imagination. When other boys would snicker and become bashful around girls, slowly starting to consider courtship, there was but one courtship that Egil Shee thought of: that of the six shooter and the cutlass.

Also, even when he became a young man he was never tempted by the wiles of whiskey, for he knew that to unsteady the shooting hand. "If that boy brings a gun in this house, I'll surely die of fright before he even shoots me." This was of course a statement from the now graying Nora.

"He's becoming too old for me to tan, my dear," said now wizening Thomas, "but I shall see what I can do by the way of logic." He would have to hurry, old Thomas would, for within two years, disaster would strike, and although it would be terrible, it would propel Egil into manhood, and would eventually lead him on a trail of gunpowder and steel and eventually to me.

3. The Fever

Long had the barbarians of the Nuine Desert prayed for rain. It had been an inordinately dry season, with no clouds, not even one the size of a man's fist, dotting the skies above the dunes and canyons. And so Ahoni, who was lead shaman of the church of Yah of the barbarians, instructed his followers to follow his example and form prayer circles around themselves. Night after night under the stars they poured forth their speech of praise. They reminded the Creator of how he had sustained them in the past and brought forth bread from the earth for them to eat.

Still, the sky was silent. No clap of thunder or lightning strike to be seen anywhere on the horizon. And still the barbarians prayed and prayed and prayed. After a month of praying and still no avail they began to fast, for they knew that the Lord would not be slow in answering as men understand slowness. They particularly Ahoni, fasted for weeks at a time through the spring and summer and on into the fall. There was even talk among the Keku tribe of desert barbarians, that they should drink from the Springs of the draught of Tet, the greatest source of magic on Wesdon Varld. But that was forbidden to all save those of the students of Tet monastery (which shall play a part in the telling of my tale later. Not to wet your curious appetites, gentle readers. Excuse me. Back to the matter at hand). But then strangely, and humorously, in a sardonic way, the prayers of the barbarians were answered.

A cloud the size of a man's hand formed over the desert in the Canyon near the center and near the Tet monastery. Water poured down in buckets as though from the very sawmill of heaven. It was not long before it reached the edge of the Nuine Desert and muddy flooding erupted like brownish red geysers from the earth. It was not long before it reached the civilized towns near the edge of the Nuine Desert.

Young Egil was playing in the churchyard with his slingshot as the first rain laden clouds blew in. He had to run for home and the only one happy about that was the gecko he would've peened in the head but whose life was saved by the forces of nature. It was the first of many victims over the coming years to have their lives extended by supernatural aid.

Egil sloshed Through the flooding downpour, barely conscious of where he was going. But luckily the Lord creator was with him that day, unbidden as he would for the rest of his childhood and most of his adult life. But nevertheless Yah saw him safely home.

The family crowded into the storm cellar to await the end of the flood. As old as he was, nearly twelve, and would have begun crying if it wasn't for his mother's soft crooning as she nestled his head on her shoulder.

> Here I sit on Buttermilk Hill
> Who can blame me, cryin' my fill
> And ev'ry tear would turn a mill,
> Johnny has gone for a soldier.
>
> Me, oh my, I loved him so,
> Broke my heart to see him go,
> And only time will heal my woe,
> Johnny has gone for a soldier.
>
> I'll sell my rod, I'll sell my reel,
> Likewise I'll sell my spinning wheel,
> And buy my love a sword of steel,
> Johnny has gone for a soldier.
>
> I'll dye my dress, I'll dye it red,
> And through the streets I'll beg for bread,
> For the lad that I love from me has fled,
> Johnny has gone for a soldier.

She little kenned that not long off in the far future, her Egil would do something similar despite all she had done for him.

Within a few weeks the rain had stopped for a time and the sun shone out bronze and sullen, a portent of things to come, mayhap?

With the coming of mud and sun and heat came the inevitable: fever. And so in her goodness, and armed with her joyous songs of praise, Nora Shee and Thomas her husband tended the sick of Pawtuckry. And when she was not tending to them or singing to them, she was preparing meals and soups to aid them and their families in their convalescence. They began to call her in town the Angel of Pawtuckry. Nothing could bring her down.

And yet to Thomas, who knew more of illnesses than his son, she began to become more pale, frail and wan. But yet her spirit did not abate. She still sang, only more weakly at times, and smiled a little less often. Yet she would not cease in her quoting Scripture and praying. But alas, and it pains my angelic heart to say so, she was confined to her bed.

And so it was that one day when Egil came home from shooting his slingshot. His father met him on the porch. Old Thomas's eyes were sullen and tired and he seemed hunched and careworn. He put both hands firmly on his son shoulders and looked him in the eye. "Son, you remember how the people village call your mother the Angel of Pawtuckry?"
"What do you mean father?" The young man asked, his eyes widening.

"Well son, this is difficult for me to say. In a way she will always be there for us, but she is… She is…"

"No… No! NO!" He tore away from his father's grasp and ran down the street blindly cursing the fever and also sadly cursing the very name of his God. That was the last time in over two decades that young Egil Shee would even have a scrap of a memory of his former joy. The great continent had sunken as in a water cataclysm.

Never would he praise the name of his God, he vowed. Never ever again.

The abysmal winter rain blanketed the town of Pawtuckry in dousing torrential sheets. The town lay on the very edge of the Nuine Desert, yet this year, it was receiving nearly cataclysmic rainfall. And with rainfall came insects and with insects, fever. The priests were delivering more souls unto Yah in these dark days than they were songs of praise or sermons.

Young Egil looked at his father's ashen face as the older man stared at the earth. "I will be fine Egil," the boy's mother had said to him when she first began to glow with the yellowish pallor. Lies! Lies! All of them, lies! Bah! He would never trust another woman as long as he drew breath. He now didn't even pretend to believe in an afterlife. His father may be softening toward these stupid black-robed priests, daft men that they were. But he never would. If there was a mad creator in heaven, the boy Egil Shee vowed then and there to exact his vengeance upon his God; he would even kill Him if necessary. Though he would not wield a gun or sword for many a year to come, it was in that moment that Egil Shee of Wesdon Varld became a vigilante.

4. The Law Man of Fury

Fury O'Flanigan's was a somewhat reputable ("somewhat" being the operative word) ale house in the Kalten port town of Glasguew. It was here that refugees from the taxation of the Kalten Isles came to start their lives anew. But they were looked down upon as foreigners. You see, Wesdon Varld though the most "modern" of all the secondary universes when compared to the primary world, it has never been under one ruler, as opposed to the the country of Irminsul in the world of Ealinde. Though some lofty minded men have sought to bring secular political order, the faith of those of Wesdon Varld is the only thing that binds them into a cohesive whole. And so barbarians and law men, Kalten immigrants and pirates, have long vied for the supremacy. This was clearly evident in this drinking establishment this night, for a motley horde of unsavory characters were crammed into the small, wooden saloon. A boy of about seventeen or eighteen, was half-mindedly sipping a sarsaparilla as he listened to a Kalten fiddler bawl out a hearty mix between a reel and a polka.

The barkeep, a brutish, hulking man with a greasy beard, looked up as the saloon doors swung open.

"Hello. Looks like we got an altar boy coming in!" Laughed the big man.

Indeed, for not only was the man unarmed (a rare occurrence at O'Flannigan's), he wore the black robe of a priest of the church of Yah. The older man walked up to the counter and hailed the keeper.

"What'll it be, Padre?" asked the barkeep.

"Nothing, thank you. I am not thirsty. I was wondering if you could help me. I'm looking for a young man by the name of Egil Shee."

"What's he to you?" Whispered the young man seated on the barstool.

"He happens to be my son. I would reconcile with him. The last I heard tell of him he was hanging around this town. I'm not proud of that. But I would bring him home."

The young man whirled on the stool to face the priest. Slowly, the light of recognition dawned on the old Padre's face.

"I haven't got a home, Da. Nay. I spoke wrongly just now. You are no longer my father, not since mother died and you entered that humhaw of a cloister."

Old Thomas's eyes misted. Leaning in closer, he softly said, "Egil, son. Listen to me. I know I haven't been there for you but I need to make that right. And now I have a way. I have been searching through the ancient tomes of our church."
"You mean to say *your* church. I want no part of it."
Father Thomas continued, taking no notice of the insults. "I have discovered a very ancient tome which makes mention of many different worlds coexisting with this one. There is a supernatural scribe who works endlessly in a library at the center of the universes, observing, reporting and recording everything, for his Master, the Lord God. I believe if I can find a way to this Nexus, I can bring your mother back to life. Please, will you help me, my son?" Old Thomas's face seemed as though it would break under the strain, so great was the irritating pressure.

It seemed as if for a second, young Egil would comply. But then his face became resolute and without a word and with one mighty shove, he pushed the aging priest to the Tavern floor. A law man came to break up the fight. He had a massive black handlebar mustache, neck-length ebon hair and a blue-eyed and red-flushed angular face that would often thrust itself unprovoked into yours to prove an ironclad point. For weapons, he bore two massive pistols in a calico green sash and two large black naval cutlasses in a massive double baldric at his waist on either side of the sash.

Unlike most law men, who preferred to wear a cowboy hat, he wore a bright green bowler of beaver felt.

"Is the Padre botherin' you, twinkle toes? If he is, Ol' Dagger-Joe Cutter will take care of 'im for ya!"

"Thank you kindly, sir! He most certainly is."
"Okay then. I'll escort him out. Say, that was quite a bold shove. I could use a young'un like you on my posse. We will sort out the details when I'm done with this. Come along, Father."

Taking one last chance, old Thomas cried out, "I am your papa, Egil!"
With an icy look, the young man replied and said something that would wound his father for the rest of the old priest's life. "I know you not, old man!"

5. Twinkle Toes

The searing midday sun palely illumined the Nuine desert. The heat waves wafted from the dunes in boiling bubble shapes, giving the appearance of the effervescence of a bottle of sarsaparilla. Upon one of these dunes, many miles south of Glasguew, a group of about twenty riders stood before a disheveled youth in flimsy sand-stained overalls.

The leader of the group, Dagger Joe Cutter, twirled his 60 caliber Westledon patent revolvers. So far as any of his men knew they were the only ones of their kind, gunsmithed by Cutter himself.

"All right, twinkle toes, if you want to be a Cutter rider, there are certain laws of shall we say 'initiation.' First of all, yous gonna learn to dance."

The big law men squinted one eye and gazed down the barrels. "Dance!" He barked. Boom! Boom boom boom! Boom boom!

The guns issued their massive reports, shattering the silence of the desert. The bullets skidded in the sand, fractions of inches away from young Egil Shee's practically bare feet, sending up little pocket sandstorms where they struck. The young man sprinted back and forth and skidded from side to side, at first scared out of his wits. But then, and almost perverse, daredevil, edge of life mentality took over his brain. He began to grin, and even work in a few antics for the fun of it.

"Good, lad." Reloading the cylinders from a satchel in his saddlebag, Cutter handed the guns to Egil. Taking a cigar from his pocket, the big law man placed in between his teeth and said. "Hey, vendego! Light me."

"Have you gone insane?" The boy blurted.

"Just do it, muffin!"

I've never even shot a gun before. I've only ever had a fork sling or a rope sling."

"It's the desert, butter face. This is where boys become men. Have at me."

The young man did best to steady his hand. He squinted his eye and… Boom! The bullet went flying into oblivion.

"Well, we all have our first try. Remember, Bucky. Ordinary men shoot with their hand but, a true marksman. A true marksman, he shoots with his mind. We will come back to that, some other time son."
And so began a rigorous training in the mastery of arms.

Out in the desert, one particularly grating time, the law man tied a railroad spike to the end of a bull whip, and began flailing it at his apprentice. "You'd better shoot it off before it's too late. But then again, bullets cost money, young'uns don't.

And there was also the discipline of the blade. He learned to fight with two cutlasses, just as his mentor Dagger Joe did. And he learned to parry and advance not in dueling way of the powdered wig Civilians but in the cunning hard knock way of a mariner of the Kalten Sea. After a while, he could even hold his own against Gus Padmo, the big rail man from Varpeton who could split a bar of led with his basket hilt broadsword.

Then, O unsanctimonious hallelujah, the gang allowed him to go on raids with them through the lands of the barbarians. In a way, though they were more heavily armed than the painted man, Egil began to respect the barbarians for their handiness with the bow and spear. Nevertheless, he began to have an even more cold and calculating heart, for he was fast forgetting the faces of home and ancestor. He sang with the men as they slaughtered the innocence clearing the way for more prospectors and taking much gold and food by ill gain, he began to have fewer and fewer memories of his mother the Angel apothecary of Pawtuckry and more thoughts baptized in the red bloody haze of conquest. And yet something was about to happen that would set him on the course to remember the face of his father.

One night, while eating in a saloon, Dagger Joe Cutter slapped down a crude cowhide map on the table. Indicating two distant makers, The law man said, "New job, boys! Now, there are two villages a ways from here betwixt us and a sweet water spring. There be a city slicker apothecary who wants the water of this spring for himself, but the barbarians think it's magic, so they won't let him have watering or mineral rights. His pockets are deep so I convinced him we're the men for the job. We depart at first light for the first village."

Strangely the next day, as the now man Egil was saddling his black mustang, he felt unsure about all this, as if there was some scruff of faith or word of God urging him to back down from this one. Could it be? Naw! Old man Cutter, whom he had begun to think of as sort of a father, would merely call him yeller. Yeah, that was it. Surely everything would be all right. Dagger Joe knew what he was doing. Maybe he just need another sarsaparilla today after all.

The barbarian village lay in a valley formed by four dunes, each on one of the cardinal points, dagger Joe pointed out that this would be good for gaining momentum for a charged. But oh, were they in for a walloping surprise.

What happened was thus, and it even surprises a being of the higher heavens such as myself. Apparently, the warriors of the tribe, had gained news of the coming of the law men. But they were all hidden. Shee thought he saw things sticking out of the sand in the valley below but unfortunately or rather fortunately as you will see, he did not mention it to Dagger Joe Cutter.

Letting out the law men war whoop, the riders of Dagger Joe Cutter stormed down into the valley, pieces poised to fire.

"Hold!" Said the leader of the barbarian warriors. The law men came closer. "hold!" They could nearly see the breath of the horses in the morning air. "Now!" The barbarians picked up Spears from the ground, long Spears, twice as long as the man informed up in Shiltron formation. Their Spears bristled forth at the oncoming horses, and alas the riders of dagger Joe Cutter, had no time to rein their mounts to a halt. Nearly all the horses were stabbed. Egil's horse reared back in pain, and the rider was thrown back hard striking his head on the ground. Blackness swam before young Master Shee's eyes and he was barely conscious of a massive body falling on him as darkness took him.

Egil Shee awoke with a groan. Summoning the last of his strength, he pushed the carcass of his dead horse off of his pinned legs and struggled to his feet. Fortunately, the barbarians had left to warn the other springs village of the attack and had not returned yet, but the wreak of rotting flesh and the swarm of carrion birds gave plain testament to what had befallen his brothers in arms. Then his ears pricked up to a sound on the wind.

"Little brother… Twinkle toes, over here."

The young gunslinger looked far to his left and saw what remained of the dying Dagger Joe Cutter, lying on his back, three iron-tipped barbarian arrows protruding from his waistcoat. His apprentice knelt by him and for the first time in almost a decade, something that smacked of sadness and tears welled up in Egil Shee's throat. "We shared our last drink today little brother," dagger Joe rasped. Listen to me twinkle toes. Don't end up like me. I now see where I'm going and it ain't good. Chart a better course than me. Save yourself…. Twinkle toes." Dagger Joe's body was rent by a spasm of bloody coughing, and then he drew breath no more.

As a memorial to his friend, Master Shee took dagger Joe's bandanna sash and bowler hat along with his weapons and slowly made his way to the nearest law men town. Though he only known him for a few years, dagger Joe had left an impressionable impact on the young gunslinger's life, one that even when he trod the straight and narrow with some help, he would never forget the loudmouth law man he had met that night in Fury O'Flanagan's Tavern.

Three Weeks Later

Brother Timothy of the church of Yah at Varpeton hurried along the thoroughfare after the young man. In his arms the priest carried a much larger robe for some reason. Finally catching up to the man in the green bowler hat he said, "Pardon me Sir, I have a message for you," the friar said. "Are you Egil Shee, formerly of the town of Pawtuckry."

"I haven't been there in years, young Padre. What are you doing asking me?"

"As you may know, your father Thomas Shee was an alchemist at our church."

Haven't seen him in years either, good riddance. What's the old coot want now?"

Brother Timothy shuffled uncomfortably. "Well, er... You see... it grieves me to tell you that he is dead."

Unexpectedly the news hit the young man like a dagger thrust in the chest. He had never wanted him to be... Why? What?

"How...? When...? Tell me everything!"

"He was researching the ancient theory postulated in the old tomes of our church on the library between worlds and the Angel that records and observes and guards it. He was convinced that the sacred draught of Tet would enable him to cross between planes and thus reach your mother, his wife. I've never seen someone so obsessed and paranoid in my life. He hadn't bathed for weeks or slept for that matter. He went to the Abbott Aderly and begged and pleaded for it. But the Abbot, seeing that he was mad and was in need of spiritual helped, prayed for him but refused him. We never should've allowed him to use hemlock in his potions. But alas the next day, the day following his return to us that it is, we found him lying on the floor dead, a now broken bottle of Hemlock near his hand. He wanted for you to have this."

he young priest held out the robe he was carrying. Egil stared at it for a moment, then without another word he seized it and, turning on his heel, ran toward the boardinghouse at which he was temporarily staying.

In a mad rage, (why why why!) Egil Shee did the only thing that was natural to him: disassemble, clean and reassemble his guns. The old man finally got it. Went mad. Now but then this wasn't his fault, was it? No it was Egil's fault. No, no! NO! It was that BLASTED angel's fault, or whatever the Daemon he was! Yes, yes, that was it. But what could he do? Suddenly a mad plan started forming in the young man's mind. If there was this library it was no good, it was evil. Altogether evil. EVIL! He would avenge his father upon this pompous scribe! Bathe in his blood if necessary! He would avenge his father's death upon him. Slowly rising, in front of the mirror he donned his father's cassock. He strapped on weapons, the sash and placed the bowler hat firmly upon his head. He was Egil Shee, the vigilante.

"I will kill you! I will kill you, scribe! I will kill you!"

"O Lord God, my Master whom I serve, you have long secluded me in this, my library, my palace of tomes. In time outside of time I have served you, recording the histories of the secondary universes other than that of the one created first and foremost for the children of Adhaam and Hava. But now, O Lord my God, I do entreat you and I take a rest from my duties, for I have sensed a disturbance in the balance of the elements, the *cosmoi* as that pagan Democritus names them. And if this library falls so too will fall the worlds and the true faith of all the free secondary races. Therefore, Lord I pray, am praying and will pray, protect us, O Lord, from the wrath of the gunslinger."

6. The Tet Monastery

A pathway leads through the stars

Thus do I follow.

"I am become Death, the destroyer of Worlds."-Kali
But rather.... of the One...That which you bind on Earth shall be
bound in Heaven...- Veritas

Abbott Aderly awoke in a hot sweat. The images of his nightmare
slowly came creeping back to him. He did not realize it, but he had
cried out, and so his attendant, Sister Audressa came with a bowl
of warm milk.

"Are you all right, Father Abbott?" Audressa asked, setting the
bowl of milk down by his cot. She had often known her mentor to
be troubled by strange dreams, and whether for good or ill, they
always came true.

"Perhaps yes and perhaps no," said the Abbott. "I dreamed again
of the man in black searching for the man in brown between
worlds. I have not had such a dream in fifteen or twenty years. The
last time I had such a dream was just before Mad Thomas came to
visit us and he, well... I have already told you that story. I have
already told a friend in the Canyon the story of my dream, and
though it may be proper to warn him again, I know he will not
leave. His tribe has guarded the way to the sacred spring for
thousands and thousands of years."

"I surely do not mean to trouble you, Father Abbott, but I heard
tell that a man with a gun dressed all in black massacred the Tet
water tribe only a few weeks ago. If he should gain the ability of
the savants, or as you like to call them, the autis...er...asper... I
cannot think of the word that they use in the original world. But if
one of them these blasphemers with guns, should have the ability
to walk to another world, simply by the sacrilege of drinking the
draught of Tet, it could cause an implosion of reality. It could...

Father Abbott, it could... Mean the end."

"I know, good sister, I know. But I have also dreamt that a certain man in black, maybe not the same one that you are talking of, shall cause a miracle, though he intends blasphemy. Maybe I should tell Bella Jessica."

"Oh, you know how that woman meditates. That is all she does when she is not playing her stringed instruments or singing. Come to think of it, maybe we should have her sing for the children again someday."

"Ah, good," said the Abbott closing his eyes. "Now you are thinking of something positive. That's the spirit, my dear. My dreams may be pleasanter yet. Good night, Sister Audressa."

***

Old Elkeen, Shaman of the Keku Barbarians, awoke early that morning. After saying his daily prayers to Yah, he went to draw water from the well. This was not the well of the draught of Tet, for that was well hidden within the center of this, the Nuine Desert. This was nothing more than cool refreshing spring water, yet for some reason the old Shaman indulged in it with gusto. He wore his best robe this morning, along with his great eagle feathers that showed him to be a Shaman. Something was going to happen to him today; he could feel it in the winds of his bones; he could smell it in the dampened sand, could hear it in the trilling of the desert gecko. *It has been many moons,* he mused quietly as he leaned on his staff, using it as a sort of shovel to form a circle of prayer around himself. *It has been many moons since my friend the Abbott Aderly came from the Tet monastery, warning me of his dream. His dream that a blasphemer will come and may even rob me of my life. However as always with every man in the sphere, my life is in the hands of Yah, the Almighty Creator.*
***

A cool wind meandered through the canyon, tossing up bits of sagebrush and sand, leaving a gritty texture in the arid clime. Law men and civilized folk seldom bothered the barbarians of the Nuine Desert. Many of these people thought that the painted wretches were quite stupid indeed, what with all their trying to resurrect the old Magicks. Even the priests of Yah, as spiritual and lofty minded as they were, cared little for magic. They didn't think of it as parlor tricks, like the wealthier politicians, but just that it was done, over with, the practice of a more powerful bygone age. But soon there would be one, who didn't know it, but he would shake the foundations of their established notions.

And so it was that when Elkeen the Shaman looked out from his medicine tent, he was surprised to find a "Civ", for that is what they called the fully-dressed civilized folk of the East, riding into the village through the midmorning sun. The man looked Civvy enough, with an oddly colored bowler hat of bright green and a calico green scarf of barbarian make around his waist. But strangely, he wore the long black robe of a priest of Yah. A man of peace, was he? A second glance denied that. Look! In the scabbard at his belt hung two heavy black cutlasses like those worn by the Mariners of the Kalten Sea. Even worse, he had two black revolvers hanging pirate-style in his sash.

His emerald eyes burned with a manic jade-fire and his curly fiery beard, sporting thick mustachios that slightly turned up at the ends like farming scythes gave him a look of the cartoonish depiction in pamphlets of the Enemy of Yah. His arms were strong and powerful (and they would have to be after a decade or more of shooting one of those massive 60 caliber revolvers he carried. His leather boot-clad shanks were as powerful as those found on oxen, yet they appear to be somewhat bowlegged from years of riding his black stallion. The man had the look of a killer, if not by his arms, then by the wild almost anti-puritanical look in his eyes.

Still, Elkeen did not run, for the law of the desert barbarian was always hospitality unless threatened.

Elkeen raised his painted walking stick in greeting, but the rider did not acknowledge. "Old man," he said in a gravelly brogue. "You, by all who's telling, are the keeper of the Draught of Tet. You're gonna give it to me now." He began fingering the grip of one revolver.

"Mista Civ. Only those truly at one with Yah may taste it. I sense the anger of the unholy one in you. Pa-Nu! Away from here!"

"Well, ye canne say I didne try, Magie."

The left pistol flashed from the sash, followed instantly by a thundering report, and Elkeen fell forward in the sand, a circular path of blood oozing forth from his punctured forehead. Not wanting to waste his time or ammo, Bloody Egil Shee struck the flint and steel that he had drawn from his saddlebag, and set the nearest wigwam ablaze, along with the entire barbarian village. All the villagers would surely perish. The wind kicked up, seemingly aiding Egil in his unholy workings.

The squas and braves of that village awoke in the everlasting halls of the One, barely reminiscent of the taste and smell of their own burning and charred flesh which they had left in death. Thus was the mercy of Yah unto those who still sought Him within that Sphere. I end the tale of the Keku Barbarians, but not the tale of the gunslinger and buccaneer Egil Shee of the World of Wesdon Varld. He rode forth, through the desert, wreaking vengeance upon me and my life's work ever in his mind. Though it might have meant, will mean, and means the end of my service, I will tell you more of him. - Lamathrath of the Nexus

News of his slaughter of the Keku travelled before Bloody Shee like the echo of a cannonade. The other tribes of painted barbarians left their homes in droves, fear-bent on an insane pilgrimage to the Tet Monastery and the Abbott Aderly.

(Ah, the Tet Monastery! I have had many a tête-à-tête with the peculiar novices-Your world would call them Cervantes. No! What is that word? Oh, yes! Savants. Excuse my fumbling...I do not often look at the Primary World, which you call planet Earth.

But back to my writing. Many of these novices, or savants have special gifts from the Master and Creator. Many of them do not say much at all. They are in their own world most of the time. But even so, many times they are in my world, which is why our dear Egil seeks them. They have tasted the waters of Tet, which gives them the ability to flit between worlds. The holy drink was given to their mothers as they labored with them and thus they fly both in mind and body to the other planes upon which I dwell. This makes them somewhat of an antiquarian race. I must say that you could find one of the acolytes the monastery both conversing with the philosophers of old and the same time running amok in the mud with nothing but a loincloth. Yet still they are geniuses, they are artists and historians, they are as all the human races of the world, only better and most gifted. It has been the cause of grief to many a mother to give up her child to the monastery, but the Abbot knows what is best and, as he is himself a cripple, he understands them most. They know, gentle readers, what it is to be alone and yet to be in the arms of God all the same. When you but join souls with one of these Maker's Angels, you discover a world all unto its own. Indeed, many worlds. Both my Angels and I know that of which we speak, especially Shannon. But I run ahead of myself. Back to the matter at present.)

Sister Audressa of the Tet Monastery looked anxiously at Abbott Aderly. Out of the corner of her eye, she still watched Shannon. The girl had thrown down her second bowl of rice and was now meticulously arranging it in patterns, squealing, fidgeting and cooing incessantly, yet happily. She began repeating "acorn, nut and tree" over and over again for the fifteenth time that morning. "With all these refugees coming in," Audressa said, "I don't know if this will still be a safe or educational place for the children. As you know from all our indicators, Shannon is the most gifted student we have ever had. If truly in the land of origin, the Promised one has come, she could be the one to open the pathways. The Scribe may even think so. She has met him you know, in one of her realm-walks."

Following the blonde sister's gaze, the Abbott lowered his spectacles and began rolling his chair across the courtyard toward the girl.

"I have had a dream again, given to me by the Creator. I will not say much of it, but this I know: sometimes an act of violence may be followed by an act of peace."
"I do not understand, Father Abbott," replied the nun.
"You shall, dear daughter, and all too soon I'm afraid."
The sound of a galloping, snorting horse echoed faintly toward the courtyard. A man dressed in black with a small green hat reined his horse to a halt just outside small gate. He was heavily armed and there was a look of murder in his eye.
"How dare you bring your foul weapons into this holy place?" Demanded Brother Giles, the gatekeeper. The horseman made no reply, but instead shot poor Giles. He leaped his horse over the gate, amid a loud tattoo of screaming sisters.

"Good morning to you, Abbott. Let's cut right past the formalities. I believe you know why I'm here."

"Quite," replied the Abbott slowly, still unflinching in the face of barreled steel. "Your name would be Shee. There was a hot-tempered lad by the name of Shee that came here many years ago. Thomas Shee, a man of Yah."
Egil spat. "Bagh! Do not speak of my father, Padre. I'm twice the man he ever was. This talk of a building between worlds cost him his life. But it shall not cost me mine. I shall take what I want by fire and steel, kefts take y'all!"
"You're a man of flaring tempers before the One. Yet he will not bow his will to you."
Drawing Shannon, close to him the Abbott said, "This young lady is but recently come into her womanhood but she is a greater warrior than you shall ever be, Egil Shee. You must listen to her song."
"Ah, so you will nay give me the waters of Tet? Very well, then."
Without another word, the gunslinger drew his revolver and sent a

bullet straight through Shannon's skull. Then a strange thing happened amidst Sister Audressa's screams. A golden light began to waft up from Shannon's body, then flew with lightning rapidity into the tear duct of her murderer's left eye. The gunslinger Egil Shee toppled from his horse.

Shee fumbled around in the sand for a moment, seized his derby and ran screaming into the desert.

The Abbott turned to Sister Audressa. "It has begun."

7. Bella Jessica

Bella Jessica sat cross-legged before her great tent, deep in meditation. The searing desert sun illumined her alabaster skin, yet it could not burn her. Her dark hair was hidden by the hood of her red punchabi.

The knickknacks of her strange trade surrounded her. Vases and vats of spices, her stringed bouzouki, the beautifully exquisite large steel dolls and statues she forged. She was a prioress in the church of Yah, though unlike Abbott Aderly, she preferred a life of solitude. Her only contact with the outside world was with the pilgrims that happened upon her abode on their way to the monastery, and with those in the monastery itself. She was quite powerfully built, for her father, it was said, had been a giant. *

*The subject of Bella Jessica's father is the subject of controversy in the church of Yah in Wesdon Varld. Her mother, a nun by the name of Baronessa, had disappeared into the Nuine Desert while ministering to the Keku barbarians. She had been discovered by her fellow sisters many months later, I saw that she was at this time heavily pregnant. She totally denied the breaking of her vows, saying that she had been married to a man for a time with the physique of an angel, but when asked to produce him for the church court she could not, merely saying that he lived in a land beyond the stars. Even after Bella Jessica was born to refuse to believe or admit that her daughter was illegitimate. (And even when she was born Bella Jessica had been a large baby. Oh no! I have given you the wrong idea. Not in the manner of great girth or being portly, but rather baby Bella Jessica was a little over 3 feet tall at birth and 20 pounds of pure muscle. But how? Giants were things of children's stories and did not truly exist in Wesdon Varld. Bella Jessica's mother told the strong girl when her daughter was old enough to understand that she had had a dream from the Lord Yah that Bella Jessica would be reunited with her father someday beyond the stars. She said that her husband had left her and sent her home after spending the summer by her side, in the manner of a honeymoon. The one good *thing, Baronessa had told Bella Jessica, that her deadbeat father had given her was an unsurpassed mastery over holy magic, as both you, and in a sense I, and Egil the Gunslinger, shall see, my gentle readers. I, being as I am like all my race, unbound by the laws of time and space, am only telling you what I know already but have yet to write. The full story of the prioress's parentage shall be told in Book II, which I shall write I warrant. And then maybe I can get around to getting finishing that annoying Paladin book. Blast it all. No. Excuse me gentle readers for my outburst. Back to the matter at hand.*

Bella Jessica had a rudimentary knowledge of herbs and healing, though her power, almost divine in nature, truly lay in her voice and her music. She was quite beautiful, but with no vanity. It was said that she could stop the pillaging Civs and raiding barbarians with nothing save her hypnotic voice and presence.

She had felt a quickening in her spirit that morning, a disturbance in the balance of the elements, and thus was in meditation, beseeching the One for guidance. Beside her stood her greatest masterpiece, a five-foot-tall statue of a beautiful fae lady with flowing golden hair. The prioress knew it not, but she would soon find the fae statue very useful. Far off in the distance, a manic howling rippled forth.

Egil Shee staggered and twitched, occasionally scraping his hair in a vigorous motion. He staggered back and forth, his head throbbing and his hands twitching, strange ruminations coming from his throat.

"Acorn, Nut, Tree. Bye-byes. Acorn, nut, tee-hee, coo…"

Why the keft was he saying…?

Shee froze for a split second. An image of a great obsidian rotunda topped with a dome of gold flashed across his sight and was gone.

Find me, vigilante…. Can you?

"Bye-Bye, Scribe…WHAT THE…!"

He ran like mad for a time with his eyes closed. He was determined to get these ruminations out of his head. And still they kept coming. Nothing he could do could get them out of his mind.

"Bye-Bye. Acorn, nut, tree. Tree, nut, acorn. Library."

"D'Yaagh!"

This continued for what seemed like hours until the part of Egil's mind that was still his to control could no longer stand it. He saw only one recourse. He withdrew one of his pistols and aimed the barrel just above his temple. He drew back the hammer. One more second and then…

"NO!"

The gunslinger whirled around and saw a beautiful young woman running towards him. Her voice seemed to echo in his mind, bringing it peace.

"Put your pistol down. In the name of Yah, man, put it down. Don't be so hasty to throw your life away, gunslinger. Come with me."

Her voice was the most beautifully hypnotic sound the gunslinger had ever heard, and so, like a young babe wanting to be fed, Shee followed. They came in time to the prioress's great tent.

"I am the Prioress Bella Jessica, though Shannon calls me 'BJ'. Oh yes, Egil Shee, don't be alarmed. I know what you did, and now you are suffering for it. The Creator showed me during my meditation."

Part of the gunslinger's mind began to reply, but in the end he could only twitch.

"When you murdered our dear little Shannon, her spirit transferred into your body, for the Creator had not finished his work in her yet. Nothing like this has ever happened to me, though I assume by every indication, you want to be rid of her. You see, however, Shannon's spirit must have a host. She cannot simply go to the afterlife in the arms of the Creator, for, as I just said, she has not yet finished the work to which he has called her. Let me see.... Ah, yes. I knew this would come in handy someday.
"Now, Master Shee. The first thing you must do to free Shannon is stop trying to fix her and simply listen. Listen to her song. It is part of the song of creation. Here, I shall help you."

BJ took the gunslinger's arms in hers and bade him close his eyes. Then she began to hum. The beautiful sweet nectar of the music assuaged the confused man's mind and slowly he began to see. He saw Shannon running to the prioress, and as the strong woman picked up the young one, he felt something sweet and strange flow out of his mouth. As he slowly opened his eyes, he saw that Shannon's life force was flowing into the steel statue. Slowly the blonde statue began to blink her eyes. Then she opened her mouth and began to sing, "Acorn, nut and little tree. Bye-bye, Mr. Scribe."

The prioress knelt down and embraced Shannon tightly. Then she released the girl and placed her index finger on the gunslinger's forehead. "Fear not, Master Shee. You have learned somewhat of penitence this day. Today the Master and Creator has forgiven your sin. Come in and I shall prepare a meal for you to eat. Surely you must be hungry after your ordeal today. Come along, Shannon."

As the three peculiar companions entered Prioress BJ's cool tent, the gunslinger Egil felt very strange. He felt a peace he had not known in years. For the first time since burying his mother, Egil's heart was at peace. It was well with his soul.

"You may rest here as long as you like," BJ said. "I foresee that you and perhaps I as well have a great journey ahead of us. We will need all the rest and resources, both spiritual and physical, that we can muster."

They ate a meal of bread and honey while serenaded by the prioress as she strummed the bouzouki. It was odd, but ever since his mother had died, the gunslinger had not had much respect for women. And yet, he was captivated by the spiritual power and wisdom of Prioress Bella Jessica. Could she possibly be, what was that word he hadn't used in decades? Yes! Yes! Truly in his heart, he believed he had found a friend. Abbot Aderly's words had come true. The gunslinger's act of violence had been followed by an act of peace.

That night, Egil Shee slept undisturbed.

***

The morning sun painted the Nuine Desert a dull purple red as dawn began to break. In the damp morning air, steel rippled through the quiet. Egil had risen early that morning, eager to reacquaint himself with his weapons. A massive 60 caliber revolver twirled in each of his hands, stopping with the hammer cocked as Shee imagined an invisible opponent. But the guns never made a report, though the gunslinger's nimble finger many times came deceptively close to squeezing the trigger.

Then the cutlasses spun forth, casting a blackened steel shadow in the morning sun. Shee's body spun through the air and he sprang to his feet, left blade thrust upward. He imagined barbarians and brawlers charging him with axes and tomahawks. His well-forged steel cut a bloody swath among them, and he could almost hear their howls of pain as he ended their miserable imaginary lives. As he was filled with battle lust, he heard a rhythmic voice breaking through his concentration.

"Egil…!"

He turned on his heel, bringing the cutlass forward and back in a draw cut.

He stopped suddenly short as he saw the prioress, a look of fear in her eyes. He realized only a second later what he had done, for the nick on her collarbone was indication. It had already begun to ooze forth blood.

With no time for panic, he immediately began to put pressure on the wound to stop the bleeding.

"Enough! Enough, Egil! I will stop it!" She exclaimed, in an uncharacteristically flustered tone.

"I'm sorry, Madame! Is there anything I can do?"

"Nothing save kiss it to make it better." This last remark was sarcastic, again very uncharacteristic. Nevertheless, the gunslinger blushed as a strange, wonderful and terrible feeling entered his stomach.

The prioress waved her hand over her wound. "Requiat." Instantly the bleeding stopped and the wound closed.

"Stars of heaven! I cannot think what makes a man like you so angry!"

"It's strange, Madame Prioress, but when I look at you, I remember the face of my mother. The fever took her when I was just a youth. To ease his grief, my father took refuge in the church. He was always fascinated by the holy magic, you see, and studied the tomes of the ancients. I believe, as I always have, that he was trying to find a way to resurrect my mother. He found mention in an ancient text of a great edifice whose keeper could see into all the worlds, both living and dead. He also found mention of the draught of Tet and those who could travel between the material planes. He went to see your Abbott Aderly, the concept of the scribe of all worlds consuming him. He pleaded for the draught of Tet, but the Abbot, misjudging his condition, refused him. And so, in despair, with the help of hemlock poisoning, my father left this world. If that scribe does exist, a thousand curses be upon him. It has been my mission to find this man wherever he may be and avenge my father's blood upon him."

"Whatever your purpose, Master Shee, for Shannon's sake, I will aid you. It is truly sad that your entire existence depends on vengeance. That is in the hands of the creator always. You cannot use your own mind to determine what is right and wrong, for the minds of humans are full of lies. Seek Yah. What he says. He is the one who has laid out the correct path. He determines the right. All we must do is hold his hand and follow his lead. I can think of a million better ways for you to honor your father's memory than to seek vengeance upon someone you don't even know. But if you seek this building between worlds, Shannon and I will look with you. Maybe, you will find who you really are. That is what I think you truly want. Let the peace of Yah guide you, gunslinger."

By this time, they were seated on the ground in front of the tent. She leaned over and kissed him lightly and for a moment his heart began to pound. But then Shannon's chatter started to come from inside the tent.

"Oh, dear gracious," BJ said, rising. "I came out to call you in to breakfast. It shall be cold now. Come along, Dear Egil. We have much to do before we set out on our journey."

And thus, a seed of doubt was planted in the mind of Egil son of Thomas, the gunslinger of Wesdon Varld. Part of him still wanted vengeance upon me, and yet he wanted to remember the face of his mother and the heart of his father. Mayhap the path to the Nexus will give him both.

Come to me, gunslinger.

8. The Draught of Tet

The noonday sun cast an alabaster light on the high dunes. Clearing a path with a knotted stave, the vigilante led the strange party forward. His horse had bolted when he fell at the monastery, so he hoped to find an outpost where he could acquire a new one. Luckily BJ had brought plenty of water. Now that Shannon was reanimated, her new form did not require sustenance, so that would make supplies last longer. Still, unless they could find a fissure of reality or the draught of Tet, they had no inkling of where to go.

"I believe," the prioress had said, "that I read somewhere that each world is linked in the center of the other. The desert lies at the center of our sphere, therefore me must seek the heart of the desert."

They walked for nearly six hours, only stopping in their tracks once or twice to quench their thirst with the canteens which soon ran dry, despite BJ's preemptive planning. This would result in desert fever if they didn't soon find water. And yet, the trio trudged on, kept moving by Shannon's singsong chatter. Normally this would have irked the gunslinger, but by now he was beginning to find it rather pleasant.

"Dooballoo, Mr. Scribe. Dooballoo. Bye bye, BJ. Bye byes, Varld. Dooballoo. Good night."

Just as his feet were beginning to falter, Egil saw a massive rock outcropping looming in the distance. Next to this outcropping, praise Yah, was an oasis. The water had a strange effervescent shimmer to it, and a pungent sweet odor. Under normal circumstances, the gunslinger would have tested for poisons, but this was the first water for miles around and thus, they had no choice. Running to the edge of the water, the prioress and the gunslinger drank deeply. "By dandy!" declared Shee. "This be better than any hard sarsaparilla ever tasted."

Suddenly, a loud twangy cry of "HOLD IT!" Rang out along with loud sharp cocking of a shotgun. The pair looked up and saw a tall, wiry man in a black cloak and a black sailor's whaling cap, sporting dark glasses. Egil Shee could by no means point fingers but the thought that instantly crossed his mind was that the man was dressed too heavily for the arid climate. What's more, the man held a heavy gauge shotgun, which prohibited the gunslinger from thinking out loud.

"Away from m' juju-water, you ignorant pukes!" the man barked in an insane drawl. "I'm Jemmaky Pullet, bane of barbarians, and I won this here spirit water fair and square!"

Bella Jessica suddenly snapped to attention.

"Oh hallelujah! Egil, this is the draught of…"

"Shut it!" barked the loony gunman. He made a move to squeeze the trigger. But Shee was faster. He whipped up his cutlass in a backhanded draw cut, cutting the side of the man's nose.

But then a strange thing happened. For a split second, the two men in black stood in a golden grassy plain, a cool spring breeze whispering among the stalks, and Shee felt slightly different. But before he could wrap his mind around it completely, they were back at the oasis.

"Where did I…?"

"I don't know!" BJ cried.

In the confusion, the gunslinger grabbed the shotgun from the insane man and sent a blast of buckshot into his chest. Strangely, the man flew back and vanished. The gunslinger and the prioress stared in disbelief, but Shannon said, "Hello, Mr. Scribe."

"I was trying to tell you, Egil," BJ said after a moment. "This is one of the Springs of the Draught of Tet. You must have traveled for an instant between worlds."

***

The gunslinger stared for a moment. "I did? He went with me for a moment. Don't know how. The question is, where in tarnation did he go just now?"

"I'd be a wild boar if I knew, Egil!" BJ shrugged

Just then Shannon started laughing hysterically.

She vanished into thin air for a split second and returned to stand in between them. Nothing had changed except that she now had an emerald-gold leaf upon her metallic head.

"Hmm… Euphoria… Heightened sense of awareness…" mused the prioress. "Landsakes… I just might have an idea. You need a time of bliss or stress to travel between planes. Come here, Shannon."

She stepped closer to the gunslinger and placed Shannon in between them. "Please don't get any ideas, Egil… er. At least not yet." She pressed up against him with Shannon still in the middle. Then without explaining what or why she was doing this, she seized his cheeks and kissed him fully on the lips. For a split second there was a flash as if his body was being torn apart. Then they stood in a golden grassy plain with mountains in the northern distance and stalks of green grass scattered here and there around them.

Shee was too caught up in the heat of the moment to notice but he felt slightly different in a way that he could not quite identify. It had nothing to do with the kiss, as wonderfully shocking as it had been, but rather the surroundings.

From a quick glance there was no sign of Pullet's body. Although there was a great indentation in the nearby grass as if there had been a tussle. But the greatest surprise was this. Shannon's new body no longer felt hard and metallic; it was instead a body of flesh, just as warm with the flow of blood as that of the girl's' companions. The vigilante scratched his head. He didn't have much time for thought for the ground began to echo with the beat of hooves.

A great retinue of armed men in mail armor came riding into view. They bore a banner of a white unicorn upon a field of silver. They formed an encroaching circle around the three and a forest of spears swung level.

The leader, a gray-bearded man with a scar under one, eye called out in a loud voice, "In the name of King Nilmeron and Queen Luaria of Irminsul, cast your weapons to the ground."

"Oh yeah?" spat Egil, drawing a pistol. "Guess again, vaquero!" He cocked and squeezed the trigger.

Click. Click click.

Nuts. The cylinder was loaded. Why didn't it fire? Different laws of nature, perhaps?

He couldn't take on a full score of armed and armored men without a gun. So he unstrapped his weapons and laid them on the ground in full view of the soldiers.

"State your business." Barked old graybeard.

"I – I am Bella Jessica Shee. And this is my husband, Egil." She shot the gunslinger a warning glance and he knew to play along.

"This is our daughter, Shannon. We are looking for a place to spend the night."

"Bah! Armed with mysterious weapons near the city of Auraheim. If it were up to me I'd try you for an assassination attempt. But the King is the final law now. So I will take you to him. Bring them, Arrec."

The Lieutenant bound their willing hands and set them behind three of the riders. They set off for a great silver city at the foot of the nearby mountains to the north.

"This world has magic, lots of magic, it's fairly teeming with it," BJ whispered to Egil through her teeth.

"What does that matter?" The gunslinger replied in a hushed voice.

"Nothing. But I may start... Oh never mind. Only time will tell, I suppose."

Egil did not understand her meaning but thought it best not to pursue the subject further.

The guard upon the battlement of the city hailed the company as they approached the massive double gate. "Who goes there?"

"Captain Bjorvar and the sixth company. I bring enemy prisoners before the King."

"They look strange but they don't appear to be Volderins. Mailbeard was slain over a year ago. His sons continue the guerrilla fighting but they don't look like that."
Bjorvar grunted. "Open the gates, Aldyr. It is for the King to ask questions."

As the gates swung inward, Egil and BJ caught their breath in amazement. Nearly every building inside the city and the stones lining the streets were smelted over with costly silver. A tall statue of a man with flowing locks and ears that tapered to a point stood watch over the main thoroughfare. Strange bold letters of a hieroglyphic form were carved into the massive pedestal. Beside it was the statue of a small young woman with braided hair that was pulled up into a crown bun at the back of the head. His Queen, perhaps?

Shee and his mock wife were so awed at all they saw in the silver city that they almost forgot to be afraid for their lives.

They were led to a great palace. Guards opened the doors to reveal a great hall of marble stretching back to a throne of carnelian upon which sat the most massive and muscular man Egil had ever seen. Yet he felt slightly miffed when he heard Bella Jessica catch her breath quickly as she saw the apparent monarch. The man was surpassingly handsome and regal with fiery red locks, aquamarine eyes and ears that tapered to a point. A massive broadsword with strange runes hung at his side

"My King Nilmeron," began the Captain. "I found this man and his wife and their child not far from the silver city. He was armed with these strange swords and these other weapons which he tried to wield against us. If you ask my humble opinion, I say he's a sorcerer, and these strange things are his foul devices."

At that moment, a pair of doors behind the throne opened and the most beautiful woman Egil had seen outside the Nuine Desert entered the room. Her figure was somewhat diminutive, her face round, and her eyes wide and blue. Her hair was tied in a soft bun of elegant braids that had the appearance of browned gold wrapped in satin. The guards bowed low but she seemed to take no notice. She walked to the throne and sat down on the King's knee.

"Luaria, *elskearion*," he laughed, kissing her softly. "We appear to have strange visitors. The good Captain here was just telling me he believes this man with the strange tools is a sorcerer of the Dark Enemy."

"An enemy you say?" she said in a soft elegant voice. "Enemies are always trying to take over our world. Despite the black robe and the funny hat, he does not look like a sorcerer of the Dark Enemy. Who are you, good sir?

"I am…" Shee began. Just as he started to speak, Shannon began to act very strangely. She convulsed and twitched and trilled and wailed, winking and repeating, "BJ bye bye, BJ No GO. My fault NO." She cuffed head in a paranoid fashion. The king and queen began to look very alarmed.

What to do, what to do? He had to do something. The gunslinger seized Shannon by the hand and began dancing a hornpipe with her, belting out a Kalten pirate sea shanty at the top of his lungs.

> "In Kalten Town there lived a maid,
> Mark well what I do say!
> In Kalten Town there lived a maid,
> And she was mistress of her trade.
> I'll go no more a-roving with you fair maid!
>
>
> "A roving, a roving,
> Since roving's been my ru-i-in,
> I'll go no more a roving,
> With you fair maid!"

During the song, Shannon stopped screaming and started laughing.

It was only when the song ended that Egil realized that the Queen had been laughing and clapping in time with his singing.

"I see, Sir Knight. You are not a sorcerer but a bard, a warrior bard."

"Yes, er, your Majesty whoever you are," he said awkwardly doing his best to take a courtly bow. "Egil Shee, warrior bard extraordinaire, traveling in your realm with my wife Bella Jessica and our daughter, Shannon. She is unique… and wonderful. As you can see."

The Queen smiled. "And I am Queen Luaria, Co-Ruler of Irminsul with my husband before you, King Nilmeron, the Elvish "usurper" of my father Kaell X before him (Gildeador rest my father's soul). My father awarded him my hand and the crown when he brought the true faith from the Elvenlands in the North. But first he defeated the wild Volderins and decapitated their greatest tribal chief, the unifier of the tribes, Kruak Mail-Beard.

"But enough of history for today. You must be tired after your long journey. I will have the servants prepare the best guest room the Palace for you."

Whew! Thought the gunslinger. *Crisis averted. And through music of all things. Never again will I underestimate the use of a good tune.*

9. A New Life

"Let his banner over me be love."-The Maid of Sharon

Egil Shee felt a curious cocktail of emotions as he left Nilmeron and Luaria. For years beyond his memory, he had told lies to achieve his own ends. And even though he was technically doing it to protect another, he found he couldn't stand it. This was not the first time in recent days that he had struggled with his own soul, which he had forgotten he even had. Nor would it be the last.

The porters led them to a great apartment. There was a large bed with marble posters with aquamarine upholstery and a divan of the same color. There was a veranda which led out onto a balcony also of marble which overlooked a garden up from which the pleasant scent of lavender and jasmine wafted.

A tray of fruit and fowl sat on a table before the bed. BJ told Shannon to eat and then set about it herself, for they had had nothing since coming to Irminsul. Egil said nothing and only nibbled at his plate slightly. After a few hours Shannon went to sleep on the great bed. Sitting down on a small chair, the gunslinger laid his head in his hands and rubbed his temples feverishly.

"What ails you, Egil?"

"Now you're starting to talk like those courtly folk. I can't put my finger on, Belley. I blow Shannon's face to kingdom come. Yah, or maybe he is this Gildeador, I don't care nothing, he leaves me alive, and so do you. And that's another thing. I almost decapitated you. And even after that you not only left me alive, you kissed me. What in the name of Kefthill's daemons is going on?"

"Please, friend, don't swear. Let me tell you a story. I'm a little older than I look. When I received my ordination, the Abbess told me, and you know that in the church of Yah at least, marriage is permitted among clergy. She told me that I would remain unmarried for years, but that one day, I would meet a man who spoke many blasphemies and yet had a diamond in the rough of his heart. It was mine and another's job, our holy vocation as it were, to heal his heart and lead him on his destiny and he would be the man I would marry. I now believe that man to be you. Ever since the lady Nora, your mother, died. (Yes, the Spirit of Yah has shown me many things), you have never loved a woman, but have rather been domineering and sexist. That is why you so easily robbed Shannon of her first body. I read in a tome once, a book belonging to the Abbott, and sought by Thomas Shee, your father, that in other planes of knowledge, as in our plane, the name of the One is praised by a different name, as in a different language. Now hear me and hear me out. This does not mean that there are many gods or many ways to God. There is but one God, who was originally called Yehovah, but those of the East called his Son Iezu, the Westerners Jesu, and the originators Yeshuah. These may sound different in different languages but yet there is but one name, the name of the son of the one mediator and creator God, by which you must be saved. We call him Yah. And those of this sphere, Gildeador. If such a man as you were to follow him, I would follow that man into Helheim itself."

Egil felt as if a mountain were rising in his breast. Taking her hand, he vowed, "To this Man of the Stars I will give my swords and my guns in my quest for the library. I give up vengeance for him and for you. And I swear to you tonight: the child will live within my care, and I will raise her into the light. I swear to you I will always be there for you."

"Then what we think of ourselves in jest. Shall it be true? Shall we let it be true?"

"Yes...yes! YES!" He could not say the last of these exclamations very well for obvious reasons.

They immediately ran to the apartment of the King and the gunslinger pounded on the door so hard his knuckles almost bled.

"What in the name of Seven Princes...?" croaked the bleary-eyed King, opening the door.

Egil Shee seized Nilmeron by the dressing gown and excitedly thrust his face unshaven and all into the King's line of sight. "Listen, sire. We are sorry that we have deceived you. Bella Jessica and I are not married, only now we wish to be, for we serve the God of all free peoples. You name Him Gildeador. So now I ask that, in the name of Gildeador, you marry us. For, being an elf, I believe I sense that your power can extend in times of war to performing marriages. We no longer wish to dwell in deceit. Will you marry us?"

"Well, I will see what I can do to remedy this situation. I am slightly taken aback at your deceit, even if it was to save your own skin. I will see what I can do about that later. But for now, here in the sight of Gildeador and of me the Lord of this land. Do you, Egil Shee, strange one, take Bella Jessica to be your lawfully wedded wife in the sight of Gildeador, now and forever?"

"I do."

"And do you Bella Jessica vow to take this man, Egil Shee as your husband and lover and partner in the work to which Gildeador has called you?"

"I do."

"Then by the power invested temporarily in me through my duties as king of Irminsul, I Nilmeron King of Irminsul, formally second-in-line prince of Gladdeas, which is now named Nilmeronel, pronounce you man and wife. You may share a kiss."

Taking up his sword from the nightstand, Nilmeron said, "Kneel, good Master Shee."

Touching the gunslinger's shoulders, each in turn with the flat of the blade, he said, "I now conscript you into my service of arms as payment for my services to you this night."

Egil Shee smiled, a familiar twinkle in his eye. "I have been doing this all my life, my King. It is but a thing that will come as second nature. Gildeador save our gracious King."

That was the happiest night of the gunslinger's life. But in his heart, Egil son of Thomas still wanted answers. Oh, how he wanted them.

Come to me, O gunslinger, knight of Nilmeron. Come to me.

Egil awoke early the next morning and followed a soldier's directions to the dining hall. He saw that his wife had arrived before him and was already in conversation with the Queen over a plate of kippers and gammon.
"Good morning, Sir Egil. I trust you found your rooms to your liking."
Egil nodded.
"You were weary from travel yesterday, so I did not broach the question. But I believe my husband, as your new liege lord, deserves to know. From what part of Ealinde do you hail?"
"I do not think your Majesty will understand. Suffice to say, and I beg your indulgence, my Queen, but I hail from a country far beyond the seas of this world, where there are many strange things, both wonderful and terrible. If I were to go into more detail it would only be confusing. Please understand, highness."
Luaria stared at him for a moment but then slowly nodded. "I shall respect your privacy, Sir. Surely, people as magical as you, can only portend well for our kingdom. Please eat."

The King joined them after a time and the man of Wesdon Varld noted that there was a certain twinkle in the Elven monarch's eye. "Strange one," he said rising and motioning to his guest. "Come with me to my personal Armory. Rondir has made something especially for you. Come now. This way."

The personal armory of the King was really a massive gymnasium of weaponry, where the personal officers of the king sparred with swords, both blunted and wooden, and elven armorers from Nilmeronel crafted magnificent masterpieces in silvered and whitened elvish steel. A rather broad-chested and uncharacteristically bald elf brought King Nilmeron some weapons wrapped in a large cloth of red silk.

"Ah! Thank you, Rondir. We took a look at your strange weapons last night while you slept and were able to contrive these. Hopefully you will find them useful."

Wrapped inside were two strangely pistol grip crossbows that were small enough to fit in each of the gunslinger's hands. They were light and nimble to the hand and yet apparently had enough draw weight to fly five hundred rods if the wind was right or so said the King. The string was from a vine in Firbolg Forest, and thus could re-cock by itself due to the eldritch enchantment. "That which the Enemy intends for evil has been used for good," King Nilmeron winked.

Egil Shee eagerly took up the crossbows and fired one at a wooden dummy, striking it dead center in the neck.

"I think I have the general idea," the gunslinger grinned.

But he was even more delighted when he saw what else he had. To him they were better than Yuletide gifts. Two heavy cutlasses of Elven steel that shimmered bright silvery white in the torchlight.

"No matter where you go, Lord Strange One, these will always out-cut mannish steel. You can bend these blades in a full circle and still they will not break, but will instead return true. Are you pleased?"

Egil beamed and grasped the Elven King's forearm in a tight grip, warrior to warrior.

"Welcome to the army of the kingdom of Irminsul, Lord Egil Shee, Strange One."

End of The Vigilante Book 1
To read further books of this series visit www.lamatrath.net

*** Further Stories ***

The Ballad of Oliver McKentry

"Over and over the world have my kilted legs trod. From Stamboul to New Providence and all the leagues between, undoing the sins of a past life. Down several generations. What mean I by that? Well, I have all the time in the God-Song, so I would not mind telling you my tale."-Oliver McKentry

The Spanish Main, the Year of our Lord 1594

The gun-stones thundered forth from the caravel as Sir Francis, more popularly called El Draco by the Spanish, barked orders from her Majesty's ship the *Golden Hind* over to the Scottish mercenaries on board the schooner *Water Horse*.

The young gunner, scarce a score years old, ignited the fuse on the cannon barrel and once again the roaring report almost shattered the beeswax in his ears. Oh, how young Oliver McKentry loved the sound of a good gun report. It stirred his dark Celtic soul and sent adrenaline pumping into his sword arm. With his Scottish mortuary sword he had slain many men. Whether they were Catholic, Protestant, or pagan mattered not. He sent them all down to an early grave. He brandished his matchlock and lit it to blast the face off the young Seaman across the rail from him. (Och! Could that be the cabin boy?) Oh well. Served the Catholic fop right, and no mistake.

The galleons were not across from each other with the schooner in between. Oliver withdrew his grappling hook from his sea chest tossed it over the rail the Spanish Galleon, and pulled it taught.

The thought of blood vengeance, though the Spaniards had done him no personal wrong, filled his lustful mind. He could almost here is that house of those sea rats as he neared the din of battle overhead, but before he could reach his victim-quarry one of the guns from the Golden Hind smashed a broadside through the Spanish Galleon, knocking the gun loose. The large iron tube smashed into Oliver knocking him into a salty reckoning in the sea below. And so, darkness took him.

Sulfur. Brimstone. Ash. These sensations. They passed through his body like a current of lightning. A trilling like that of the Beast of Job pounded in his ears. A light, ruddy yet unholy, burst in a splash of chaotic color before his eyes. In a flash, his entire philosophy changed and the so-called fairy stories of his grandmother began to make sense. Mayhap the life of a mercenary did not seem quite so appealing a choice after all. "There is a way. A way out, Signor." A brawny bronze-skin man with muscles like Heracles and wings of silver gray, clad in armor like unto the Polish hussars. Similar, only much more magnificent, and embossed with Greek and Hebrew lettering. The Sanish Angel man stood before Oliver, barring the Scotsman's way to the fiery pit. "I, a lieutenant of Christ, in my former life the Conquistador Don Elayo de Mendoza was once offered this chance that I now give to you. To become an indentured servant a soldier in the Secret Angel Army, for eight score and two years. At the end of your penance, you will merit entrance into the third heaven. We are the Legionnaires of History. The Lord Jehovah passes us through time, but only are appointed spans, to accomplish his will by encouraging those to submit to it and sadly, mitigating the effects of those who won't. You, man of Glenfinnan: Will you serve your time?"

McKentry, his mind blasted by this time, could only nod mutely.

"Very well," said de Mendoza. "I shall be your supervisor. You shall be sent back along with all your equipment and this. He handed him the now angelic Scotsman the cannon barrel that had served McKentry's death knell. It now had a strap and a pistol stock and surprisingly the Scotsman found that he now had the supernatural strength to lift it and set it on his shoulder. "Also," said the Spanish Angel. "You probably will be sent to India at some point and you'll need this. He wrapped a brown turban, like those worn by the Sikhs of India, around Oliver's head. "It renders the wearer invisible when needed. Now, let us go with the blessing of God." As quickly as it had come, the vision of hell's pit was gone, and both the experienced and the novice Angel were again in the land of mortality.

The Lay of Sigurd of Outremer

After the days of the Norse shield wall

But twenty--one years before Pope Urban's call

In The frozen lands of the North

A new babe, the son of a Jarl came forth

At the height of it all, Lady Signy stood on her legs

And screamed forth a call of "Grat Gudde Vhair est deg?"

The baby came forth and his father praised God.

And yet, as the months wore on, it was odd.

He was not turning or crawling about

And all he could do was flounder like a trout

"Is my son but a ban-child of sin?
Will I ever see him bear arms with his kin?"

As the boy Sigurd grew, he much feared the church

As he saw his friends play with their swords of birch.

Ever the cloister would be in his gaze.

That was where he thought he'd spend all his days

One night at age of knighthood it did rain

And the rush of the fjord winds addled his brain

He went high on a hill and stood out on a tor

Where his ancestors said there thunder-raged Thor

"God, if you give me full use of my legs,

I'll die in your service! Grot Gude, Vhair ist deg?"

The lightning crashed down and struck upraised arm

The thrall in the barnyard saw all the harm

And carried him home in his strong stout arms.

Erik and Signy prayed long by his bed

That their son would not go to be with the dead.

And when his head lifted, they praised their great God.

But then, there was something quite wonderfully odd.

His arms were no longer stiffened and weak

but now for a broadsword soon would they seek

He stood upon his two legs now quite strong

Jumped up on the table and laughed loud and long.

Surely a miracle had happened now

But then he suddenly remembered his vow

Like the sword Gram, his heart was now shattered

For to be a warrior was all that now mattered

but lo! All the young man's hope now was not lost

For news from the South on the sea swept across.

During this time Sigurd had trained at arms

And was the best of all in art of war-charms

A call to the faithful to unsheathe the sword

And free the Holy Land from the paynim horde.

Now young Sigurd could die for the Lord

by fighting and bearing holy cross and sword!

The night before was to depart for the East,

His father, Jarl Erik, held a great feast.

And at the feast presented his son with a gift

That was very sharp and heavy to lift.

It was his great-great-grandfather's sword.

Passed down from the days of the Viking hordes.

The steel was far better than a modern blade

and would serve Sigurd well in the crusade

It was inscribed with Ulfbehrt, the legend'ry Smith

And had long protected their kin and their kith.

Bidding family goodbye Sigurd took the cross

And by ship across the Hellespont tossed.

He wore conical helmet and gleaming Norse mail,

Bore sturdy kite shield to turn Seljuq-nail

Unlike most ridders, however, he wore

A deep wine red surcoat with rood white pallor.

His horse was as black as the sin that men fear

And, nodding back to old times, was named Sleipnir.

He came to Antioch with Bohemond's men

And saw in great shock, holy war? Nay! Sin!

Moslems and Coptics, roasted like sheep.

Jewesses and Orthodox tramped in the streets.

This was not the power of Christ's resurrection.

Sigurd's soul had one recourse: insurrection!

Slaying crusader and Muslim alike,

He fled Bohemond's evil puissant pike.

Quothe he then, "I can only bring peace.

I want none of this carrion, brute, battle-feast!

Those who slay the innocent in this land will

Feel this sharp justice: my Norse watered steel!

As long as I walk the earth as a true swordsman,

I'll defend all: Byzantine, Moslem or Norman

I can neither go home nor give up my sword.

I surely surrender my fate to the Lord."

A Namir in the Desert

Farzan spurred his Arabian mare farther and farther from Cairo, hoping desperately that he would outpace his but recent Hash-Ashin brethren. He cursed his ill fortune but above all he cursed his cowardice for not with-taking of the sacred flower that gave the practiced killers an advantage over the Franj. He did not care that seventy-seven virgins no longer waited for him in the afterlife; all that mattered was prolonging the first one.

But now, three days into the desert, the cries of his pursuers came to him on the wind. And in the evening gloam on the windswept Eastern horizon came dots as black as the abyss, that grew larger and larger. Cries of "Allahu akbar! Apostate, apostate!" Swept toward him. He could see the riders, the assassins, as the Franks called them, their slender Damascene swords drawn. They were almost upon him, and so he closed his eyes and breathed a prayer, strangely to another God, other than Allah. And then….

A cry pierced the desert twilight in a language must rougher than the tongue of the Franks. "Gratte Gud, for fraid!" A giant of a man swooped down on a small, hairy black steed. He bore a much heavier sword but could wield it as easily as the slender blades of the assassins. The fittings were strange but the blade was of Damascus steel; odd for it was unknown among the Franks. Besides this he was dressed as much similarly to the Frankish warriors. The man fought with great skill and easily dodged the licking Saracen Blades. Assassins usually rode lightly armored, but still the men knew the places to perform cuts, draws and thrusts. His watered steel was soon stained with the blood of the assassin riders. Had Farzan been able to think, he would have turned and spurred his mount in the opposite direction, but he was too awed at the strange knight's prowess.

The strange warrior cut down the last of Farzan's pursuers and afterwards did something very strange. He began to weep and muttered something that sounded like a prayer in that same strange language. "Grotte Gud, nie giltas…"

Not expecting an answer, Farzan asked, "who are you, Sir, and why did you rescue me? Those of our creeds hate each other."

Farzan was taken aback when the Frank answered in perfect Arabic "the peace of Jesus, to you, my friend. I follow Jesus, not the misguided ones who claim to be his followers. I am on the side of peace. As for my name, I am Sigurd Eriksson, known among your people as al-Namir. You are free to go. Salaam."

Al-Namir. The tiger of the desert. Hunted by both Godfrey, defender of the holy sepulcher, and Kilij Arslan. They said he was a demon who road Shaitan's black horse, slaying all in his path. And yet, why did he spare Farzan's life. Maybe there was something to this Jesus.

"If you'll permit me good Sir, I want to stay with you neither my brother assassins, nor much less the other Franks have ever show me any kindness. If kindness is the way of this Issa you serve, I should serve him to. Will you tell me more of him, al-Namir.

"Gladly, little brother. I have prayed for forgiveness. Come let the desert bury the dead. May the Lord have mercy on their souls. I pray that the light and peace of Jesus may once again illumine these lands."

The Stag Man

Past the Isles of True Gramarye

On the shores of the Evergreying Sea

The keeper, the Stag Man waits for the ships of you and me.

His figure is tall, his hair is white.

So are his eyes like the full moon night

Yet his skull is not that of a hag,

For protruding from it are the horns of a stag.

They are white like bone or ivory

His eyes are blind, and yet they see,

The white ships rolling in from the sea.

He is waiting for you and me

With the message of the King hanging on the tree.

Beyond him are the windswept doors of the great hall called
Eternity.

Before you walk its timeless halls

In the presence of both kings and thralls

Before in there you come to be

In the Hall called Eternity

The great stag man makes his plea,

To touch the King upon the tree.

For if come to bound you do not be,

With Crown, Cloth, and Wool Robe three,

You shall pass to Eternity

Held by the Dark Gramarye.

I, for one, shall answer the plea,

That the stag man makes of me

Before the day I come to be

In the hall called Eternity.

The Raid on Rockshale

Norwald of Skraelinen sat in the middle of his great hall, surrounded by his many mail-clad warriors, his fiery blue eyes staring intently into the fire. He had built a small empire of fire and gore during his reign as lord of Skraelinen. What he truly desired was to carve a name for himself on the monolith of time. In his view, it was far better to be remembered carrying a merciless sword than a philosophic pen or codex of just laws. He had gained more land and wealth than any previous lord of Skraelinen. Yet still, an insatiable hunger for more: more power, more wealth, more blood, drove him onwards with a vengeance. His blade had drawn the blood of many valiant warriors, most of whom were more honorable than he. Today, he had called his thanes to the hall, for a mad, blasphemous scheme was burning in his brain.

"My lord?" ventured his undercommander, a bald bearded man named Broridar, "why have you called us here? You only conscript us when you are thinking of raiding. The stone veil is fast approaching, and the dark stones shall rain down from the sky crushing our crops. Why raid now?"

"Because, fool, our target shall be the Abbey of the Stag at Rockshale. Therein is kept the greatest treasure of all: The Golden Book of the Stag. The jewel-encrusted golden pages of that tome could provide a feast every night for the rest of our lives. He stood, raising his hands as a sign of exuberance. "And I shall be able to look up into the heavens in defiance of Fate and say that I, Norwald, warlord of Skraelinen, wrested it from the hands of the superstitious ones."

"But, my lord," Broridar cautioned, "the religion of the Sisters of the Abbey is powerful with magic. If we kill any of them, and most assuredly if we kill Matriarch Svanleina, we may be cursed by their God."

"Bah!" The warlord spat. "I do not fear any of the gods. I have lived my entire life in defiance of them." He struck the arm of his chair, causing the links of his blackened mail to rattle. "We go for the book, or, I swear, I will kill you all where you stand." All the assembled warriors doubted not what their capricious master said, for they had seen him do far worse than that of which he spoke.

And so, within the hour, the huge raiding party departed for the Abbey of the Stag. Unbeknownst to Norwald,

Lord Wendenel, a follower of the true faith, had come with his army on pilgrimage to the Abbey. When Norwald and his raiders arrived at the Abbey they were met head-on by the massive army of Lord Wendenel. Miraculously, Norwald fought with the tenacity of a caged beast, littering the granite-strewn ground with bloody corpses. He broke through to where Matriarch Svanleina stood.

He pointed his broadsword at her neck. "Give…me…the book!"
She shook her head. "Though you die here a lost man, you shall serve the true God, for the Stag Man shall come for you."

Norwald never saw Lord Wendenel drive his massive blade into his back. Seeing their leader fall, the raiding party fled, leaving Norwald, warlord of Skraelinen to bleed to death on this, his granite tomb.

The Choice of the Warrior

As I lay among the rocks

Bleeding from many wounds.

I lay among those I had slain

Upon this granite tomb.

I saw a figure robed in white

Shining like the moon.

He looked like someone I did know.

His eyes and beard were white as snow.

His hair was long like a wool rag

And from his head grew the horns of a stag.

Upon his staff was a jeweled crown

And a linen cloth as white as down.

In his other hand was a robe of wool.

Above the stars shone pale and dull.

He spoke a little verse in rhyme,

And it echoed through the doors of time.

He said, "Norwald, I have come for thee,
Across the Evergreying Sea

For your time has come to be

In the hall called Eternity.

Much glory have you sought,

But it was a prize dearly bought

Many men have you slain

And brought the King on the Tree pain.

But that King has paid the price

For you to dwell in paradise,

Freed from the Dark Gramarye.

Now wouldst thou bind unto thee

The crown, the cloth, and wool robe three,

And touch the King upon the Tree?

Would you now accompany me

Across the Evergreying Sea

To the hall called eternity?"

The answer welled up in my breast,

And I answered with a resounding "Yes!"
I reached out with my fingertips

And pressed the items to my lips

Then the stag man spoke a word

And I received new mail and sword

The true Norwald was revealed

And all my many wounds were healed.

I set sail on that magic sea

With the stag man beside me

With my new Master soon to be

In the hall called eternity.

Henri L'Foy

Poor little Henri L'Foy!

Yes, he was a sickly boy.

He had no chums or schoolmates,

The illegal son of Charles the Great.

The saddest boy on Frankish earth,

He had been crippled from birth.

In a dark convent room he lay.

Death would soon take him away.

When the novice held his hand,

It was hot as a firebrand.

Then his feverish eyes saw

A sight that made him stare in awe.

A mounted man before him stood

His shining mail was bright and good.

He was therefore a paladin,

But not one of Frankish ken.

His short mane was of the night's hue.

And his eyes were a sea spray blue.

"I am Norwald, not of this land,

Champion of the stag man.

And now you must come with me.

To the hall called eternity.

For you have already

Touched the King upon the Tree.

Now, lad, will you come with me?"
The boy gave the knight his hand,

No longer a flaming brand.

They galloped upon the white steed

Until time was of no heed

They rode on through the air.

Little Henri did not know where.

They came to a misty shore

With an old man standing tall before

A great mighty wooden hall,

Where there dwelt the faithful all.

The stag horns from the old man's head

Did not fill Henri with dread.

When with him he began to talk.

Henri found that he could walk.

He had been blessed eternally

By the King Upon the Tree.

The Knight of the Stag

When the Spanish friar at Henry's court was to be burned for
a witch,

The knight of the stag bore him off on his horse

As silent as a lich.

The Knight of the Stag came riding, riding, riding.

The Knight of the Stag came riding

Throughout the halls of time.

When the chosen of God were driven out for fear of the
racks of Spain

One moment there, and then not

They felt a horse's mane.

The Knight of the Stag came riding, riding, riding.

The Knight of the Stag came riding

Throughout the halls of time.

When a bloodbath came on the Eastern Church in Jerusalem.

The Knight of the Stag rode by on his horse.

His mail-clad arm saved them.

The Knight of the Stag came riding, riding, riding.

The brave Norwald came riding.

He rides in this dark time.

The Knight of the Stag came riding, riding, riding.

The Knight of the Stag came riding

Throughout the halls of time.

Chooser of the Slain

The April breeze rustled through the quiet Gaelic camp.

Before the tent of Brian Boru, the ground was cold and damp.

One moment the ancient High king was bowing his head in prayer.

Another moment he saw a strange warrior standing there.

His first thought was to call for his Goll-aglach

But the man raised a gloved hand

And so the king held back.

The man was tall and clad in mail of a silvery sheen

And unlike Brian his face was beardless and shaved clean.

His mane was short

And was black as raven's down

His eyes were sea blue as the waters before Dublin town.

"Peace, High King," he said at length.

"I am Norwald, a man of strength.

Not Gael, nor Norse, nor Norman Lord.

I was in my home a great warlord.

I'm worth far more in the attack

Than even twenty Goll-aglach.

I'll fight without pay, I am thine.

Only let those that I kill be mine."

The Boru agreed out of awe.

He understood not what he saw.

The next day as battle engaged

The elderly Gaelic king sage

Saw the strange man fight beyond ken.

For no weapon swung could touch him.

His broadsword sang a silvery song

And cut a swath through the Viking throng.

For every foe that he did smite

He performed strange last rites

That were melodious to hear.

Then the slain would disappear.

A Viking mercenary said,
"My King, that man with the dark mane

Is a Chooser of the Slain."
"No," said Brian with shaking nod.

"A servant of Almighty God."

When the Norse began to flee,

The strange man they did not see.

He had gone back to where the king soon would be

In the hall called Eternity.

Mariana's Destiny

The Novice of the Stag,

A girl called Mariana by name,

Stood before the matriarch,

Excitement shaking her small frame.

Underneath her gray veiled hood,

Above the top of her blue-gray dress

Her raven curls fell to her shoulders

A softness was in every tress.

Her eyes were as light blue as the misty veil

That encircled all Rockshale.

Said Svanleina, "You've come to be

Bound to the circle of three.

And a master have you found

In the King upon the Tree.

"Now we must open the Golden Book

And have the tenacity

To upon its leaves have a look.

You'll serve in that capacity."

When she opened up the book

She found she could not ignore.

When she took a closer look,

She saw something not seen before:

A mail-clad warrior on a steed.

His sea blue eyes she could not read.

His hair was somewhat long and as black

As that of the novice standing back

To speak Svanleina could not begin

For it was Norwald,

Felled Lord of Skraelinen.

The Mirror of Three

"Your companion is a ghost,"

Old Svanleina said.

"You must pass through the Mirror of Three

To become like the dead.

You have already come to be

Bound by the Circle of Three

Who is the King Upon the Tree.

By Him you will be led."

Mariana stepped through the glass

And from the flesh of this life passed.

She walked through the land of the dead

Upon the gray, misty tread

Until she came through the veil

And saw a mounted knight in mail.

His hair and eyes were the hue of hers.

The sign of the stag was upon his spurs.

Before she started her life anew

She mouthed the words "I forgive you!"

The Apothecary's Son

The apothecary's son

Had drunk hemlock, poor little one.

Now his face did show alarm

As he hung limp in his mother's arms.

He saw a mist-enshrouded door

With two figures standing before:

A mail clad knight upon a steed,

Mighty in both word and deed.

The other was a priestess, of a kind

In a blue-gray dress, soothing to mind,

With blue eyes, dark tresses, and a comely face.

In her hand she held a wooden mace.

The handsome dark-haired knight spoke,

The one tall and strong like oak:
"Do you wish to come with me

To the hall called Eternity?

For you have already

Touched the King Upon the Tree."
The beautiful priestess spoke

Raising high her mace of oak:

"Or do you wish to stay here,

Dwelling with your mother dear?"
Immediately the boy chose the other,

For he intoned the word "Mother."
Mariana gave a laugh

And tapped him on the head with her staff.

He flew back to the land of sin

Into his mother's arms again.

The City Called Eternity

Said the Stag Man to Norwald,

"The time shall soon come to be

For the triumphal return

Of the King upon the Tree.

Then our hall will be no more,

And we shall dwell forevermore

In the city of Golden ore,

The city called Eternity."

Song of the King's Mariner

On a strand, 'neath a sky of thunderous crowds

Of black, ominous, foreboding clouds

The King's Mariner did there remain,

The rain lashing his silvery mane.

"I am too old and frail," thought he

"To set my course on the foreboding sea."

But then the Voice of his King spoke,

As steadfast as a stalwart oak.

"Do not fear to set thy prow,

Even though the winds of doubt howl.

I'll send a Dove to comfort Thee,

And guide thee o'er this stormy sea.

A Dove down from the sky did float,

And led him to his battered boat.

And so the sailor took his heading

Though the journey he was dreading.

For countless days he sailed in the squall

In troughs and crests of foaming waves.

When he was sure this him death would bring

The Dove on the tiller began to sing.

Courage to him it did impart,

And gave a peace unto his heart.

He listened closely and heard more:
The songs of those that went before.

Then suddenly the squall abated.

Its foaming breath he had outwaited.

On the horizon, his eyes sore

Beheld his destination shore.

The Adventures of Ben-Herev the Danite

'Tis out of the foolish things
The LORD Most High does make kings.
In history, many a story
Of humble ones brought to glory.

I. The Adder on the Shield
(The City of Dan, 1263 BC)

Dan shall judge his people, as one of the tribes of Israel. Dan shall be a serpent by the way, an adder in the path, that biteth the horse's heels, so that his rider shall fall backward. (Genesis 49:16-17)

It was a dark and gloomy night in the city of Dan. The full moon cast a pale light on the vacant streets as rats scurried here and there, ever searching for crumbs of bread. The only other source of light came from the few lamps barely illuminating the dingy taverns that lined the crooked streets. Above the door to one of these haunts was a tiny sign bearing the sketch of a lion. Inside The Black Lion, several Sidonians* lay sprawled in drunken sleep over half-empty wineskins. Several other customers laughed and shouted loudly as they gulped down mouthfuls of barley beer. A few overly-intoxicated ruffians regurgitated into wooden buckets in the corner.

Jephthah, the proprietor of The Black Lion, was busy scrubbing the stone counter when suddenly, out of the corner of his eye, a figure caught his attention. He shifted his gaze and beheld, sitting in a far corner, a giant of a man, clad in Assyrian lamellar armor. On his feet were boots made of otter skin, and an Assyrian helm adorned his head. In his right hand, he held a bronze buckler and on his left hip rode a short bronze-hilted sword in a bronze scabbard. The man was tall and stocky, with bulging sinews and powerful legs. He had a great curly black beard and dark brown eyes that pierced like iron spear points. His face and attire marked him as a Danite mercenary, but he bore himself like a prince. Catching note of the tavern keeper's stare, he grunted, "Well, why do you stare?"

Jephthah motioned for the man to come and take a seat at the counter. The man came, sat himself down on a stool, and waited as Jephthah filled a skin with wine. "From whither came you?" he asked.

"I have been serving as a mercenary in the army of Shalmaneser of Assyria. The blood of a warrior flows in my veins. My father fought under Joshua when our people first came into this land, and he fought by my side when our fellow tribesmen took this city seven years ago. Since then I have been wondering throughout the land, seeking adventure."

"What think you of Shalmaneser?" grunted the tavern keeper.

"I am proud to say that he is the most honorable Assyrian I have ever encountered, and I have encountered many an Assyrian these last seven years."

"Honorable! Bah!" the tavern keeper spat. "If you call blinding fourteen thousand prisoners after his defeat of Shattuara honorable!"

"But Shattuara had blocked all the surrounding wells. He had no other alternative. We were dying of thirst. Would you not call this little deed of wrath honorable after almost dying of thirst?"

"Honorable, you say! That pig of a king you call honorable is the lowliest worm to ever crawl the earth."

"You dare …!" thundered the Danite as his hand shot to the hilt of his sword. But the wary tavern keeper had sensed this outburst coming and made good use of the wine jar in his right hand and, with a great upward motion of his arm, brought the jar dead-center into the unsuspecting man's face. The world around the Danite blurred and soon all was utter blackness.

Darkness. Utter darkness. Pools of color formed and receded, formed and receded. The Danite felt as though he was bobbing up and down, up and down incessantly. The dark mists cleared and the man found himself lying on a floor of pure lapis lazuli at the foot of a broad staircase. He suddenly heard, clearly and distinctly, a voice that was like the sound of many rushing waters.

"Ben-Herev, Son of the Sword, hearken to me!"

The voice seemed to be coming from atop the staircase. Slowly, Ben-Herev began to ascend the stair. Each step was carved with the eight-pointed star of the Amorites and the Assyrian winged god Asshur. As Ben-Herev's foot past over these engravings, they crumbled into dust.

Finally reaching the top, Ben-Herev gaped in awe as he beheld the most powerful man he had ever seen. He sat upon a great carven stone chair. His hair was long and as red as burning coals. His eyes pierced the Danite like arrows. His sinews were like iron chords, bulging from beneath his garment. He was clothed in a great white toga. An iron muscled curaiss protected his chest, and a large iron falcata hung in a gold sheath at his waist. Opals laid in gold adorned his golden belt.

"Ben-Herev!" thundered the giant. "I have come to you with a message from the LORD Most High: 'Behold, I have called you, as I called Abraham your father before you, to be a wanderer upon the earth, biting the heels of the unrighteous, like an adder by the path. This is My sign to you.'"

The seraph drew his sword and scratched the symbol of the Adder, the battle standard of the tribe of Dan, upon the shield.

For a moment, Ben-Herev stared down at his buckler, dumbfounded. Then he lifted his head and looked at the seraph.

"But why me?" he asked, bewildered. "I am no one of consequence."

"Centuries from now, it will be said that the LORD uses the foolish things of the World to confound the wise. Now, Ben-Herev, awake!"

Ben-Herev sat up, rubbed the swollen knot on his forehead, and looked around. He was in one of the rooms in The Black Lion. The tavern keeper had apparently summoned all the strength he possessed, and had carried the Danite up the stairs.

He looked at the bedside table whereupon lay his equipment. Upon the boss of his buckler was inscribed the symbol of an Adder snake. The dream had been real!

As Ben-Herev was pondering this, Jephthah walked into the room, carrying a trough with a loaf of bread and a pitcher of goat's milk upon it. Upon seeing the man, Ben-Herev cautiously cleared his throat.

"Sir, I hope you will forgive me for the way I acted last night."

The innkeeper smiled. "Think nothing of it, man. Your head was full of the drink and you knew not what you did. Be assured of this: you shall always have a friend in Jephthah of Dan."

Ben-Herev got up, donned his armor, paid the tavern keeper, and sallied out from the city of his people, as Abraham his forefather did before him, following the path to which the LORD had called him.

*Philistines

II. The Brotherhood of the Adder

The next day, Ben-Herev journeyed northeast into Sidonian territory. He had no idea where he was being led. All he knew was that the LORD was his guide and he trusted in Him.

Ben-Herev stopped in a small hamlet that evening and purchased a horse named Balaam. The next morning he continued northeast. At midday he stopped to break his fast. As he was sitting under a hyssop tree he heard the sound of iron scraping against bronze. He turned his head, hand slowly moving towards hilt. But when he looked behind him, there was nothing there. He had barely turned back to his food, when he heard a piercing cry of "Aaai!" Suddenly, there was a wiry figure upon his back, its nails digging like a vulture's talon into his neck. He threw the man forward over his head onto the dirt road. It was then that he felt an iron point on the back of his neck. Slowly, he turned around. As he did so, he came face to face with a Cushitic man with an iron spear swung at throat level. He stepped back two paces and saw that the two men were not alone. There were two other wiry men armed like Ben-Herev's attacker, with iron-bladed daggers. They were Hebrews by the look of them. They wore red tunics covered with boiled leather. There was a huge Sidonian of bulging thews who stood about a head taller than the Danite. He was clad in an Assyrian lamellar shirt and carried a large Cretan double-bladed battle axe. The Nubian, who was holding Balaam's lead, wore a bronze scale mail shirt with a white tunic underneath and a cylindrical bronze Egyptian helm.

"You have no doubt heard of the five lords of the Philistines," the Philistine said. "We are the five lords of Philistine thieves."

"Try to steal from me and I'll cut you to pieces," hissed the Danite from behind clenched teeth.

"Then perhaps we should come to a different understanding," said the Nubian. "Share your resources with us and we will share in your adventures."

"Fair enough," said Ben-Herev. "But how am I to trust you?"

"Though we are thieves," one of the lithe Hebrews said, "our word is our honor."

"Very well. What is your name, then?"

"I am Akuba the Nubian. And this," he said, motioning to the giant Sidonian, "Is Abimalech of Giresh. These," he said, indicating the Hebrews, "are the sons of Zakar: Issachar, Naphtali and Reuben."

"You are all scoundrels," mused the Danite. "And I like you all the better for it."

The men sat down and had some food. When they had finished, they began discussing their plan of action.

"We could go back to my city for the night and make our plans in the morning," suggested Abimalech. "I'd live there permanently if it wasn't for Phichol."

At the mention of this name, anger welled up inside the Danite, and he did not understand why.

"Who is this Phichol?"

"The lord of the city. A more tyrannical one you will never find. Just the other night, he murdered one of his concubines for resisting him."

"I like him not," said the Danite. "But it is a good plan. Let us go."

***

The market of Giresh was alive with the buzzing noises of buying and selling. Customers haggled with merchants over prices of dates, wine and melons. Merchants yelled out the quality of their goods to passersby. The whole area was alive with the sights and sounds of trade.

As Ben-Herev and his new companions passed by a baker's shop, they heard the sound of a scuffle. Going around the side of the shop, they beheld a girl, evidently the baker's daughter, struggling against two brawny guards.

"Give us a kiss, pretty!" one of the guards snarled.

"No! No!" the girl screamed, kicking and flailing wildly.

Ben-Herev grabbed a nearby clay jar, and, with all the force he could muster, hurled it at the back of the guard's helmeted head. It came crashing down, causing the guard to crumple to the ground, blood flowing freely from his head. Akuba ran forward, swung the butt of his spear in a great semi-circular arc and brought across the teeth of the other guard. This knocked the man down to the ground on his back. Another guard came around the corner and saw the stunned men.

"Stop!" he screamed.

The small party ran around the corner and tore towards the gate, the guard following at their heels. As they came towards the gate, they were met by a battalion of guards entering the city.

"Stop them!" the pursuing guard screamed. "They wounded members of the royal guard!"

The entire battalion pounced on them and overcame them by sheer weight. In the blink of an eye, they were bound in shackles and were being led away to the judgment seat of the city.

They were taken to a large courtyard of sandstone. In the center was a large fountain flowing crystalline water. A large seat of carven sandstone sat up against the northern wall, facing the fountain. Upon this throne sat a Sidonian. He was of powerful sinews, though not nearly as strong as the Danite or his Philistine companion. The man's hard, cold brown eyes seemed to bore through the Danite. A cold sneer was upon the man's stone lips. A silver circlet sat upon a disorderly mat of brown hair. The man was clad in a black satin robe with a silver sash. He wore gold-threaded sandals on his feet. He beheld his audience with a discriminatory air and said, "My men tell me that you have wounded two of my personal bodyguards. Is this true?"

"It is sire," said the Danite, inclining his head slightly. "But they were attempting to ravish a girl. We were only trying to protect her."

"I allow my men to do as they like. Therefore, you stand in contempt of me."

He clapped his hands twice, and the guards that had escorted them there came forward.

"Take them out to the town square and flog them."

The guards grabbed the Danite and his companion and took them forcibly out of the courtyard.

***

Thwap! The spiked whip tore into the Danite's flesh and stung like the adder's bite. Thwap! The blood poured down Ben-Herev's back. Thwap! The Danite gritted his teeth and starred straight ahead.

From a divan on the opposite side of the square, Phichol watched the proceedings with cold mocking eyes.

"Enough!" he commanded, raising his hand. "Unbind them, give them their weapons and let them go."

Ben-Herev and his friends were untied from the whipping posts and given back their weapons. As soon as Akuba received his spear, he started toward Phichol, a look of vengeance on his face. Ben-Herev quickly caught him by the arm and said, "Hold! I have a plan!"

They walked in abject shame from the city. Turning back to it, Ben-Herev vowed that he would one day exact his vengeance on Phichol.

That night they camped near the hyssop tree where Ben-Herev had rested. The Danite ate and drank his fill, and then fell into a deep sleep. Lightning flashed in the sky of Ben-Herev's troubled mind. Suddenly, he stood in the courtyard of Phichol, but it had changed. The walls, floor, fountain and throne were covered with lapis lazuli, and upon the walls laid in gold was the adder of Dan. Upon the throne sat the seraph that had come to Ben-Herev in Dan.

"I have come to you with a message from the LORD," the seraph said in a deep, resonant voice. "Thus says the LORD: 'Behold, I have brought you out of the city which your people call home and to Giresh. I give it to you now. It is your destiny to become its lord. I have given you allies whom you can trust and have given you great strength with which to accomplish your purpose. This is my sign unto you.'

Thus saying, the seraph reached out and touched the adder upon the Danite's shield. It instantly fell onto the floor and became a living creature. It slithered stealthily across the floor, apparently looking for something. Then, from behind the throne slither great cobra with the symbol of a Sidonian trading galley emblazoned on the back of its hood. It slithered up behind the adder and poised itself to strike. Then, the adder whirled around and sank its teeth deep into the cobra's neck and held it until the cobra fell dead on the floor. Then it slithered back to the Danite and dissolved back into the shield boss.

"Now," said the seraph, "awake and return to your city and gather your friends about you."

***

Ben-Herev awoke with a start. He sat up and saw that the first pink rays of the sun shown in the east. He looked around him and saw that the others still slept. He hurriedly awoke the others and said he had something very important to tell them.

He stood on top of a great stone and shouted, "Now hear me! I have received a message from the LORD Almighty. He tells me that it is my destiny to overthrow the tyrant Phichol and rule as the new lord of Giresh. We could very successfully make raids on Giresh in the night, and escape back to the city of Dan before morning. I know just the man we can trust. He is an innkeeper in the city. Are you with me or against me?"

For a long moment the group stood silent and irresolute. Then, stepping forward with a bold air, Rueben said, "I am!"

"As are we!" his brothers exclaimed.

"I am with you!" bellowed Abimalech.

"And I," said Akuba.

"So be it!" the Danite said, stepping down from the stone. "Let us be off!"

The small party mounted their steeds and took off like bolts of lightning toward Dan. They thundered through the gate, making such a ruckus that the guard upon the tower thought an earthquake had struck. They dashed through the crooked streets as if there were wolves biting at their mounts' hooves. At last, they came to screeching halt in front of *The Black Lion*.

Ben-Herev immediately dismounted and began banging heartily on the door. After a few seconds, the door opened and a bewildered Jephthah stared wide-eyed at his muscular caller.

Grabbing the poor man's shoulders, Ben-Herev exclaimed, "Jephthah, my old friend, I have heard from the LORD!"

"Wait! Wait!" blubbered Jephthah, by this time very flustered.

Regaining his composure somewhat the Danite said, "I am sorry my friend! It is just that the LORD has made my destiny clear to me."

He went inside, sat down at a table and motioned for the others to come and sit.

"Jephthah," said the Danite panting, "These are Issachar, Naphtali, Rueben, Abimalech and Akuba. I met them yesterday on the northern road. I went to the town of Giresh and met its lord, the despicable Phichol. He had us flogged for helping a poor girl who was being taken advantage of by two of his bodyguards. That night, the angel of the LORD came to me, just as he did here two nights ago. He told me it was my destiny to rid Giresh of Phichol and become its lord. If we can base our operations here, we could carry out raids on Giresh at nightfall. Albeit it would only be a thumb in Piccolo's eye, it is at least a beginning. What say you?"

A smile spread across the innkeeper's face. "I know you to be a God-fearing man, Ben-Herev. If that is truly your destiny, I would be honored to take part in it."

The innkeeper then stood, walked behind the counter and returned with an Assyrian bow.

"I was quite a shot in my day. I believe it's time I try my hand at it again!"

"Excellent!" The Danite laughed. He went outside and came back with his buckler. Placing it on the table he said, "let us swear an oath: to fight side by side for justice until it is attained."

"We will fight!" swore the others, placing their hands on the shield.

"Good!" said Ben-Herev triumphantly, slapping his hand down on the boss. "Henceforth, we shall be the Brotherhood of the Adder."

III. The Assyrian Riders

And the might of the Gentile, unsmote by the sword,
Hath melted like snow in the glance of the Lord! Lord Byron

The torchlight flickered upon the tapestries in the palace of Phichol. The distraught lord sat on a divan, nervously sipping a goblet of red wine. The massive bronze doors swung in and the captain of the guard stepped through the doorway. He bowed and then delivered his report.

"Another kilo of gold has disappeared from the treasury, sire," he said apologetically. "Another symbol was found in its place." So saying, he produced a piece of wood with the symbol of an adder snake etched upon it.

Phichol snatched up the block, and with apparent disdain hurled it to the floor.

"What am I to do, Malech?!" he screamed. "This accursed Brotherhood of the Adder has pulled my beard too many a time! I have set traps for them, sent out battalions to annihilate them, and yet they still plague me! That Ben-Herev has become a legend in Dan! I must get rid of him! But how?"

"Send a message to Hemar, lord of Akesh, requesting his cavalry units. The next time they make a raid, we will trample them like dust with five hundred cavalry."

"That is the first intelligent thing you said since I met you," Phichol snickered. Outside the palace walls, a blind peddler disappeared into the shadows.

***

Akuba rode swiftly back to Dan. Coming through the door of the Black Lion, he said, "Phichol means to trap us. He has sent for the cavalry units of Hemar of Akesh. The next raid we make, he will send them down upon us."

Ben-Herev stared into the fire burning on the hearth. He sat pensively for a moment, and then stood. "I know how to deal with this complication. But I do not know if I have enough time."

The sun shone down upon the as Ben-Herev rode to the bandits' camp. The camp was full of Assyrian horsemen. An Assyrian with a scar underneath his left eye looked up and saw Ben-Herev coming.

"Ah! Ben-Herev! I have not seen you for many months! Not since Shalmaneser gouged out the eyes of Shattuara's men! What do you here?"

"I have need of your men and horses," the Danite said.

"You must prove yourself again!" the Assyrian shouted, running up and striking him with clubbed fists.

"So be it!"

The Danite gave the Assyrian so hard a blow, it sent him flying backwards.

"You win!" the Assyrian yelled. "I shall be your ally!"

***

The town of Giresh lay quietly asleep. At the gates, Phichol waited at the head of five hundred cavalry. A solitary figure rode through the open gate, carrying a ram's horn. The gate was open because Phichol thought he need no longer fear the Brotherhood of the Adder. Ben-Herev reined his horse to a halt in front of Phichol.

"I will give you one chance, and just one, to surrender."

"Ha! Surely you do not think me that foolish, Hebrew!"

Phichol opened his mouth to give the command to charge, but before he could the Danite's horn blared in the night. Two thousand Assyrian horsemen poured through the gates and surrounded Phichol's horsemen.

Ben-Herev dismounted, drew his sword, and came forward. He declared, "I claim this place in the Name of the LORD God of Israel!" Thus saying he pulled Phichol off his horse and ran him through.

By this time, the townspeople had gathered about the front gate. They heartily cheered their new lord. Suddenly, Ben-Herev beheld the young woman he had saved from Phichol's guards several months before. He came to her and said, "What is your name?"

"Ankara, my lord."

"You shall be my queen and this town shall worship the true God!"

That is how Ben-Herev became lord of Giresh. How the city prospered under his reign. Ben-Herev won great renown throughout the country of the Sidonians and Israelites. But these are also other stories.

Barbarian Brothers

Before the fall of mighty Rome, there were barbarian lords. Their city walls were large round shields, their towers blades of swords.

(Chalons, AD 451)

Barbarians stab Rome in the chest
As her golden sun sinks in the West.

"The king is dead!" The shout echoed across the blood-washed field. Athanaric wiped his sweaty brow with the back of his hand. He looked behind him, and there he saw it. The body of Theodoric. Theodoric, the greatest Visigothic king since Alaric, was dead, killed by a Hunnic spear. For an instant, the entire regiment was in a state of panic. Then confusion abated and the entire front line ran forward in a red haze of fury. A monstrous cry of "CHARGE!" burst from the throats of the Visigoths as they charged downhill and broke the fierce Hunnic horse line. Their Roman allies followed suit, swinging spathas-an elongation of the *gladius*, or Roman short sword-and throwing pilums, their long, keen spear points inflicting deadly wounds on the Hunnic horsemen. The Hunnic line fell back like stalks of wheat before the scythe. Attila, their king, tried again and again to rally them, waving his so-called sword of Mars above his head like a battle standard. But the Hunnic line could not stand against the combined force of the Roman legionnaires and Visigothic warriors. The line was driven back and back, until it finally broke into a full retreat. The Battle of the Chalons was over.

***

I came solitarily
To the fields of Chalons.
But, when I left the place,
I left it not alone.

-The Song of Ilka

Athanaric's moved silently through the corpse-strewn field, as carrion birds searched for prey and insects scurried among the bodies. What the Romans said was true: "*Cadavera Vero innumera*": truly countless bodies. Athanaric paused and looked at his reflection on the blade of his sword. It was a long-bladed sword, the Germanic kind that would give rise to the swords of the middle ages. Its guard was short, and its pommel was semicircular, similar to the pommels of the swords used by the Visigoths' "cousins", the Vikings and the Saxons in the centuries to come. He was a fine-looking boy of sixteen. The steel cap on his head partially covered his light brown curly hair. Hs brown eyes sullenly stared at his reflection. He was about five feet tall with broad shoulder and powerful legs. As he stood gazing at his bloody visage, Athanaric suddenly became aware of a slight rustling sound. He looked to his right and saw, to his horror, a Hun struggling up from beneath a Visigothic shield. The man was clad in a leather scale mail hauberk and wore a fur-lined conical Hunnic helm under which his tangled raven locks fell in a disorderly fashion. Hard brown eyes above a bloody black beard stared at the young Visigoth. The man was about nine years the young man's senior. A single-edged Hunnic sword, which looked more like a long knife, hung at his side and a double-curved bow of wood and bone hung from a baldric on his back. He had a look of terror and bewilderment upon his face.

For a moment, the two stared at each other, neither one daring to speak. Then the Hun started and exclaimed, "Please do not kill me!"

Athanaric had learned something of the Scythian dialects from his travels with his countrymen, so he was able to understand the man's speech. Athanaric took off his sword and laid it on the blood-stained ground as a sign of peacemaking. The Hun understood and smiled.

"I am Ilka," the Hun said. "What do you call yourself?"

"I am Athanaric, son of Amalric."

The man drew his sword, and holding it on his palms, knelt before Athanaric.

"I make a sacred vow to you. I vow that I will fight by your side for the rest of my life and love you as a son and as a brother."

Athanaric nodded solemnly and offered the Hunnic man his hand. They grasped each others' forearm tightly. The man stood to his feet and they both walked back to the Visigothic encampment. Little did Athanaric know how much his life was changed in that moment.

***

And now upon the Western lands
There comes a mighty Eastern man.

Athanaric and Ilka picked their way through the Visigothic encampment. The warriors were busy casting lots, eating meat, and cleaning their blood-stained weapons. As they walked by, several men glanced warily at Ilka, but he paid them no heed. They finally came to the tent of Thorismund, Theodoric's son.

The new king sat on a chair covered with purple cloth. He was clad in a golden scale mail shirt, and a small golden circlet adorned his head. Behind him trailed a cape of purple satin. Although he did not look it, he was only a few years the boy's senior. Athanaric knelt before him and inclined his head.

"My lord, this is Ilka, a valiant warrior whom I found while scouring the battlefield. If it pleases you, Your Majesty, spare his life, for he has sworn an oath of loyalty to me."

The young king paused for a moment, deep in thought. Then, slowly, he rose from his throne.

"Athanaric, your sword has been of great value to my father's forces, and as it is customary for kings such as myself to give boons to their soldiers, I see it fitting to grant your request. He has the look of a fighter," the king said as he beheld the man, "and his skill with the bow would be very useful to us."

"My lord," said Athanaric, "I have served three years in your army, and it is now my desire to go out into the world with this man and win my fortune."

"And so you shall," said the king with a slight smile on his lips as he placed his hand on Athanaric's shoulder. "But wait until my father's soul has entered Valhalla."

***

The sun was low, setting in the West as the funeral pyre of Theodoric was prepared. Battle chants from ancient Gotland and Germania were sung and many fine works of gold and silver were placed upon the pyre.

The king was born out on a stretcher by four of his retainers. He was clad in a scale mail hauberk and a purple cape hung about his shoulders. His battle sword was laid across his chest and his crown was upon his head. His burnished helm was laid beside him. The battle standard of the Visigoths waved slightly in the cool evening breeze.

Thorismund came forward, bearing a torch. They were going to cremate the body, for, though Arian, a select few of the Visigoths held to the old tribal Germanic beliefs of their forefathers. The body was placed upon the pyre. Thorismund walked to the pyre and, for a moment, looked at the surrounding warriors. Then, he threw his head back and with a loud cry of "Woden!" threw the torch upon the pyre. The wood was soaked in pitch, so it caught fire quickly. Then the air was split by the sound of ten thousand swords upon ten thousand shields. Battle cries soared to the sky like screaming eagles. One of the greatest warrior kings to ever live was going to Valhalla that night.

And now upon the plains of Gaul
There come two alone
Who find, one day,
That they may
Live off the fat of Rome.

Today upon the plains of Gaul
It is now told
How Hun and Goth did speak of
The songs and deeds of old.

***

While upon the plains of Gaul
I was a'riding,
I was told of warriors bold
And of a mighty king.
-The Song of Ilka

Athanaric walked quietly to his tent that night, donned his hauberk, helm, strapped on his sword and slung his shield on his shoulder. He then went to the stable and saddled his horse, Athaulf. He picked out a great black stallion for Ilka, and came back to where he waited. Ilka had picked out a blackened mail coif from the armory and came out with it upon his head. It was now time to depart.

Athanaric looked back over his shoulder at the Visigothic encampment, and, strangely enough, tears welled up in his eyes. For three years Theodoric's legions were all he had known. Those men were his countryman and he would never forget them. But the compulsive yearning for adventure and excitement that lies in the hearts of all men tugged at his heart, and, he turned his head and tightened the saddle.

The two young men mounted their horses, spurred them, and set off at a canter. After they had ridden several miles, Athanaric glanced at his companion and said, "Ho! Sing me a song of Scythia, and I shall sing you one of Germania." "As you wish," Ilka said. He looked up at the sky and cleared his throat.

"Out on mists so gray and grim,
The War God whets his sword
Every hour expecting the coming of the great lord.
The Four Winds blow,
The mountains grow
To quite a monstrous size.
The red blood runs,
The King of Huns
Comes riding 'neath the skies
And yet the fire does not cool
In the Great War God's eyes.
Empires are ours
Greater than Rome
And built of blood,
And not of stone."

"That is a mighty song, my friend," Athanaric said. "Now, I shall sing to you the ballad of the great king Hermann, who slew the mighty legions of Rome long ago."

"The River Rhine runs red with blood
Of many a legionnaire.
Their many pleas and frightened screams
Ripple through the air.
The sons of Thor are led to battle
By mighty Hermann.
The sound of his name

Rings with fame
To every good German.
For on that day the Dragon's blood
He spilt upon the stone.
With upraised sword, the battle lord
Slew the giant of Rome."

"That is a great song indeed, my friend," Ilka mused.

"It is passed down from generation to generation among my people, and other nations as well. Of mighty Hermann and how he crushed the legions of Octavius centuries ago."

"Tell me the tale of your life, my friend," Ilka said.

"I was born in Germania, just beyond the Gallic border. My father and I joined Theodoric's army three years ago. We left to fight with the Romans at Orleans. He was killed during the siege, and I returned to the army continued to fight until I found you."

"Attila raided my village when I was a lad," Ilka said softly. "His warriors killed my mother and father and I was raised by his horsemen. I fought under him from the beginning of his campaign, and continued to do so until I encountered you at Chalons."

"And come what may," Athanaric said, "I'm glad to have you with me, my friend."

***

They rode on and continued south. Evening came, and they came to the city that would later be called Troyes after the invasion of the Franks. Little did they know that they had come to the place where the Frankish kings would be crowned in centuries to come. They came through the north gate of the city and were proceeding down the main street when they heard shouts coming from the left side of the street. Looking in that direction, they beheld a small brawl taking place in the doorway of one of the wineries lining the street.

Four Roman guards were engaged in combat with a strange priest. He was endeavoring to shield an old beggar from the Roman onslaught, and was holding his own quite stoutly. The priest was clad in a dark brown habit and a plaid sash hung over his right shoulder. He had the look of a Gaul of Julius Caesar's day. Long brown hair flowed down from his head and a short moustache sat upon his upper lip. He had the look of a druid of ancient Gaul. He was armed with a gladius, the kind used by the legionnaires of Rome in centuries past.

Spurring their horses forward, they galloped toward the fray. Ilka slid his Hunnic bow from its baldric and took an arrow from his quiver. Thwang! The arrow sailed into a Roman neck, forcing the man down to the ground, gurgling blood. Athanaric whipped out his sword and sent it up and down, up and down in a bloody arc. The battle fury of the Germanic peoples engulfed his mind, and all was a red haze before his eyes. Forcing his way through the knot of soldiers, Ilka grabbed the priest, hoisted him up, and set him on the saddle behind him. Once this was done, the three riders bolted back through the north gate and galloped down the rode until they had left the city far behind them.

**

And now upon the plains of Gaul
There comes a holy man.
His mission is to spread True Light
Throughout all the land.

"Thank Jesu you came!" exclaimed the priest. "I surely would have gone up to third heaven had you not come to my rescue."

"Think nothing of it, father," Athanaric said. "My companion and I are friends to the helpless."

"I am Vercenius, a wanderer on the earth and missionary to the entire empire. Many years have I journeyed the world, proclaiming the word of the LORD."

"Then you are in strange company," mused Athanaric, "for we are men of war, not of the cloth."

"A warrior's heritage is mine, nonetheless," said the priest. "My ancestors fought under Vercingetorix when Julius Caesar first came into this land. But I have been redeemed by Jesu's blood. I am now a warrior of the cross."

Athanaric was familiar with Arianism, as it was popular among his people. However, he had never heard someone speak of Christ with such fervor and devotion. He was, no doubt, intrigued by this man.

Athanaric had also heard of the Roman defeat of which the priest spoke. A Germanic prince, a certain Aermanric, who was of far greater fame than Hermann, had made a pact with wolf demons in order to defeat the Romans in battle. He had later been captured years later and put to death, but the people of Germania still sang songs of his brave deeds and his great iron war hammer.

"Whither go you?" asked the priest.

"We know not. We go where our wandering hearts lead us."

"A life without purpose is an empty thing. Such was mine before I encountered the Grace Everlasting. But now I know that the LORD will guide me where he wants to go."

"How can you trust so blindly in this God of yours?" Athanaric asked.

"Why should I not? For He is the One who laid the very foundations of the earth, and set the stars in their place."

Athanaric smiled. He was beginning to like this priest in spite of himself.

***

After all these years of blood and tears
Of war and constant strife,
Comes clarity and purpose,
Meaning for my life.

-The Song of Ilka

They continued to ride north, camping at night on the plain. Athanaric observed the priest carefully. He kept an eye on him as he fingered his rosary beads and said his evening prayers. He had never encountered a man such as this. He truly practiced what he preached. Once, when they saw a small group of Ostrogoths bearing a silver chest, Vercenius stayed Athanaric's hand as it shot to the hilt of his sword. The man could fight, but whenever he could, he abstained. He had a soft demeanor which could touch the heart of the most savage barbarian. And he possessed a certain power which commanded respect from all he met. Athanaric felt a strong tugging at his heart that he did not quite understand whenever Vercenius was near. A strange feeling of longing enveloped Athanaric like a misty shadow. A confused mess of thoughts constantly raced through his mind. He had gone out into the world to make his fortune, hadn't he? And yet, there was something in the priest's manner that made Athanaric desirous of that special something, that secret source of joy and inner peace Vercenius possessed. Because of these thoughts, he had difficulty sleeping at night. Ilka, it seemed, was likewise affected. However, the two warrior never spoke of it.

***

One night, as Athanaric was eating supper, the priest came and sat down beside him. Ilka was sitting on the other side of the fire, sharpening his sword. "Athanaric," Vercenius said, "where do you think you will go when you die?"

"If I show myself to be brave and courageous in battle, I shall go to the halls of Valhalla as my fathers did before me."

"And what is the fate of those who do not die in battle?"

"They suffer for eternity in Nephliheim."

"A rather bleak prospect to be sure," the priest observed. "Far better to lay faith in Jesu and His blood."

"I know the doctrine, priest," Athanaric scoffed, casting his eyes to the sky. "Mankind was sinful so the Father created the Son for our redemption."

"But you do not understand, my boy," Vercenius chided. "The Son was with the Father before the foundation of the world. They are One, and have always been so. Because sin entered the world through a man, it must be by a man that sin is conquered. Such a man must be pure and only God is pure. Therefore, by becoming a man, God made it possible for us to enter into his forgiveness."

"How can you believe this without proof?" Athanaric asked, bewildered.

"My LORD said once that blessed are those who do not see and yet believe."

At that moment, Athanaric felt that strange tugging at his heart intensely. He fell to his knees, and, in tears, said, "baptize me father, I want my sins to be forgiven."

"And I as well!" Ilka exclaimed, suddenly standing to his feet.

The priest left for a moment and returned with cupped hands full of water.

Athanaric and Ilka knelt on the grass as the priest sprinkled the water on their bare heads.

"I now baptise you *en nomine Patri et Fili et Spiritu Sancti*." The young men felt like leaping for joy. Never in their lives had they felt this way before. It was as if a huge burden had just been lifted from their souls, and was replaced instantly by an overwhelming feeling of peace.

After celebrating and giving thanks to their new God, they went inside the tent and went to sleep.

Athanaric was awakened by the sound of savage yelling. He snatched up his sword and raced outside. Outside he beheld a small band of Franks, riding horses, the first of many to invade Gaul in the coming years. They were yelling wild battle cries, waving their franciscas above their heads wildly, the bearded axe blades shimmering like silver in the moonlight. Ilka emerged from the tent and proceeded to launch several arrows into unsuspecting Frankish throats. Athanaric yowled a fierce battle cry and plunged headlong into the fray. Vercenius emerged from the tent, swinging his gladius franticly. In an instant, the three were caught up in red haze of battle, hacking and slashing wildly. Slowly but surely the Franks gave way, finally breaking into a full retreat.

Panting and wheezing from exertion, Athanaric and Ilka stumbled back to camp. They were met by a horrifying sight that stopped the blood, ice cold in their veins. There lay Vercenius, gasping for breath, drenched in a pool of his own blood, a francisca protruded from his back. They ran to him and supporting his weight between them, carried him into the tent and laid him upon a blanket.

"Athanaric," the priest gasped, grabbing the young Visigoth's mail shirt, "the torch has fallen from my hand. I pass it on to you. Swear that you will take it, both of you."

"We swear," Athanaric said, tears welling up in his eyes.

"Good," the priest said. "Then by the crystal sea shall I see you."

Thus saying, his body grew stiff, and the calming touch of death stole over him.

Epilogue: A New Life

And now, upon the plains of Gaul
There come two alone,
Their hopeful eyes fixed heavenward,
Their purpose set in stone.

They bore the body out upon the open plain and buried it where Vercenius had fallen. After saying a prayer and a psalm, they bid each other farewell and went their separate ways. Athanaric returned to Germania and Ilka to Scythia and there they spread the True Light among their people, never forgetting each other, or the kind priest they met on the plains of Gaul.

The End

The Song of Ilka

When I was young,
A group of Huns
Upon my village came.
Killing Mother and Father,
They set the huts aflame.

The hot red tears
Came flooding down
My dirt-ridden face.
They had killed my people,
These men of my same race.

I was raised upon the steppes
By warriors of the Huns
They treated with fairness
As one of their sons.

Then there came mighty Attila,
Uniting the tribes
Some were won by the sword,
Others won by bribes.

Then I fought
Under his banner
'Til we reached Chalons.
Roman and Goth
Drove him back,
Fleeing to his home.

I came solitarily
To the fields of Chalons.
But when I left the place,
I left it not alone.

A strapping strong young Visigoth
Was my new ally.
The reason he befriended me,

I do not know why.

While upon the plains of Gaul
I was a'riding,
I was told of warriors bold
And of a mighty king.

Then upon the plains of Gaul
A wandering priest we met.
Though I did not know it,
My life would better yet.

The good message
Of Jesu's blood
He did with him bring,
And of the resurrection
Of the Mighty King.

After all these years of blood and tears
Of war and constant strife,
Comes clarity and purpose,
Meaning for my life.

So now back to Scythia
I shall ride.
I am now a warrior
On a different side.

I go back to Scythia
The great True Light to bring,
And the awesome message

Sir Vaelen and the Angel

Sir Vaelen donned his hauberk and great helm

And his yellow surcoat with a green tree of elm.

He took up his lance, and his yellow shield,

And rode forth for honor over the green fields.

He rode till he came to a darkening wood,

Where the trees like bastions before him stood.

He steeled himself and rode ever on,

Till he could not tell the night from the dawn.

He rose through the mist coming up from the ground

Until he heard a high and shrill sound.

Coming to a clearing like unto a glade

He saw to one side a beautiful maid.

She was clad in white, in a gown of lace.

Fear was written plainly on her face.

On the other side, trying to burn

Was a terrible fire-breathing wyvern.

Uttering a cry of "For the right!"

Sir Vaelen charged forth, the wyvern to fight.

Swinging down his sword, which was named Darkbane,

Sir Vaelen split the beast's head in twain.

He raised his shield up emblazoned with the tree.

The woman said, "What do you ask of me?"

Sir Vaelen fought for the King of Light.

He replied, "Naught do I ask for this fight."
The lady smiled. "You have spoken true.

Therefore I have a gift meant for you.
I am an angel of the King of Light.

I bestow upon you holy gifts for the fight."

She touched his hand and gave him power

To give him strength in his darkest hour.

He found that then nothing he feared.

Then the fair angel, she disappeared.

Vaelen rode forth, seeking more wrongs to right.

He had received the Baptism of Light.

Gefellanernacht

This poem is for my sister, Greta, who held my hand while my mind sojourned in darkness. I can think of no better way to tell of my very real adventures while separated from the rest of the world than in verse. On June 1, 1918, while fighting on the Western Front, I sustained a severe shrapnel injury to the head. I awoke a week ago at the Army Hospital in Salzburg. Greta told me that she and mother had been praying and praying for my recovery, and at times it didn't seem that I would last. I know why I held out.

And this is why I write.

Siegfried Baumer, November 11, 1918

I woke up in front of a cave

In a mist-enshrouded land.

Before me on a horse was an old man

Holding a shining brand.

He was clad in bright plate mail

Shining like bits of white shale.

And his beard was long and white,

Shining like the moon at night.

He bowed and said,

"I am Gotz von Engel.

Paladin of Konig-Engel.

The deed you must do now, though you are shocked

Is slay the dragon Gefellanernacht.

You must do this thing, then

For you to see Greta again.

Take my equipment, I'll go with you.

The armor will give you strength anew."

I couldn't slay a wyrm or even a calf

And yet what choice did I have!

I took the battle gear.

'Twas amazingly light!

We went into the cave to the fight

We pressed on for an eternity, the sword gave us light.

It pierced the darkness throughout the whole

Even the dark night of my soul.

We came upon the serpent of fire

Who opened his maw in anger and ire

And yet I did not know fear,

For Gotz sang hymns in my ear.

I felt caught in a stormy sea

And the belly of hell belched fire at me.

Just as I thought I'd soon be dead,

I hewed off the fell wyrm's head.

I looked at the knight of muscled girth

Who laughed aloud with much mirth.

"Very well, faithful young hind.

You've passed through the dark night of your mind."

Faded from view the holy brother,

And I saw my sister and mother.

Sharpening the Blade

In the halls of heaven,

Where await the Seven

For the word of the Lord,

The Commander Michael whets

The blade no holy smith regrets,

Redeemer of unholy debts,

The holy seraph sword

To be delivered to the Son,

The only holy righteous One,

The day of battle to be won

Wielding the blade of His Word.

The Lamb, mighty in word and deed,

Fire coming from his steed,

Shall cause the Enemy to bleed.

All shall be restored.

Hare-Strider

Prologue

Steelclaw, the great falcon, flew over the icy mountain-backed landscape. A cool breeze clipped his wings as his keen eyes scanned the village below, searching for his master. Rays of light from the seldom-seen summer sun painted the village of Badgerstede a golden hue. These beams and sparkles of golden cheer caused the hearty badger folk to abandon their grave, slightly volatile demeanor, for the sun seldom showed her face in their icy, mountainous homeland of Ykkelunde. The country was, after all, aptly named the land of ice.

Steelclaw circled the village of the badgers as he screeched into the wind. The village was surrounded by a great palisade of pointed stakes of ash wood. In the center of the north wall was the only entrance: a gate formed by two doors that swung inward on iron hinges. These could be barred in case of a siege.

In the center of the village was a badger builder's masterpiece, the Great Hall, the longhouse of the Lord of Badgerstede. It was built of hardened ash braced with polished steel. The doors were carven with the image of a great battle hammer crossed with a double-bladed axe, the badgers' battle standard. Steelclaw flew in through the great hole in the thatched roof of the Hall.

The elders of the tribe were in deep discussion with Cerdic Steel-Arm, Lord of Badgerstede, concerning their plan of action for the coming winter.

The auburn falcon alighted on the leather-gauntleted wrist of Cerdic Steel-Arm of Badgerstede. The chieftain was extremely tall and had shoulders almost as mighty as those of an ox. His chest was broad and muscular beneath his mail. His eyes burned with the fire of intelligence and shrewdness, qualities of a tactful, able king. Over his hauberk he wore a heavy curaiss of boiled dark brown leather. In a baldric on his back hung a great two-handed broadsword with polished bronze fittings. His bloodline had ruled Badgerstede since the downfall of the Titans centuries ago.

He was seated on a great carven throne in front of an open blazing fire. Chairs were arranged in a semicircle around the fire, facing the chieftain. Upon each sat an elder of the village. One hand fingered his braided whiskers, while the other ran through his long white and black mane. His brow creased with worry as he listened to conflicting counsel.

A middle-aged badger who had lost a hand in battle was speaking. The injured warrior, whose name was Wyffa, fidgeted about in his chair as he presented his case. "My Lord Cerdic," he said in a voice that was always rather hoarse. "Strange winds have been blowing from the east across the sea. It is a sign of woe. I move that we muster every fighting beast that we can to repel the coming attack, whatever that attack may be."

"That is but idle child's prattle, Wyffa," barked another elder leaning on a long-shafted axe. "Your desire for battle clouds your vision. Can you not see that our crops are failing? You say the warriors should muster for a battle that may not even come to pass. I say that, for the time being, we turn our blade smiths into farmers so we might store for the winter that will soon be upon us."

"Why, Athelstane-" Wyffa began to retort, but Steel-Arm silenced him with an upraised paw.

"Have we gone back to the time of the Titans, that we put faith in superstitions?" Cerdic demanded in his deep authoritative voice. "Eldendag, the Ancient of Days, did He not say in His Word that He has freed us from the bondage of curses?"

This solicited a smirk of victory from Athelstane.

"How dare you?" bellowed Wyffa, his hand shooting to the hilt of his dagger.

"Peace, thanes, peace," interjected Anlaf the Ancient, the priest of Eldendag, and the keeper of records. Everyone in Badgerstede respected him for his seniority and wisdom.

"I have been studying the stars, as is my way," the wizened badger continued. "They told me that the Wielder of Three Swords shall come soon. He shall save us from looming oppression and His reign shall be long. It will be one of peace and prosperity. My counsel, therefore, is to take care of our needs and always be vigilant, but whatever we shall do, we must do always looking for the coming of our greatest chieftain, the Wielder of Three Swords, whose battle glory was prophesied many centuries ago. As you know, this prophecy came not long after Lord Cerdic's line began to rule in the wake of the destruction of the Titans. But it still rings true. I feel that the Ancient of Days would say that he shall come within our lifetimes. Therefore, I say to you: be ready. Be vigilant. Now, put up your weapons, lest there be none of us left when the Wielder of Three Swords is born.

The subject of the Council then meandered on to lesser matters for a time, but to Lord Cerdic's relief it soon adjourned. Cerdic sighed inwardly, deposited Steelclaw on his perch beside the throne and retired to the royal quarters in the back of the hall. On the walls of the steel-braced chamber hung wine red tapestries with knotwork and other linear designs of gilded thread. In between these tapestries hung broadswords with lobed pommels, as the will of the axes with huge single-bladed heads. Torches at intervals illuminated the chamber dully, and the light reflected off large, round shields painted bright colors.

Upon a great featherbed surrounded by tapers in the center of the room lay Svanhild, the pretty wife of Cerdic. The badger lord leaned down and kissed her lightly.

"Are you well, my dear?" he asked gently.

"Yes, my love," she replied, smiling weakly. "The baby shall come any day, now. It is a strange thing however, that I can never feel the baby kick." She heaved a long sigh. "Ah well, I guess it does not matter. Maybe, with Eldendag's blessing, our son shall be the foretold Wielder of Three Swords."

"May he be, my love," the badger lord said, smiling with hope. "May he be."

Cerdic Steel-Arm doffed his armor and sat near the bed for a time, praying fervently that his wife had spoken a truth that was soon to be realized.

1. Your Son Will Come Soon

Five days after the council, Lord Cerdic Steel-Arm left the skalli, which was what the folk of Badgerstede called the longhouse, to inspect the cavalry. The badgers had always ridden upon faithful hares that dwelled within the forest. In the days of their wars with the muskrats, many skalds, or badger minstrels, had composed great lays about the mighty thundering cavalry charges. Whenever a hair mount died, the warrior would skin it and wear it as a cloak to remind him of the bond that he had shared with it. Today, Lord Steel-Arm was wearing a cloak of the skin of his first mount, which his wife had dyed a deep royal red with holly berry juice to denote at his rank.

As he walked up and down in front of the ranks of the hair riders, they saluted by presenting their long spears. Each member of the King's personal guard was clad in shining mail and bore a large buckler which was painted red, with a silver boss engraved with the crossed hammer and axe of Lord Cerdic's house.

Satisfied that his huscarls were ready for battle, the mighty badger lord made his way to the stables, for his morning visit with his favorite steed. The hare steed Greritter was nearly as old as Lord Cerdic himself. He had been a gift from Cerdic's father, Ulfar Great Axe, the day that young Cerdic had begun his fifteenth year. His fur was silver-gray and he was well-advanced in years, yet he was still swept and mighty. Cerdic greeted him heartily and scratched him behind the ears.

"We have come a long way since we first met those many years ago, my friend," Cerdic chuckled, patting Greritter's side. "I am a came a king now, and shall soon have a son to rule after me. Much different than that foolhardy boy you once knew, eh?" He patted his steed once more.

"Your son may be here sooner than you think, my lord," an unseen female voice said.

Cerdic turned to see Belgla, the midwife, standing in the doorway. "Things are going smoothly as far as I can tell," she said. "Your son should be here by midnight at the latest.

Lord Steel-Arm fought back the impulsive urge to whoop for joy. He was forgetting himself. A princely birth required a princely gift. He hurried off in the direction of Regin the blade smith's forge.

The smithy of Regin Hammarson was a large dome of overlapping oak beams, with a wall constructed of white stone. Smoke poured from the gaping hole cut out of the center of the roof. As Cerdic neared the forge, he heard the sound of hammer on anvil and a strong loud voice singing baritone.

"And so the mighty Halfdan, he

Scaled the slope of Ben Manni.

The fortress he sought to raid

For to gain a Titan's blade.

Though the mountain him hath slain,

Yet he shall come down again."

The lay was that of Halfdan the wanderer, who, centuries before, had endeavored to scale the tall, treacherous mountain of Ben Manni, to the legendary fortress dating from the time of the Titans stood. Halfdan had never been seen again, but some said that he would come back someday.

Cerdic cupped his hands around his mouth and shouted, "Halloa."

The hammering noise ceased. Out came Regin, the burly weapon smith of Badgerstede. He was tall and broad shouldered, and his scruffy man had been pulled back in a long braid. He was several summers older than Cerdic, and had forked whiskers and fur that were starting to become splotched with gray. His chest fur was thick and white and stained in many places with soot from the fire. He wore a worn leather apron that was torn in several places from years of use. His favorite weapon, a great maul with a silvered head, rested on his gray shoulder. The muscles of his arms were large and strong from years of swinging the great weapon in mock combat. When he saw his lord, his fierce eyes sparkled with delight.

"My good jarl," he said lifting his free paw. "What business have you at my humble forge today?"

"Hail, Regin smith," cried Cerdic, returning the greeting. "Belgla told me this morning that my son would arrive before the night is over. A Prince needs a princely gift."

"May Eldendag smile on his coming," Regin said jovially. "I shall labor to produce the best weapon possible, as befits the son of so great a king."

"Name your price. What will it cost me?"

"Nothing, my liege," Regin replied. "You can repay me by letting me spar with you. It has been many years since that sword of yours has seen battle. I see that you are already armored. If you will give me a leave to prepare, my lord."

Cerdic nodded his approval and the older badger went back into the smithy. While the badger lord waited, he unfastened his cloak and allowed it to slip down behind him onto the snowy ground. Then he unsheathed his great broadsword.

Regin returned a moment later, clad in a mail shirt with an iron-bound leather cap upon his head and carrying a round nasaled helmet forged from burnished strips of steel, in his other hand. He handed the spangenhelm to Cerdic and took a fighting stance. Nodding to one another, the combatants then ran forward, swinging broadsword and hammer aloft. Cerdic was careful not to let Regin strike to his blade directly, as the force of such a blow would cause even the fine, tempered steel, to crack.

Despite the crisp air, the two warriors were soon panting from their exertions. For a time, Lord Cerdic seemed to gain the upper hand, pushing his companion-in-arms further and further back was leaving horizontal blows to the section of the shaft just beneath the head of the maul. But just as Cerdic was about to weigh Regin down to his knees, the graying yet muscular smith bellowed and pushed back with the leather bound haft of his maul.

This caused Cerdic to falter, staggering backward one or two steps. With a hoarse whoop, the exhausted Regin rained down two more crushing blows, which Cerdic quickly parried with desperate strength. The aging smith bellowed and, with one final downward sweep, knocked the badger lord's broadsword from his hands. Regin had struck with more force than he intended, for the downward stroke caused him to stumble and fall flat on his face in the snow, dropping his maul in the process.

Lord Cerdic helped the smith to his feet. Regin stood there for a time, shaking his face from side to side, muttering and spitting slush. "I think we shall call it draw," he panted at last. "I know right well what I am going to forge for your son: a small warhammer and a dagger in remembrance of this friendly bout."

"Many thanks, brother. You serve your chieftain well." Cerdic gripped Regin's forearm tightly in farewell and left the smith to his work.

2. An Unlikely Heir

Cerdic turned away from old Regin's forge and trudged back through the snow toward the Royal longhouse. His pace quickened as he drew nearer, as both anxiety and excitement increased in unison. After all his years of waiting and praying, he would finally be a father and would have an heir to rule after him.

On impulse, he ran into the stables and flung open the door to Greritter's stall. Saddling the aging beast, he swung up into position. As he dug his heels into Greritter's sides, he happened to look over his shoulder and noticed that one of the gray hare's mates would soon give birth to a baby hare. Good. This would be a fine present for his son.

Clucking to Greritter, the badger lord urged his mount forward. "I shall have a son, my friend, and your son shall have a master," Cerdic whispered merrily in Greritter's ear. The gray steed bounded through the village toward the skalli, causing the villagers he passed to stare confusedly after their lord. Cerdic reigned Greritter to a halt in front of the skalli, and so sudden was his stopping, that the beast kicked a sudden tattoo of snow in the air. He flung open the doors to the Great Hall and raced back to the royal quarters.

The royal bedchamber soon became so overcrowded with midwives and apothecaries administering potions, and servants running to and fro with pots of hot water that Belgla soon made Cerdic leave the room. In the few glimpses the poor father-to-be caught of his bride her breathing was labored and husky and sweat poured like a fjord down her brow.

For the next several hours, Cerdic paced like a caged feral animal, up and down the Great Hall, wringing his hands, and casting nervous glances this way and that. In that moment, the mighty King was no different than any other husband: anxious for the safety of his wife and child.

He prayed fervently again and again, "Hear my cry, I pray, O Ancient of Days, keep the beloved one You have given me in the palm of Your hand. Protect her and keep her safe. Ease the pain of her labor, I pray. Also protect the life of my child yet unborn. You knit him together in his mother's womb. You set the number of his days and the purpose for his life before he was even conceived. Let him pass safely into this world I pray. You have entrusted to him to me and to my wife and we shall give him back to You and teach him Your ways. I place his life and destiny into your hands. Hear me, O Eldendag, I pray."

At the midnight hour, Cerdic Steel-Arm heard Svanhild cry out in agony. Then he heard the unmistakable wailing of a newborn babe.

"Sire, come," cried Belgla. "Make haste."

Her voice was laden with a sense of urgency, almost dread. Cerdic's body tightened with apprehension and he bolted into the royal bedchamber. Belgla was holding a baby wrapped in swaddling close, but her eyes were wide with horror. Another midwife was endeavoring to wash and bandage Svanhild's stomach.

As if she feared his wrath, Belgla handed the babe to Cerdic. Cerdic's eyes widened in shock as he beheld his son. From head to hip, the child was like any other badger baby. But below the hips, there were but only two small stumps.

Cerdic's son had no legs.

Cerdic closed his eyes and a tear ran down his cheek. Why had Eldendag given him such a son. What had he and Svanhild done wrong? How had they sinned?

Then he heard the soft, gentle voice of his wife calling to him weakly. "Cerdic, my love. Come here."

He walked over to the bed and laid his free hand on that of his wife. She was pale from loss of blood. "He is your son, my love. Though he does not appear to possess the qualities of a chieftain, I sense that the hand of the Ancient of Days is upon him. Promise me, Cerdic. Promise me that you will not lose hope in him, but will train him up in the way he should go. Eldendag has spoken to me and told me that our son has an incredible destiny, for he shall be the Wielder of Three Swords. Promise me."

"I promise, my love."

A look of peace came over Svanhild's face. "I go now to dwell with my ancestors in the halls of the Ancient of Days. Do not grieve overmuch, my love, for we shall meet again on the glorious day. I love you, my lord." Her eyes glazed. Then the spirit of Svanhild Svensdottir departed for the halls of Eldendag.

Cerdic wept softly for a time. When he had dried his tears, he looked at his newborn son. "I promise you, my son," he said almost inaudibly. "As Eldendag is a shield for all who call upon His name, so shall I be a shield for you. I shall train you in the way you should go and do my utmost to ensure that you grow into the full-grown beast that Eldendag intends for you to be. This I promise, with the Ancient of Days as my witness."

Cerdic called Belgla the midwife to his side. "Belgla," he said softly, his voice heavy with determination. "You must do this for me. Gather the apothecaries and midwives to prepare the body of my wife for her funeral, and go find a suitable nurse for my son. Say nothing of the child. I shall reveal him when I know it is at the proper time. Tomorrow we celebrate my wife's Hall-Walk. Have faith, mother midwife. Eldendag will show me how to deal with the Council of Elders."

The new father took his crippled son and lay with him on a settle, rocking him slowly and quietly crooning songs of his dead mother into the baby's ear. "I love you, my son."

The next morning at first light, Cerdic rose and tended to his son. He took a cloth and, using his swaddling close, wrapped his son in the deep red fabric. Then he called for the Council of Elders to assemble along with representatives of all the families of Badgerstede.

When they had all assembled, Cerdic Steel-Arm stood before them, carrying the babe against his shoulder. "Last night, after giving birth to our son, the Lady Svanhild went to dwell forever in the Golden Hall of Eldendag." Exclamations of shock and grief followed this statement.

"We shall celebrate her Hall-Walk in due time." Cerdic drew his other paw up toward the cloth and grasped it. "Regin

Hammarson, blade smith of Badgerstede, will you bring forth the royal gifts you crafted, please?"

The hulking Smith came forward, holding a bulging bag of sapphire blue cloth in one fist. The other gripped the haft of his ever-present maul. He emptied the bag on the floor before the King: it contained a blued battle mallet with a handle wrapped in brown leather and entwined with silver thread. There was also a poniard with a rune-marked fuller and lobed pommel.

Regin remained where he was in front of the king. Cerdic nodded approvingly in Regin's direction. "You have done well, Regin smith." The weapon smith inclined his head respectfully but did not move, as if he knew by instinct that Lord Cerdic would soon need him.

"Now I introduce you to my son and heir, Morcar." Cerdic spoke gravely but with a touch of pride in his voice. With one swift motion, he swept off the wine red cloth. There were several exclamations of shock and surprise as the people of the village finally beheld the prince's unusual physical quality.

The mighty badger opened his mouth to speak again, but before he had a chance, Wyffa interjected. "Such a beast cannot lead us. If he rules, it will be our downfall. Heed my words well. You should kill him."

At this remark, Cerdic Steel-Arm raised himself up to his full towering height, squared his shoulders, drew a deep breath and bellowed forth, "What? Would you have us go back to the time of the Titans? We are not mindless murders. It is written that the life of every beast is sacred to Eldendag. The gift of life is the most precious gift the Ancient of Days has given us. I cannot and will not take that away from my son. You say he cannot lead our people after I die. You do not know that for certain. One could just as easily declare that you cannot be a warrior, for you only have one hand."

Wyffa's eyes flared and his face reddened, but he did not reply.

Satisfied, Cerdic turned to the assembly and commanded, "Prepare to commemorate the Hall-Walk of your queen."

As the badgers filed out of the Hall, Regin, leaned in close and whispered into Cerdic's ear, "I would not trust Wyffa. He has the heart of a rat. I promise you this: I shall do my best to watch over your son with a ready hammer and will not hesitate to brain those who would harm him. He is an unlikely heir. But he is your heir, nonetheless, and I will serve him as faithfully as I have served you."

A great pyre was built in the field in front of the Hall. The body Svanhild was bourn on a stretcher made from a red tapestry. She was clad in a dress of evergreen hue. Gold bracelets were on her wrists and a silver circlet set with a large pearls alternating with royal blood red runes was upon her head. She was placed on the pyre, and as the torch was applied to the kindling, Anlaf led the folk of Badgerstede in the chant of the Hall-Walk.

"Upon the sky-road I come

Through the pearled north-sea,

Up to the Sun-Dust hall,

For to be with thee.

And we who are still here

Shall sing the song

To fading memory."

When the song ended, Lord Cerdic saw that Regin the weapon smith was standing beside him. Placing an iron hand on the lord's shoulder, Regin said, "Now an arduous task lies before you. You must raise your son without Svanhild. You must raise him alone."

"Not alone, my friend," Cerdic replied, gazing at the flaming pyre. "Not alone, for I have the Ancient of Days."

3. Tales of the Titans

Morcar's eyes fluttered open. Turning his head, he saw that the tapers dully illuminating the royal bedchamber were still smoldering. The pale cool of early morning made his skin prickle. By his calculation, it was only just dawn, but Morcar didn't give a care. He was excited. For today was a special day. It was his fifth birthday, and today his father would take him to the Hall of Records to teach him the history of Ykkelunde. Morcar hoisted himself using the wooden bar that hung on a thick iron chain above his bed.

"Father," he told softly in the direction of the large royal bed. "Father, may I get up?"

"No," came the slow, groggy reply. "It is not even light yet. Go back to sleep, son."

"But it is dawn, and it is my birthday, and you told me—"

"Very well. Very well," Cerdic said as he slowly forced his legs over the side of the bed, and rose, back rasping, into a sitting position. After opening his mouth in a gigantic yawn, the great badger stood and walked over to his son's bed.

"Come on, then." Cerdic grinned as he tossed his son up in the air and caught him. The father lovingly nuzzled his braided whiskers against Morcar's cheek.

Taking Morcar in his arms, Cerdic put his son on his shoulders and walked out of the royal apartment. Knowing full well the Morcar would not wait at all for breakfast, Cerdic grabbed some bowls of cold stew, the remains of last night's supper. Wrapping himself and Morcar in warm cloaks, he stepped outside into the brisk early morning air.

He made his way in the pinkish light of dawn to the stables and stopped before the pen of a young hare with a gray hide splotched with patches of brown. This was Egil, sired by Greritter shortly before the old hare had passed on. Egil served as Morcar's legs. After making sure that his son was securely fastened in the homemade harness that kept him in the saddle, Cerdic nodded and said, "There you are, Morcar Hare-Strider." Father, rider and mount then made their way to the small hut of Anlaf, the priest of Eldendag.

Cerdic rapped on the door with his massive paw. There was no sound from within. The badger lord knocked a second time. Still no response. This time Cerdic struck the door so hard the very walls of the dwelling seemed to vibrate.

Father and son heard some incoherent muttering from behind the door, accompanied by the tapping of a walking stick. The door creaked open to reveal a drowsy Anlaf, still in his sleeping robe, and eyes heavy from curtailed dreaming.

"To what do I owe this early pleasure, my lord?" The priest asked, yawning."
"Forgive the intrusion, Anlaf, but my son awoke early this morning, refusing to allow me a moment's peace until I took him to the Hall of Records for his first lessons in our history."

"So, my lad," the priest said rubbing his eyes and smiling down at Morcar, "you wish to know of the time of the Titans. I remember when I first learned of those dark days. Very well. Come along now." The old badger threw a warm cloak about his thin shoulders. The small company left the priest's hut and continued on in the direction of the Hall of Records.

The Hall of Records was different from the other buildings in the village in that, instead of wood, it was built of stone. It stood there like an edifice built of a single gray brick. The rectangular building had but one entrance and egress: two great carven oaken doors. The doors and the frame of stone that encased them were decorated with interweaving designs consisting mostly of knotwork and animals.

Cerdic pushed open the great doors with his massive arms and the three companions entered the hall. Morcar caught his breath in awe. The floor of the hall was of polished oak, coated in an enamel so brilliant that seemed to be of burnished gold. There were great enclaves carved out of the stone wall. Inside each of these enclaves were huge scenes carved in bas-relief. The first few of these scenes depicted strange warriors. They were much taller than badgers, about six feet by Morcar's calculation. They were clad in huge coats of mail, and what Morcar could see of their bodies puzzled him. Their paws and faces were smooth and, strangely, were not covered in fur. The only things they possessed that looked vaguely like fur were their long, braided whiskers and long manes. Their weapons seemed to be gigantic versions of those used by the badgers

"Who are they?" Morcar asked, pointing at one of the scenes.

"They are the Titans," Anlaf replied, walking up to the first carving. "They ruled this land in the ages before the awakening of our kind. Great and terrible they were. They knew not the Ancient of Days, and worshiped many dark gods of battle and thunder. Their minds were plagued with the love of battle and bloodshed.

"Their wars continued for many years. The number of those slain in battle far outweighed that of the children that were born. They continued killing and killing until there were only two great tribes left: one ruled by a king named Cerdic Thorfinnsson and one ruled by a king named Morcar Silkbeard.

Morcar looked questioningly at his father.

"We bear their names, son. Nothing more."

Anlaf continued. "There was a great battle between the armies of Morcar and Cerdic. So great was the bloodshed that none survived. A great snowstorm came and buried the bodies of the Kings and their huscarls."

Anlaf moved on to an image of a great badger, clad in mail and carrying a maul in one hand and a double-bladed battle axe in the other.

"After He had buried the dead by His own hand, Eldendag breathed the breath of life into a badger whom he named Andag. Eldendag gave Andag His Words so that the badger's descendents might follow Him.

"Andag tamed and rode the first hare, and built the Great Hall of Badgerstede. He bore a maul and an axe to ward off wolves. His weapons became the standard of his house and his lined has ruled Badgerstede ever since. And even though you may not think it possible, I foresee that you shall continue that line, Morcar. You may even prove to be a greater ruler than even Andag himself."

They walked to the door. After Cerdic opened it, they saw that the sun had risen fully in the eastern sky. Old Anlaf stepped out into the cool morning air and yawned. "Now if you will excuse me, I am by this time starving, and must see about getting myself some breakfast. My jarl. My prince." Anlaf began to walk slowly back to his hut.

"Come, son," Cerdic said gently. "We had best be going home." Father and son departed from the Hall of records for the Great Hall. But young Morcar could not stop thinking about all that he had seen and heard that morning.

4. A Plan for Me?

As Morcar grew older, he became steadfast friends with a tall badger youth about two years older than he whose name was Eirik. Eirik was the son of Wyffa, but unlike his father, he did not distrust the young Morcar. Whenever it seemed as if the other boys of the village were about to taunt Morcar, Eirik would stand beside him and silently discourage the ruffians simply by his tall stature and imposing build.

"There is little stumpers again," The taunters would holler repeatedly, but before Morcar thought much about what they were saying, he would hear the tramping crunch of Eirik's boots as his friend walked up to stand behind him. He would transfix the revelers with a dour gaze and they would suddenly think of a task that needed doing and run off in the opposite direction.

Physically, Eirik had the makings of a chieftain. He was tall, able and strong, and no other youth could best him in the practice of arms. His sword arms were as thick and corded as those of a full-grown warrior. He was also very handsome. All of these attributes and him much respect from people of the village. They were willing to obey him. Every time when he went off to the hunt, a crowd of cheering youths and youngsters would follow him to the gates of the village, cheering his name loudly.

One day when Morcar was thirteen years old, he and Eirik went, as they often did, the training ground to practice the use of their weapons. As they approached the training ground, Morcar saw to his dismay that Olaf and Ganmund were there sparring with each other. These puffed-up twin brothers were numbered among the worst of Morcar's tormentors.

When he saw the two friends approaching, Ganmund stuck out his bulbous chin and called to his brother, "Ho, Olaf. Look who has come for training today, Eirik Wyffasson and his other half."

Morcar's cheeks stung as the two bullies burst into fits of raucous laughter at the cruel jest.

"Hold your tongue, imbecile," barked Eirik, coming to a halt. "You are not half so skilled as you think. I know for a fact that Morcar here could best the two of you with a cudgel."

"Aye? And how could he stand against us?" Another cruel laugh followed this question.

Eirik's fur stood on end. "I will show you. Come on, Morcar."

Eirik unstrapped Morcar and placed his crippled friend on his shoulders. He then handed a cudgel to Morcar and held onto his stumps. The twins selected sturdy cudgels of their own and believed forward, trying to strike Morcar down from atop his perch. But, try as they might, Olaf and Ganmund could not bring Morcar down from atop Mount Eirik.

Morcar then gave vent to his anger as he brought the cudgel down upon the heads of the twins with several resounding thuds. After a time, the twins began to mutter discontentedly to themselves. Then, as if they were thinking with one mind, they struck simultaneous blows at Eirik's paws. Morcar felt the muffled weight of the blow.

"Yow," Eirik cried, instinctively losing hold of Morcar's stumps. The poor badger fell onto his back in the snow.

Rubbing their swollen heads, Olaf and Ganmund burst into fits of laughter. Faintly, Morcar and Eirik heard Olaf softly snicker in Ganmund's ear, "One thing is for sure: that cripple will never be the folk leader."

Picking Morcar up and brushing off the snow, Eirik said, "Pay no heed to what they say, my friend. Their minds are full of nothing"

Eirik took Morcar back to the Great Hall and said goodbye for the day. For the rest of the day, Morcar's mind was filled with a confused mass of angry and sad thoughts. What was the purpose of his existence? Did he really mean anything? Would he ever amount to anything at all?

Cerdic noticed his son's low spirits. At the dinner table, he laid a paw on Morcar's shoulder and said, "Something has been heavy on your mind, today, my son. Whatever is the matter?"

That was all it took. The young badger poured out his heart to his father, concluding by saying, "please do not punish Olaf and Ganmund. If you do, it will only cause them to hate me more. Oh father, how can I ever be chieftain? Is there a plan for my life?"

Cerdic drew in a deep breath and said, "Son, many times the way in which Eldendag will accomplish His will in our lives is hidden from us. Many times we need to simply hold on and trust Him. Little by little, He will show us what to do. We must never grow weary in doing what He has called us to do in the different seasons of our lives, though it is tempting, at times, to stop. Though you see no hope in the present, my son, you must hold onto the promise that the Ancient of Days has a plan and purpose for your life, even though you do not see the manner in which it will unfold. It is growing late, and we should be going to bed."

Morcar tossed and turned that night, pondering and wrestling with all that his father had said. He finally resolved in his heart to trust the Ancient of Days to bring his plan to fruition in his good time. All that Morcar would have to do would be to follow the voice of his Master.

The Skald Queen

Prologue:

"Me not want to sleep," the baby said, propping himself totteringly up on his bed. "Me want hear story first."

"Oh, very well," the woman said. "I shall tell you the best story I know. But then you must be a good boy and go to sleep. Agreed?"

"Yes."

"The story begins a long time ago, in a land far across the sea…"

Reachra Island, Ireland, 795

1.   The Dragon out of the Sea

Niamh walked along the edge of the hill overlooking the bay. The rising sun cast its golden bronze rays upon her face as she gazed down upon the crashing surf below. The dark cliffs at the water's dully listened with ocean spray that was turned from white to amber. She closed her see blue eyes and took a deep breath of the salt-laden air.

Ah! She was forgetting her purpose in coming. Her father had sent her there to gather thyme for a mixture he was preparing. He was the apothecary for the monastery built on the small island. He was not a monk, of course, but the abbot gave him his own land in exchange for his valuable services. Conchobar's wife had died when his daughter Niamh was but two years of age. Niamh's father had raised her on four maxims: the teaching of Scripture, the knowledge of herbs, the sayings of the saints, and good tales of the old lore. Niamh had known a relatively peaceful existence for most of her ten years of life. She had been tutored in the Scriptures not only by her father but also by the good brothers of the monastery. They even deemed her worthy to learn a bit of Latin and writing. She could quote both the epistles of Paul and of Patrick and Columcille by heart.

As the short blonde Irish lass gazed out over the water to the horizon, she beheld a strange thing. She saw what at first she thought to be a water horse, like unto the one St. Columcille had blessed when he had come to Loch Ness. She stared at it in wonder for a moment, not comprehending what he saw. Finally, the old rumors came flooding back to her. A Dragon ship. Word had come across the water two years ago of the slaying of the Saxon monks in their island monastery of Lindisfarne off the coast of Northumbria. Those not put to the sword had been sold in the slavery by the cruel men of the North. One thought filled her mind: <u>run</u>. She dropped the rush basket she had been carrying, turned, and fled back down the hill, her terror lending speed to her legs. Bolting across the green field toward the small earthen hut outside the walls of the monastery where she and her father lived. Panting with exertion, she flung herself through the open doorway and nearly knocked over a stool on which sat a mortar and pestle. Snatches of the pungent powder flew into the air and dispersed as the bowl violently rocked back and forth. She looked up to see her father's worried face. Her eyes were wild with fear, her chest heaving up and down.

"Niamh, daughter," he said, laying his massive hands on her trembling shoulders, "What is it?"

"A ship…" she panted, "…the dark strangers…the <u>Dubh Gailis</u> are here."

For a moment he stared at her, too shocked to speak or react. Then he straightened, a determined look in his eye. Gathering her up in his arms, he said hurriedly, "We must warn the brothers."

Running out of the earthen hut, he sprinted to the enclosed garden near the side of the monastery, from which the brothers obtained their meager food. A young monk, a novice, was breaking up the soil with a wooden rake as Conchobar raced into the garden. Seeing the urgency in the apothecary's eyes, the novice dropped his gardening tool. Without wasting time in greeting, Conchobar said swiftly, "Brother Milluic, listen. Raiders have come. Northmen. If you value your life you will ring the warning bell. Now."

Uttering a small exclamation of fear, Brother Milluic ran inside the monastery. A moment later the frantic, clanging cry of the great bell rent through the early morning stillness like a sword. From all around the monastery grounds, monks came running, their robes blowing in the wind. Although the coming of Conchobar's warning had come just a moment before, the Vikings were swift in coming, so one or two of the slower brothers fell, a throwing ax or a spear protruding from their backs. Niamh froze with shock at the sight of her slain friends. But her father had seen the maraudings of bands of his own countrymen before, which in some cases surpassed and cruelty the reavings the Norsemen would bring, so he did not allow himself to be overcome with shock. Thinking coolly he breathed, "I must save my supplies from destruction. Covering his daughter's eyes, the young apothecary ran back in the direction of his hut. He stopped short just as he ran through the door. For there, towering above the Gael, standing clad in mail, long sword drawn, was a Norseman.

The Viking stared at Conchobar for a moment, undecided. It was at that moment that the apothecary noticed that the dark-bearded man's arm was bleeding and that his blade was stained with blood. One of the brothers had met his death trying to resist him. Instinctively, Conchobar soaked a cloth in a bowl of salve. Then, he gingerly tied it around the Northman's arm, as the warrior eyed him warily. For a moment, the Viking winced as he felt the salve burn his raw flesh. It seemed as if he would fell the apothecary with his sword. Then he relaxed.

At that moment, a tawny-haired raider armed with a great axe burst into the hut. He looked at the dark-haired man. "Why do you not kill him, Bjorn?" The blond man asked in the tongue of the Vikings.

"Helgi, this man put magical water on my wound and eased the pain. He must be skilled in healing magic."
"But what good is he to us?"

"I am from Jutland. In the far north of my country, there is a powerful jarl named Gunnar. He is so far north that he does what he pleases, and does not pay many taxes to King Sigfred. He is very rich. But he has also been very ill of late. Therefore, a healing man could be worth his weight in gold."
Bjorn motioned for Conchobar to follow. When he tried to take Niamh from the apothecary, he shook his head violently to make them understand that he would only go if they did not harm his daughter. They would have to kill him before she came to harm. Bjorn understood. Casting up his eyes he nodded. Altogether, it would be good to have another slave to sell.

As they were led down away from the monastery to thore, Conchobar's heart was saddened as he saw the poor brothers being cast down from the towers of the monastery to their deaths. He said a silent prayer for them, yet he did not weep. He knew that the Lord had a greater purpose for them through all this. Conchobar resolved then that he would simply trust in the Lord, as Patrick had done of old. They boarded the longship and thus left their happy life in Ireland behind, their faces turned north on the foaming sea.

2. On Board the Dragon

The longship was a craft both beautiful and terrible. It was a living testament to the shipbuilding ingenuity of the Northmen. Although not large, it still qualified as a ship, for it had twelve oars. It was constructed around a sturdy keel, with each row of planks overlapping the next. The planks were hammered together with large iron nails and washers. The planks were also coated and caulked with animal fat to prevent leakage.

A huge tiller was attached to the back of the keel. As Niamh looked aft she saw that a graying man was a blackish white beard braided in the forked fashion of some of the Northmen leaned against it. He had but one bluish gray eye. He reminded the Irish lass of Balor, king of the Formorians.

The Viking called Bjorn, who had spared their lives motioned for Conchobar to sit down by the tiller. Conchobar complied mutely, casting suspicious glances of the navigator, holding Niamh closer to him. Over the bulk of her father's shoulder, Niamh saw the fork-bearded man staring at her in amazemen. He reached out his hand and said something that sounded like, "Sigryn". Seeing this, Conchobar edged farther away from him.

Bjorn walked to the graying man at the tiller and said, "Thorstein, ganga."

The other Viking shifted the tiller and barked a short command. The men gripped the oars firmly. The large, square sail was unfurled from the masthead. The beautiful yet terrible dragon- headed prow, meant to both frighten away spirits of Hel and to strike fear into the hearts of victims, was propelled forward, away from Ireland and the isle of Reachra north into the unknown.

At this time, the Northmen were afraid of the open waters, believing that to be populated with sea dragons and other monsters. For this reason, the longship hugged the coast of Brittania for the first few leagues of the journey. Niamh was able to observe the seafaring life of the Northmen. The Vikings lived on small basic rations while at sea. Each man sat upon his box of provisions and equipment while rowing. Mail and helmets were only worn by the very wealthy. Most men wore their regular clothes along with perhaps a cap of boiled leather. The typical tools of battle were a hide-covered buckler, sometimes braced with iron, along with a sword or axe.

Although Niamh still spoke the tongue of the Gaels to herself and with her father, she began to understand the hard, rolling speech of the Northmen, which was quite unlike the soft, flowing language of her homeland. She first began to understand, due to the talk of the helmsman, who oddly seemed to have taken a liking to her.

One night, as she was chewing a hard piece of bread that Bjorn had given her, the man at the tiller looked at her tapped himself on the breast with a large index finger and intoned, "Ic Thorsteinr." Then he pointed at her. She pointed to herself and said her name. The big Northman smiled.

Over the next few days, Niamh spent much time with Thorstein. She would point to an object on the ship or the horizon and he would tell her the word. She learned very quickly and even taught the old Viking some words in Gaelic.

"Why are you so gentle with me?" she asked him one day.

"You remind me of my daughter, Sigryn."

"Where is she?"

The Northman looked away and was silent for a time. "Loki took her from me."

"I am sorry," she said softly, laying her small hand gently on his massive fist.

One day when she was sitting with her father, the apothecary said, "I do not approve of you talking with that Northman. You shall soon forget the tongue of your people. As you forget your native tongue, you may forget your native ways, and even, though I pray not so, your native faith."

"But Athair, you must remember, that the native tongue of the blessed St. Paul was Hebrew, yet when he spoke with the churches in Greece, he spoke Greek, and when he was in Rome, he spoke Latin. This did not cause him to abandon the true faith."

This seemed to satisfy Conchobar, and he said no more. He seemed so satisfied, that he asked her one day, "Niamh, my daughter, will you not teach me some of the words you are learning from the Northman? I will probably need to be able to communicate wherever they are taking us." Niamh laughed slightly and assured her father that she would be happy to oblige him. With her assistance, he became comfortable with the strange language.

The ship was making its way to Jutland, so after hugging the coast of the islands, they made their way south to the coast of

Brittany and east along the coast of the empire of the Franks. At this point, Niamh began to entertain the hope of rescue.

"Athair," she would say excitedly, "do you think the Frankish King Charles will rescue us?"

"Oh my child," her father sighed, "Charlemagne is too occupied with the wars on the continent to give a thought to a lone longship filled with a small band of Northmen. We must trust in the Great King over all to protect us and preserve us from the wrath of the Northmen."

With the passage of time, the dragon vessel came in sight of the southern end of Jutland. This land, unlike the Viking lands of Scania, was very flat, consisting mainly of plain, but also a few rolling hills. The summers were cool and the winters cold.

The men did not bother stopping at Sigfred's court, but continued along the coast north to Gunnarstede, the home of the powerful jarl, Gunnar, son of Anlaf. King Sigfred was far too occupied with the internal affairs of his own kingdom to pay a single longship heed. One day, Thorstein helped Niamh climb the sealskin rigging, and she saw through the mist a sight that she would not soon forget, a high Viking hall, and in front of it, the many thatched roofs of the Norse settlement. They had come to the island of Zealand and the village of Hroskilde or Hroar's Spring. Conchobar and Niamh had finally reached their new home. What her fate would be here, Niamh did not know, but as the oars were stowed, she prayed a silent prayer.

Athair ar Neamh, I put my fate in your hands.

Chain-Mail for Vulfhelm

The morning of Midsummer's Day began just the same as any other day for Vulfhelm Gunnarson, the dwarf hunter. You may ask yourself how any dwarf's morning can consist of anything usual. Well, granted, he lived in a now long-forgotten world that his people called Gormolduin the land of the gray-green hills, and dwarves had lived there for hundreds of years. Being a dwarf in a land now long forgotten, he did not have a mommy or daddy to wake him up and send him to the schoolhouse, and he could not go to the grocers and buy a plump chicken for dinner. Rather he got up early every morning by himself, took the throwing axes that he used for hunting, and went out to see if he could find a wolf, bear, or if he was lucky, a deer. He would then skin his kill and sell off the excess meat to Thorkel the butcher or Bjarni the tanner.

Gormolduin lay on a broad hilly plain surrounded by tall blue mountains. No one knew what lay beyond the mountains except tidbits of information gleaned from small hints in old wives' tales. It rained on Gormolduin in spring and late fall, and the green hills were white mounds in winter. But now it was summer and the sun shone down brightly.

The dwarves lived in small houses of gray stone with domed roofs. They proudly called these dwellings brughs. The foundation of each house was dug out of the hill. You may ask what would be particularly pleasant about living with your feet under a hill, but as far as the dwarves were concerned, it was very normal for them.

The interior of Vulfhelm's brugh consisted of only two rooms: a large central bedroom, and a kitchen. The floor of the bedroom was strewn with the pelts of a few of Vulfhelm's many prizes. You may think the dwarf hunter very cruel, as you may prefer to see bears and deer and elk in a zoo or park, rather than lying arms and legs outstretched on your bedroom floor. But they were the only way that Vulfhelm could have food and warmth, so perhaps you should make an allowance for him. He slept on a great oaken bed in the middle of the room across from a rectangular window with neither panes nor a frame. The bed was now draped with deerskin, as it was summer and deerskin was lighter than bear or elk fur. The kitchen consisted of a stone stool and table upon which was set an earthen basin of precious rainwater for washing and a stone mug for cider.

Vulfhelm awoke with the early morning sunlight streaming onto his face. Something was different about today. He could feel it in his bones, for you know, whenever a dwarf has a feeling or inclination, he feels in his bones first. Perhaps he would bring down an elk today and that would bring him many pieces of gold in the market, and enough hide to make a new cloak. Anything could happen on the day of the Midsummer's fair.

Vulfhelm leaped nimbly out of bed and walked over to the wall where the opal mirror hung. You may wonder how anyone could afford a mirror made of opal. But it must be said here and not forgotten that in addition to being great masons and weapon crafters, dwarves are also renowned miners.

He looked at his reflection. He was rather tall for a dwarf, almost four feet in height. He was also bald, a rarity among his race. His beard was long and as brown as mud. Even while sleeping he wore the leather vest and kilt of the dwarf hunter. If he distinguished himself at King Kundulf's wolf hunt at the end of the festivities, he could gain the auspicious honor of wearing mail instead of leather. Having a long shirt of metal rings would be much better than just wearing a leather vest.

The dwarf king held the hunt in times of peace, to keep his warriors seasoned in case of an outbreak of another civil war. There were a few hours left before the festivities began, time enough for hunting.

Vulfhelm strapped on his skinning dagger and shouldered his satchel of throwing axes. After quickly downing a bowl of cold bear steak stew and some cider, he ambled, whistling, toward the mountain foothills at the western edge of Gormolduin.

The morning mist was rising off the rocky foothills like the drawing back of a vaporous veil. Cresting one of the hills, the

Dwarven hunter paused as he caught a scent on the air. He took in a whiff. Ah, he knew the odor well. Wolf.

Slowly drawing out one of the throwing axes, he turned slightly, looking up above him. He froze with shock mixed with a bit of delight. There, above him on an escarpment, was the largest black wolf he had ever seen.

For a moment they stood very still, eyeing each other. Then, before the dwarf had a chance to react, the wolf pounced.

Vulfhelm could never quite recall exactly what he did just then. As the wolf sailed toward him he closed his eyes and then heard a <u>shunk</u>.

He opened his eyes and was staring straight into the pupils of the wolf, both sides were frozen in a look of hunger. Vulfhelm breathed a sigh of relief.

He turned the wolf over and retrieved his axe. Then a strange thing happened most of the wolf vanished in a wisp of smoke, leaving only the head, in the form of it hood, attached to the hide, which was like a cape.

You know, surely, that if you were in Vulfhelm's place, you would run home and tell your mommy and daddy, because you would probably be scared.

But dwarves are raised from babyhood on tales of the fantastic, so Vulfhelm was excited, not scared. "Surely this must be a gift from the Unknown One," the dwarf hunter thought. So he picked up the cowl and put it on his head.

As soon as it had touched the bald surface of his head, it began to burn. He tried and tried to take it off but it was as if it had attached itself on purpose to his head. Yelling an angry yell, he stormed toward the smithy of Gormolduin to have Eirik the weapon smith pry it off with his tongs.

Old Eirik was cooling some spearheads he made for the wolf hunt when poor Vulfhelm came crashing into the floor

"Oi," cried he in a gruff voice. "You stupid walking dog. You knocked those blades off the bench."

"Eirik, it's me, Vulfhelm the hunter."

"Now don't growl and huff," the smith said, not understanding and taking a better look at him. "Aha, you are a nice fellow, and you can stand on your hind legs and grab things with your paws. You'll be a perfect attention grabber. Come on, if you're a good boy, I'll give you a haunch of meat."

Eirik was much bigger and much stronger than Vulfhelm, so the poor hunters saw no point in resisting, so he just rolled his eyes and decided to play along. He followed the Smith to his stall near the edge of the fairgrounds, wondering why Eirik could not understand him.

He begrudgingly allowed Eirik to put a leather leash around his neck and tie him to one of the front legs of the stall.

Vulfhelm spent the morning juggling swords and daggers in front of Eirik's stall. As a boy, he had often played throwing games with his knives, so it wasn't very hard. Many people came to see the strange wolf man, staring and gawking at him. His spectacle made for good business for Eirik, but Vulfhelm did not care in the least.

Several times boys and girls would run up and throw apples at him. He would have growled fiercely, but he was afraid of being caned by Eirik. The smith gave him a haunch of raw meat at about noon, but of course, Vulfhelm refused to eat it. Just when he thought he could take no more, he heard the horns of the king's men blowing.

King Kundulf rode up on a large elk, accompanied by his bodyguards, who were called huscarls. He was clad in shining chain-mail, and a long red cape fell down from his shoulders. A battle hammer of silver white metal hung in a sling at his waist. A round helmet with silver eagle's wings on the sides topped his red mane. A round shield was slung on his back.

He stopped in front of Eirik's stall. "Eirik blacksmith," he said, pointing to Vulfhelm, "Where did you find that?"

"This strange dog stumbled into my forge this morning. I thought he'd be good for business."

"That is no dog. That's a berserk. There haven't been any berserks here since my grandfather's time. He'll be perfect to lead the wolf hunt."

The king took a bag of coins from one of his huscarls and tossed it to the smith. "I believe this will cover the expenses."

The Smith stared open-mouthed at the gold, not believing his luck.

"This is wonderful," said Kundulf. "Now the wolf will attack him instead of us."

What? If there was one thing the dwarf hunter didn't want, it was to be bait.

"No, no," he cried, "you can't do this to me."

"Oh, look at him," said the king, "he is excited."

"My king," said one of the huscarls, who happened to be very fond of animals, "do you think that we should put him in a hauberk first? I mean, for protection."

"Well," the king hesitated, "I suppose... oh, fine, fine, fine. He can have one of my spare ones."

Vulfhelm, by this time feeling very flustered, was led to the great castle, called a skalli in the Dwarven language and dressed in a shining mail shirt that reached down past his knees. It must've been worth a full year wages. This was the one part of the day that he fully enjoyed.

The king's bodyguard then took him to join the army on a field near the edge of the mountains. All of the Dwarven warriors were there, dressed in chain-mail and round helmets with nasal guards. They carried with them swords, long axes, and long spears.

"Berserk," Kundulf ordered Vulfhelm in a commanding, kingly voice, "lead out."

His life flying before his eyes, everything from his training by his father to his first kill, Vulfhelm ran up toward the foothills to the first crags, grumbling about the blasted wolf pelt that had pushed him into this mess.

Suddenly he saw a flicker of white out of the corner of his eye. He heard a cry of "White wolf" behind him. Suddenly a spear whizzed past him, almost nicking his mail. There was a great cry and the army surged forward. For you see, having a white wolf pelt meant much the same to a dwarf, as having that special something from Father Christmas would to you or any of your friends.

Afraid for his life, Vulfhelm dove behind the crag. There he came face-to-face with a white wolf. So that was the one that the army had seen. The wolf looked hard at him. He froze the hunter with his stare.

"He is looking into my heart," Vulfhelm said silently.

Suddenly the wolf transformed. A beautiful white lion with eyes that burned like coals of fire stood before him. They were both hidden by the crag so the army didn't know what was happening there.

"You were right," the lion said softly. "That wolf cowl and pelt was a gift from the Unknown One, for I am He. I am Kyrie, the Creator of this world and of all the free peoples. For, you see, this world is vast beyond your comprehension. There are many more peoples than dwarves in this world.

"Yes," the Lion continued, "the cloak separated you from your fellow dwarves, just as your sin separates you from Me. Do you want me to bridge the gap and do you want to accept your mission? Part of what I want you to do for me is to show your King how not t judge people by their appearances. I shall give the words to speak."

For a while Vulfhelm didn't know what to say. Then joy at the thought of finally being free and of knowing the Unknown One flowed into his heart.

"I accept with all my heart, Master," the dwarf said.

"Then be free." The Lion breathed upon the dwarf. Then a wonderful thing happened. The mail that the hunter wore turned white.

The Lion then said, "You must go home now, for your task is not yet begun."

Kyrie vanished. After a time, Vulfhelm left the crag. He felt as if he had a daddy again, a real Father he would never lose.

When he climbed out of the crag, he encountered King Kundulf and the rest of the Army, who were looking for the wolf.

"Ah, berserk," said Kundulf, eager for the hunt, attempting to coax him with a piece of meat.

"Stop," cried Vulfhelm. "I am not an animal. I am a dwarf of flesh and blood like you. It is not the will of the Unknown One that dwarves or any other being with a soul should be treated like an animal. Listen to me, please."

Then, the eyes of the Dwarven king were opened and he understood the hunter's words.

"Oh, Vulfhelm," said the king, apologetically. "We are all very sorry for the way we treated you. Please forgive us. You've earned the mail you're wearing, that's for sure. Let me help you take that hood off."

"No, sire. I'll keep it. It reminds me of what I've learned today. I'm a dwarf with a purpose now, no mistake about that. It's funny that my name means 'wolf helmet', now isn't it? I won't wonder about that anymore after today."

Pwyll the Hunted

Prologue

This is a brief chronicle of the history of Sarum. Three hundred ninety years after the coming of the faith of the Light to the native elves of Sarum, the pagan dwarves sailed down from the North in many longships. The Raiders did battle with the fair folk, enslaving and killing many. The elves were driven into the far west of Sarum and many sailed a short distance across the sea, to an island that was smaller than Sarum, which they named Erinnar. They established a kingdom there and named the island Erinnar. For over six hundred years, the bellicose dwarves ruled Sarum, eventually embracing the faith of the Light. But then, in the six hundred seventeenth year of the dwarven kingdom, Sarum was taken from the dwarves. Through diplomatic treachery, the human paladin Lord Wulfgar of Strongrock obtained permission from the High Prelate of the Light to invade Sarum. The last dwarven king of Sarum, Hrothulf, was killed by an arrow through the eye in battle against the humans. Since then, the human lords of Strongrock have ruled Sarum. There has been much enmity between the dwarves and their human overlords, and between the humans and the elves still remaining in Sarum. A hundred years after the human conquest of Sarum, Lord Wulfgar's great-great grandson, Harrick, sent many knights across the sea to conquer Erinnar. The elves were soon overwhelmed, and Harrick named his younger son, Jarl, overlord of Erinnar. Now only the small elven nation of Wyllecost in the far west of Sarum, is free from human dominance. The house of Strongrock rules all of the parts of the Isles. Two years after the conquest of Erinnar a babe was born near the border of Wyllecost to Madog, Lord of Langershire fief, and his elven wife, Sionan. They named him Pwyll. They knew it not, but he was to become one of the greatest heroes of our age. He was like a son to me, and I Am honored to be the recorder of his tale.

Gilliam, Abbot of Langershire

The Breaking of Wittandrassil: Paladin Rising

"Tell me again ancient one, why do we need the Knights of the order of Tree?" The Speaker who posed this question was a young man, scarce eighteen. His name was Torith Donan, the youngest initiate in the Order and he had been born long after the war with the demons.

"Ah, young sir," chuckled old Galeth, twenty-ninth Sage of the Warding Staff, as he stroked his long white beard and leaned upon the sacred artifact. "That is a tale as old as the Valley of Crystal itself. Long ago, when the balance of magic was unstable and the earth belched forth fire and spume, the demons rose from their unholy halls and wrought arcane destruction upon the Valley of Crystal. My ancestor, Aronoth, beseeched the High One, and He entrusted my ancestor with the Warding Staff, and with the power of the staff my forefather conjured forth twelve magic swords, holy brand's blessed by the high one to banish and vanquish demons. Aronoth selected twelve men, of pure heart, to fight the demons. Together with the enchantments of my forebear they drove the demons back to the pits from which they came. The High One stretched forth His hand and sealed them away, planting a mighty tree Wittandrassil to bind them with its holy magic so that they may never rise to destroy the Valley of Crystal ever again. The power of the tree is harnessed through the wittenstone, the holy gem at the root of the tree. Let us pray that it never becomes dislodged, for if it does, the demons will break free of their bonds. But now let us go back to the village and eat."

Being the youngest member of the order, Torith was given the duty of watching Galeth's granddaughter, Annandaila. At first, he thought this duty merely one of a glorified nanny but slowly a change came over him. As he saw her dancing in her white silk and gossamer dresses before the great white tree, his heart began to melt and a new strange feeling came over him. One day as they sat before the white tree, Annandaila, who was quite naïve to the magical workings of the Valley, looked down and said, "Torith, there is a white jewel stuck in the roots of the tree. Give me your dagger and I will pry it out. It will make a fine brooch."

"Annan, you mustn't!"
But the girl did not listen. She snatched up Torith's dagger, flew over to the white tree, and began to carve out the wittenstone. The moment it was in her hand there was a great rending and crashing as the white tree Wittandrassil split asunder. Annandaila fell with a scream into the fiery void. The demons rushed forth from the fiery void like a black, crimson tide. Lava belched forth from the earth, turning the lush vegetation of the Valley into ash and cinders.

The warning horn baled the call to battle. Paladins in shining mail and plate armor rushed forth, swinging flashing broadswords pouring forth holy light. Even with the skill and faith of these holy warriors, the demons pressed on, bathing the Valley in darkness and flame. Their desecration was complete. The battle had been like a fog enshrouded dream for Torith. But he did, unknowingly, strike a blow for the cause of righteousness. One of the twelve primary paladins, Gildras, wielder of the holy sword Faea, had fallen back, scarred to the heart by a demon claw. Feebly lifting holy blade and offering it to Torrith he whispered, "The old order is dead. A new paladin must rise. Today you become that Paladin. You are our last hope." Then he died. As Torith was staring speechless at the blade, a demon pounced upon him, knocking him on his back. His instant reaction was to hold the sword in front of him. The holy brand pierced the demon to the heart, the blade glowing with a white fire as it touched the tainted blood. Then the demon was banished back to the fiery void.

After the battle, the demons escaped out of the Valley, to wreak their destruction on the outside world. There was only one other survivor of the battle, Galeth the Sage of the warding staff. His face was grim and as cold as a statue's as he walked toward Torith over the torn earth.

"You have lost your innocence, boy. This is your last day in this paradise, for this paradise is no more." Handing the young man the wittenstone, the old Sage said "The gem is drained of its potency, as is my staff. You are all that is left of the order of the tree. You must gather all the lost vestiges of the holy magic back into the stone so that my staff may have power again and Wittandrassil might be replanted, but first you must rescue Annandaila, for she is held prisoner in the void. This is your destiny, and though you did not choose it, you have been chosen for this sacred task. Go. And may the High One be with you."

At first, Torith Donan thought he might weep, for his sadness was deep and overwhelming. Yet he gritted his teeth and marched off into the distance, hoping to find his destiny and his redemption.

By Blade and Covenant

1.   A Witch Shall Be Saved

Glencoe, Scotland, 1637

"Burn her! Burn her! Burn her for a witch!" Ellery McTavish
looked out in dead silence at the screaming crowd of ruffians,
trying for her death. Oh but that she had not chosen the calling of
an apothecary, but her dying father had had no sons to make
poultices for him so she had had no choice but to break tradition.
Her fiery locks blew in the wind barely covering up the beauty
Mark on her neck that the Inquisitioner had deemed a "devil's
teat". Had she been but a wee bit taller, perhaps her highland legs
could have carried her into the hills away from the mob. The court
held before the village elders had been but a mockery. Her
sentence had been sure the moment they caught her. A huge mud
caked men wearing a mask of black leather shoved her over to the
stake and bound her there with tight cords. Father McCusker came
forward bearing a crucifix and a torch. "Ellery McTavish, you have
been found guilty of practicing magic and consorting with the
Queen of elfland. I willne allow ye last words, lest you cast a spell
on us. She began casting her eyes this way and that, breast heaving,
tears running down her mud-ridden cheeks, praying that anyone,
even a trow or water horse of legend would save her, she could feel
the crackling heat of the flames as it neared the brush and kindling
at her feet. Then suddenly…

BOOM! There was the sound of a pistol report, only seven times
louder than usual. The burning torch fell harmlessly into a pile of
mud and the old priest slumped forward, brains and blood oozing
from a gaping wound in his head. Ellery knew practically nothing
about weapons, but no ordinary flintlock, she knew could wound
like that or have that accuracy, for it seemed that the shot had
come from a great distance. She heard the neighing of a great
Highland stallion, saw the glint of steel out of the corner of her

eye, another shot, strange, for a pistol could not be reloaded that quickly. there seem to be a path clearing among the ruffians as discord an invisible force sowed discord among them. There came out of the pandemonium a Clarion Highland voice. "Faer the Laird and the Covenant!"

Ellery heard a great *thwak* and suddenly realized that her hands were no longer bound. An arm as thick and strong as an iron brace scooped her up onto a galloping horse as she and her unknown savior rode away into the Highlands.

The galloping hooves beat the Highland ground. Ellery shocked eyes saw both hill and glen race past. Suddenly the horse paused. Mighty yet gentle arms lowered into the ground. "Catch your breath, lassie." For the first time, young Ellery looked up to see her rescuer. He was a tall man of about twenty-one years of age. He had very plain garb, wearing dark black breeches and worn riding boots. A highland targe hung on his back, and his torso was protected by a heavy plate cuirass such as the forces of King Charlie wore. Long black gloves that stretched down to the elbow were on his hands. A sharp basket-hilt broadsword hung at his waist. The only ostentatious things about his appearance were the bright red sash about his waist and the flintlock that hung from. It was more beautiful than any firearm she had ever seen. The grip was casting in brass and was as bright and shin as white gold. An old man's face was engraved near the barrel and many lenticular designs were carved behind it, such as French leaflets and flourishes. Ornate signs were even sketched on the barrel itself. But even the firearm was not as beautiful as the man who wielded it. His face was hardened and strong like the Highlands fierce blue Celtic eyes seemed to bore into Ellery use very soul and bespoke a faith that was as essential to the man as bread and water. A thick goatee decorated his mouth and chin. Curly locks cut in the

Puritan fashion yet slightly longer were visible underneath his slouch hat. "Who-who are you, sir?"

The man smiled broadly and dismounted. Removing his hat in a courtly bow. He said with a thick brogue. "I am Killian McGeldenwytt, servant of the Lord, and protector of the covenant, and I am at your service, milady. Like Abraham, I follow the path where the Lord leads me, protecting the weak and innocent and only taking a life when it is absolutely unavoidable. Thus have I said a prayer for the soul of that misguided priest and that the Lord might absolve me of the sin of taking the life of that man of God. For he was a man of God, though I do not agree with his theology. Obviously, I cannot take you back to your village. Therefore, you must come with me. I swear by blade and covenant that I will keep you safe. Please, do not fear me. What is your name?"

"My name is Ellery McTavish of Glencoe. I am in your debt for saving my life. I can see that you are a man of faith. Though your appearance somewhat frightens me, I see no other alternative than to journey with you. I cannot return to my home, for they would kill us both. I can see that you are very fond of the Scriptures, and are of the Covenanter lot. As Catholic as I am, you have opened up my mind to new things. I am indebted to you in the Lord. Therefore, where you go I shall go. And as St. Ruth with the woman Naomi, your faith will be my faith. Perhaps the Lord has orchestrated for our paths to cross for a reason. Unless God takes me to heaven, I will nay leave ye."

"And by the Holy Book and covenant, lass, I shall protect ye in like manner as David did for Jonathan and Abigail. Come. We ride where the Lord leads."

Blades of the New World

Father Joao Tiago

Alternate World: the Japans, 1565

Nagasaki, Jesuit trading post

And now, here upon the Japans

There comes a mighty holy man

Of fiery faith

Arm of the Lord

A man both of the cloth and sword

Jouncing in the cart, Katsuka relived the events of the past few days. She had been a former geisha turned street performer. The man in charge of her performing troupe, a short fat man with a rather volatile temper had announced that the keeper of the black ships, and head of trade for the orange robes, or Jesuits as they called themselves had bought their contracts and was sending them as courtly entertainers to the court of King Fernando Matteo-Alonzo of Portugal, and thus she had prayed to Izanagi, Izanami, Momotaro and anyone else under the Dragon-laden sky who happened to cross her mind that she would not live to see such an event come to pass.

Through the silk-lined latticework, the young woman could make out two distinct figures, one of her master, the other of a Portuguese merchant, and she could hear the rattle clink of coins. Slowly a third figure, so tall and broad shouldered, it seemed almost like an oni of legend, materialized near the edge of the scene, unobserved by the other two., The seeming oni suddenly gave voice to cry that showed the blood of every woman in the cart. Though her butchered Portuguese was somewhat lacking, she thought she heard the massive figure say "In the name of the Father, Son and Holy Ghost, forgive me for what I must do." There was a swooshing sound and the heads of both buyer and seller rolled to the ground. Massive hands thrust open the doors of the cart. A face with the close cropped beard of the Jesuits and eyes that burned with a manic yet compassionate fire bore into her like the blade of a katana. He grabbed her by the wrist and barked in perfectly eloquent Japanese, "If you want to live you must come with me now, *wakarimaska?*"

She nodded, too shocked to form the word.

To the others he yelled. "Flee! Ima! Flee for your lives!"

He hoisted her onto his shoulder and used his fine hand-and-a-half katana to free one of the horses. The confused girl and her unlikely rescuer galloped away from Nagasaki into the coming dawn.

Once they had ridden several miles the man stopped by a small pond next to some tall bamboo plants.

It was only then that the freed slave girl had a good look at him. He was a tall man standing at six feet. He had the look of a Jesuit but did not wear an orange robe, having a black kimono instead in the sash of the kimono was a katana worn in the proper samurai fashion, with the blade facing upward in the scabbard. Thus, it could be drawn in one sweeping motion by bringing blade away from scabbard and scabbard away from blade simultaneously in an upward stroke so as to most likely strike a killing blow. And for the markings of a fine workshop though Katsuka, being a commoner, did not know much about katanas, preferring to use the Japanese dagger, or tanto. The man wore the broad-brimmed black hat of a Jesuit, though this along with his skin tone and grooming styles was the only thing noticeably European about him. He smiled slightly as she looked at him.

"Forgive me, ona-gozen. You must, as the shepherds who found our Lord, be sore afraid. You do not even know my name. Allow me to introduce myself. I am Father Joao Tiago, lately of, but not quite, the Society of Jesus."
"Then what are you doing here? And why in Izanami's Realm did you rescue me?"

"Oh. Well… that is a long story, that one. I was cast out, for nowadays the church run by the vicar of Peter does not smile upon the science which acquires gold. And so now do I travel the land acquiring the gold of heaven by speaking for those who cannot speak for themselves and defending those who cannot defend themselves such as you. I do not know what have life you had back there but I do perceive that you'll be much better off with a protector, rather than an owner, for I can plainly see that as far as your life back there is concerned, as we say in my homeland long lost, Innes is dead. What is your name, young one?"

"Katsuka. I owe you my life and the life upon this unknown road is better than being bought and sold like chattel. Lead on." She bowed slightly.

"I vow that, as I protect my own life, I will protect you, Katsuka-san."

Katsuka gasped. Never before had any man spoken her name with such honor.

"Where do we go from here, Yashto-san?" Katsuka asked after they had breakfasted next day. Yashto was her name for the former priest, for she could say neither Joao nor Tiago. At which the father smiled and said she would never be able to memorize the disciples of the Savior.

But to the question he answered. "To Osaka village and Castle. There are several good things for alchemy to be obtained at the market there. Also there is talk of a new daimyo. I believe his name is Ieyasu and he comes from the Tokugawa clan. I have never been one to compromise my principles but that is not say that in turbulent new times such as these one should not be in the good graces of powerful friends. I just hope that a certain Jesuit, Rector Miguenillo, is not there. If so, he should watch his purse."

"Wakarimasen."

"Oh. He is a very avaricious man. That and his testimony against me cast me out of the Society of Jesus. I should very much like to see him…Ah, no. No. Ie. I have vowed to take lives only when necessary. For if a man needlessly sheds the blood of another man, by yet another man shall his blood be shed. So it says in the Law of Noah and Moses."

But let us not talk of such things. It is nearly mid-day and not a fleck of brown rice or orange chicken has danced on my lips."

"I thought the society only ate the best European breads and pork shanks," said the younger woman with a thoughtful air.

"Every stomach in the world must bloom where it is planted. I know you're probably not going to like this. But when we going into the inn in that village you must pose as my servant. A Jesuit traveling in the company of a former geisha would arouse suspicion. Sin? That is to say, Hai?"

The girl nodded.

The Orange Shishi was a small inn with a dilapidated sign depicting the eponymous Asian mythological lion dog carved upon it, much of the orange paint now chipped away. Going inside, the Jesuit and his "servant" found a sweaty man behind the counter with several dust ridden people eating bowls of rice, beef and chicken and speaking in hushed voices. "Watered down sake and a bowl of brown rice with orange chicken. The same for my servant please." The rice paper door swung open and shut and four burly men reeking of sweat and sake staggered into the room.

"Say I, *hick*, know who you are," burped the leader, the stench of his breath nearly curling Joao Tiago's beard. "You are a Jesuit. Probably have the alms for that new Christian temple in Osaka. Let's have a look."

All four men's hands move toward concealed wakizashis. "Hide under the counter, quick," he hissed to Suka and then barreled his massive shoulders into the line of drunkards.

Once they were all outside, the Jesuit samurai drew his katana and crouched in a defensive position. "Say," the leader said, "that's a Masamune style blade. Very rare nowadays. Should fetch a good price with a ronin."
The big man charged. But the lively Jesuit was too quick and brought the blade over and across in a lightning quick motion across his attacker. Just as the leader started to fall, gurgling up blood from the wound, the Jesuit pushed the dying man into the two other attackers, causing the ruffians to teeter off balance. Decapitating one, the Jesuit then cleft the other from shoulder blade to hip. The last took flight and the Jesuit did not follow. Instead the father cleansed his blade, sheathing it. Kneeling, he crossed himself and prayed, "O Lord, have mercy on the souls of these prematurely departed. They knew not what they did. Forgive me for the taking of their lives. I did not will it so. Amen."

He picked up one of the wakizashis that the bandits had dropped, stripped the dead man of the scabbard and went back inside the inn. Everyone had taken cover, for fear that the Jesuit had been outmatched and the bandits would be returning.

"It's all right. You may all come out now."

"Domo Arigato. Thank you, thank you, kind sir." Said the innkeeper. That Ingeko and his band have been disturbing the peace in this village for years. Now at last we are rid of them. Rest assured, you always find friends here. And your meals are on the house."

"Truly it is the best orange chicken I have ever eaten."

"What is that for?" Suka asked, indicating the shorter sword.

"This is for you," the Jesuit said. "Not the best craftsmanship, I'll admit, but it shall serve its purpose."

"But it is forbidden for women to carry swords."

"It was also forbidden for King David of Israel to eat the shew bread. You are no ordinary woman," the Jesuit said softly.

"But I don't know how to wield it."

"Then I will teach you. Come, we have finished our meal. Let us go."

Toyokata Village, 2 days later

"Well, bless my Greenwich armor! Father Tiago, you buccaneering confessor!"

Tiago whirled, taking the Tokimune stance, placing himself in front of Katsuka. From the shadows of the dusking alley stepped a man about a head taller than the Jesuit. His mouth was curved upward in a flash of a grin and his ruddy-haired head tilted slightly to the side, but his form cried out far more than a simple fop. Beneath his azure plate armor were corded Saxon muscles, far superior to those of Norman influences. A fine side sword of Toledo make hung in his baldric.

"Good evening, Roger Haverland," Joao replied in Portuguese. "I knew not that you had license to privateer this far east, that is if you do still pilot *The Green Man's Revenge*."

"Aye. I am both pilot and captain now, but privateer no more. My homeland can fight the Spanish on her own."

"What of your homeland? Does Bess Plantagenet still rule England?"

"She does. The Huscarl Council still governs in her name. Robert Bruce V rules the Kingdom of Scotland, Rodrig X rules Wales and King Patrick O'Brien stills sits enthroned over the Emerald Isle."
"The last time I saw you, you were about to sail to a parley with young Captain Drake off the coast of Hispaniola."
"Tisk, tisk, well that did not end well. This is not something you would say, but the young brat can kiss my codpiece. I seriously doubt if he will ever amount to anything. However it did end better than the time I saw you almost flayed alive by that corsair Onibakka and his band of cutthroats."
"They…tried. Unsuccessfully, obviously….No matter. When you first accosted us, I thought you were an attacker. But where are my manners…. This is my ward, Katsuka-san."

He then translated an introduction for the captain to the girl.

"Truly she is far fairer than the White Lotus. I would suspect you were thinking of leaving your holy vows, priest?"
Tiago's eyes flared, hand moved to hilt. And he did not translate Haverland's latest witticism.

"Peace… Peace, friend Joao. It was but a jest. Where are the winds of your fury blowing you at the moment?"

"We are headed to Osaka to investigate the young Tokugawa. Hopefully Oda Nobunaga will not discover I am there."

"Hopefully it won't be like Kyoto last year, when the town guard nearly crucified us. That was my last time masquerading as a tuga. My ship is anchored near here. I'd be more than happy to carry you to the port nearest Osaka."
"I have never cared for your profane manner, *Anglais*. But the Lord looks at the heart. Lead on."

The Green Man's Revenge was a refurbished war galleon: 52 guns, a lean and trim prow that was spiked and could also be used for ramming and a keel that could cut the water like a razor. She was capable of an incredible 500 kn. Mister Kiernan, a half-drunk Scotsman with a leg made of blackthorn, kept an armory of 5000 Spanish cutlasses, 3500 pistols and 1000 boarding axes and hooks. Though most of the crew were seventh sons of Europe, there were several who were from that region of the world. The cook was from Siam, Mongkut by name, a short man with quick reflexes, bald save for a tail of hair tied at the top of his head. Though most of his cutlery with used for making khrua and other such dishes, he wore two Siamese sabers, and he excelled in their use. He was the friendliest to the Jesuit upon introduction, for he had been baptized at the hands of Xavier himself. And also there was the quartermaster, Harsha Sandeep, whose family had been followers of Christ since the days when St. Thomas came from the holy land. His family had dwelt long in Tamul, and he retained the dark-hued skin of that region of India. Although he was a follower of the true faith, he had trained long in the Sikh martial arts and wore their turban, always black in color, but instead of putting the khanda broadsword sigil upon it, he had pinned to it a crucifix. He excelled in the use of buckler and Indian saber and always wore a cuirass made from overlapping strips of black boiled leather. The others were half breeds with little known lineage to their name, and sons of Portugal Spain and Italy, all of whom, though they had blackmailed, drank and gambled their way to this Eastern Tortuga, were fiercely loyal and worth every ounce of their salt in a sea battle.

Three days out of the harbor an Asian gale came roaring in from the east and drove the ship North. For days it seemed as if the helmsman was reeling like a drunk man

Black Flag and Black Book

Trinidad, 1646

Well, they call me hangin' Johnny.

Away, boys, away

They call me hangin'' Johnny,

And it's hang, boys, hang

Topangan looked with dead eyes out upon the world. Topangan. He now doubted if that even was his name, for he had been call "you" and "boy" so many times since the Song-Mali had swept down upon his village from the north, enslaving and raping as they came. They were Mohammedans, forcefully converted from the docile Coptic faith by the edge of the scimitar some centuries earlier. Topangan and his people still kept to the primitive animistic faiths. Therefore, the Song-Mali saw them as animals to be slaughtered and enslaved for jihad. But desire for trade and profit is a universal urge in the hearts of doomed men, so Topangan and his fellow hunters were sold to British plantation overseers for work on the sugar plantations in the West Indies. Two burly, whiskey-rife overseers stood on the river dock next to the slave, waiting to ferry him across to the plantation, the last order of the day. They were armed with slightly rusted hangers in case one in their charge happened to struggle free and bolt for the surrounding foliage.

Suddenly, Topangan's ears twitched as they caught a whistling sound floating on the warm Caribbean breeze. It was the tune of *Hangin' Johnny*. Topanga thought he saw he something descend from the overhang. It was a hulking mass, but moved with the skill of a spider monkey.

"Wilcox," slurred one guard to the other. "Was it my ears only, er do you hear... *Gurp.*"

Long blades protruded forward through the chests of the overseers, then unseen hands withdrew them. The young African was in a shocked stupor as his wraith-like rescuer hurried him into the dense brush.

"Are ye hurt?" A resonant, brogue-laden voice asked.

It was only then that Topanga fully saw his savior.

The man was well over six feet tall. He had fierce blue eyes and a dark beard, short and manicured but thick. He wore a black slouch hat, as one would typical find on a cavalier. Despite the tropical heat, he wore gloves, a heavy jerkin and thick traveler's boots, all of brown leather. A long black coat with red cuffs, the inverse of those worn by the new professional English soldiers, the grenadiers, was draped about him.

From his belt hung two swords of rare damascene steel. One was a long saber with a flambeau guard; the other was a hanger with a heavy blade and almost non-existent basket. Above these, two flintlock pistols hung in a bright red sash.

Endeavoring to save the black man from shock, the stranger smiled and whispered. "Do not worry, brother, I will neither harm you nor enslave you. It is written spiritually in the Book of Romans, in the Great Book that guides my wandering path that whom Christ sets free is free indeed. I am Ehud McKiernan, of the Covenant, a friend to all the oppressed in these parts. You my friend, are the snowflake that starts the avalanche. Now, you may tell your name later. But, I cannot free your brethren across the river alane, so I must know: Will you help me?" Topangan managed a nod.

In a pistol flash, the mysterious Scotsman led the former slave deeper into the Jungle. Topangan had no time for any thoughts save one: Surely this God of Love and Mercy was different than the god of the slavers. Topanga wanted to know more of him.

Fathoms of the Bowl

"From Galla we get brandy

From Borinkeen comes rum

Sweet oranges and lemons from the Tougains come

But whiskey and cider are Bretland's control,

Bring in the punch ladle, we'll fathom the bowl."

The old bar song rolled forth from Sally Brown's ale-stained lips. She was the entertainer in *La Pajara Linda*. Governor Zingaro thought that it served only privateers, but in truth there were always more than a few full-fledged Pyrates present. (Letters of mark mattered little in Borinkeen.)

One such ruffian had been keeping his wandering eye fixed as well as possible on the robust young lady for quite some time, and, as soon as the song ended, barged his way over to the counter, slurring, "I'm thirsty for the wine of yer lips, lass." His flailing hands reached for Sally, as a look f terror spread across her face.

Suddenly a cry of "Bakka!" rang out and a katana, such as those used by the samurai of the Jahappans cleaved the drunkard to the breast bone. Sally had time enough to see her rescuer before he stole out into the night. He was a tall Tougain with the gaze of a priest in his eye. He had a goatee and mane of short dark hair, and the mane was partially covered by a featherless black musketeer hat. He wore a black kimono and his samurai blade was of watered steel.

Sally whispered a prayer of thanks for her silent gallant, Father Joao Tiago, for that was his name, though she knew it not.

Ehud McKiernan Walked through the open air market with his Ouaitiin friend Tapangan. Ehud and his black blood-brother were searching for the same thing, the Norbretman's slouch hat. For, despite thee excessive Karribbean heat, the brogue-tongued McKiernan liked the handsome figure he fetched in his brown leather jerkin and pants. Fully armed under his red-cuffed black silk waist-coat, he felt quite the privateer, or rather, I truth, liberator. But he was incomplete without his famed brethren slouch.

"Ah, koowan, (*brother*)," Boomed Tapangan, "That Tougain clown there has your hat."

Approaching fromabout a hundred yards away was a rather mismatched and ridiculous looking Tougain sporting a black slouch incongruously paired with a Jhappanian kimono, albeit black.

"Ho, sirrah, lira lee," Brogued McKiernan, "Ye've absconded with m'hat. Return her or taste highland steel."

The Tougain raised an eyebrow. "The Holy Writ says that wine is a mocker and beer a brawler and I don't know how much of either you've had so early in the morning but this hat is mine, thus I bid you both good day. *Pax Vobiscum.*"

"A papery, are we?" sneered the Bret, drawing his watered steel cutlass and saber, but honorably leaving his brace of flintlocks. Sheathed. "Well I am of the Heeland Covenant faith. Have at you!"

"Wait!" Cried a third voice. A rotund, disgruntled, barkeep pushed himself in between the two would- be combatants. "Father, please. before you kill this man allow him to pay his debt to my establishment. What's more, he left his hat behind. Lucky I didn't keep it as collateral, eh?"

Tapangan and Ehud began to laugh and even the usually stoic Tougain half-grinned. "Where are my manners? Ehud McKiernarn's my name, and this is my blood-brother, the machete-wielding Tapangan, very handy in a rough spot, I might add. I apologize for all this. Let me treat you to breakfast While I fathom the bowl."

"Yours truly, Father Joao Tiago, Thanks you, my friends.

When all intake had settled, Father Joao asked, "What, if I may make so bold is your business here? Privateering?" McKiernan leaned in close and lowered his voice. "You are a man of the cloth, so though our theology is different, I believe I can trust you. Tapangan and I are clandestinely working to end the slave trade in these islands."

The priest chuckled softly. "Not many would approve of your methods…or mine. I have many secret connections here from years of being a blade for the Lord. After several aimless years, I have again found a cause to call my own. We shall forge freedom here by crossed steel."

"Thus we are named priest, the Crossed-Steel Brotherehood." "Aye<" asserted Tapangan.

Thus that day a new family was born as three hands were struck together.

1. Bullies in the Alley

"Help me, Bob, I'm bully in the alley
Way hey, way hey, bully in the alley.
Help me, Bob, I'm bully in the alley
Bully down in shinbone al."
-Borinkeen halyard shanty

Tapangan's eyes fluttered open to see the dawn light reflecting off the bluish green palm thatched roof of the bungalow at the *Boar's Eye*. He and his two compatriots had been staying in the shoddily built inn for about a week. Joao had received word through his clandestine sources that a shipment of slaves was due to arrive on board a Bretland captained by one Brian McSheyten. If rumors held true, Master McSheyten was one of the cruelest sea dogs to ever call port in Borinkeen. His colors were of a Keltik Raven perched atop a skull. His heart was black, but there was one color that mattered more to him: the color of gold.

There was the sound of booted feet upon the ladder and McKiernan appeared carrying a platter of coconut halves and limes along with several small bottles of light ale.

"Eat quickly friend. McSheyten's foul auction takes place within the hour."

He threw down a cloth laden with several braces of pistols, a blunderbuss, powder and shot.

"I procured these from several trustworthy friends. We may need them at the auction stand. Tiago is waiting. Come."

By Prayer and Piracy

Introduction

My dear lad,

Now do I lie on my death bed, with no things save these hands and these memories. It is for thee, Benjamin, my dear grandson, that I write this account of my life, and though many things within this record may seem altogether too fantastic, you must suspend disbelief for the love of old father Ankyrk.

I, Brenford Ankyrk, was born in the Year of our Lord 1549, the son of Jamison Ankyrk and his wife Tabitha. That was the year as you know of the prayer book rebellion against the representatives of the young King Edward. As we had many Catholic neighbors, and our family was of the first buddings of that stock now known as the separatists, or more recently, Puritans, we feared for our lives. We sojourned from Cornwall to live in London until the time of the ascension of that witch-maid, Mary Tudor. During her many persecutions of those of the true faith we hid, like the unnamed Saints of the book of Hebrews, in hovels and holes in the ground.

Then, after the ascension of Elizabeth, who reigned even until recently, we moved near the Romney Marshes when I was 16 years of age, in the late fall of the Year of our Lord 1565. And there, upon that silt-misted landscape, is where my whirlwind of an adventure with Certain Gentlemen, the act of which I am both proud and ashamed, truly began.

1.   A Capstan for my Cross

One evening, I was meandering down by the shoreline after evening prayers. I told father it was easier to say my psalms there. But in reality I went to the sea to skip stones and watch the gulls. Suddenly, I saw a strange light bobbing toward me out of the darkness like a lightning worm in the sea. As it came near, I grew afraid and hid in the brush. Two men with long stocky legs like those of a flamingo in New Spain came walking down near where I hid. Their pantaloons were dark, dirty and rent. And I could see up through the reeds that one bore a somewhat small rapier and his companion bore a mortuary sword. They were talking in hushed voices. "Wine's comin' in aboard the Gemini tonight. The Clagger's not been good on his dues lately. Devil can take the old snake as far as I'm concerned. I never much trusted Welshmen or half breeds and he's both. Well. It's a good thing I brought along me old da's pig-sticker, just in case things have a mind to turn unsavory. Hullo? What's the… gottya."

Having noted me, the fellow with the mortuary sword, reached down into the brush and hauled me out by the collar of my shirt. "What 'ave we here? This one's a somber-clothed young rat. Smells clean. What's that black book you got there, bilge-pump? A psalter? Bah! Thought as much. One of them separatists, for sure! He'd rat us out and no mistake. The magistrate would be down on us like maggots on bread. I say we slit 'is pretty little throat."

"Hold, Warwhite," said the other, the one with the rapier, who was much taller than his stocky companion. "I may just have an idea. As you know, old Clagger always be lookin' for new cabin boys to make the wine runs. We could we use a little bit of a discount on that shipment of wine sailing in tonight. Do you follow me, old man?"
"I say, Bingley. Truer words were never spoken. Not even by the blessed St. Paul himself. And ho! Look! Here comes the old devil of a sea dog of 'oom I was speakin' just now! Good even, Captain Clagger! "

The smuggler, the one called Warwhite, who was still gripping me by the collar, cuffed me on the back of the neck so that I fell in the packed, grungy sand. I opened my eyes to find that I was staring at a pair of seaweed-caked seamen's boots of Bristol make. I raise my head and looked up at the face of a man who my old dad would surely say was Asteroth of the Inferno himself. Up from the boots, the iron-built legs were clad in smelly breeches of brown burlap, two matching heavy wooden-hilted rapiers with brass guards and pommels hung in the brown steel-studded belt. His off-white sleeves were billowy like those common to the royal Tudors and their courtiers. But the torso sported a sort of brown leather gambeson to deflect sword cuts. His arms now akimbo, the captain's hands were clenched into tight, grimy fists that could just as easily rain down a blow as grasp a grog bottle. Worse yet, the mammoth man's nails were horribly un-manicured to say the least.

His bald head was topped with a beige slouched sailor's beret, but oh, to this day I can still remember that satanically evil face. Several scars from encounters with the Tatars in the Eastern seas adorned it like grim battle trophies. His eyes were of blue fire, like the base of a flame just upon the wick of candle. He had a raven beard shaped like that of John Calvin, but it was unruly and dripped often with barley beer, as I would soon come to know. Even when he smiled wickedly, it seemed as though he was sneering with malice and hatred. He was not holy enough even for the deepest circles traversed and seen by Dante. Little did I know it, but that man, demon or sorcerer though he may have been, would shape the course of decades of my life.

"We've got a cabin boy to sell ye, Cap'n. In exchange for a little discount on this month's shipment, that is."
Clagger's hand moved for a moment toward the hilt of one of his swords. Then he lifted me high into the air and began sniffing me, which felt like being jerked through the bowels of hell on the back of Ceberus. Poking and prodding me with his spike-like finger.

Then he set me down with a snarl and a grunt.

He spat and barked. "Seems fit enough. A little bony perhaps, but there is nothing that the nine tails and a few turns of the capstan

won't improve. All right then, Warwhite. You blokes have yourself
a little deal. About the price now. This boy is probably worth five
shillings at best. You owe me fifteen for the wine and the madeira,
and that's not to mention that I had a little trouble procuring this
round of stock. You can have it for ten."

"Nine."

"Nine and a farthing. Not a hay penny less."

"You bleed me, Master Clagger. But… I suppose 'tis fair. Done,
then."

The one called Bingley handed over a bag of coin, and the two in
turn begrudgingly gripped Clagger's sword arm to seal my fate. The
hulking captain dragged me to his dinghy and I left behind
everything I had ever known, and what little I knew of God, and
went aboard that cauldron of hell that sailed upon the waves, the
contraband ship Gemini.

"Poor old death came riding by

And we say so, and we know so

Poor old death came riding by

Oh, poor old man

The ship Gemini was neither a fortress ship nor a sloop but rather
a foundling of the two. The fo'csle was very low and old man
Clagger's cabin was very high. Her Bowsprit sported the carved
images of two twins joined at the shoulder with no right or left
arm. The free outstretched arm of each figure held a bared cutlass.

An old barnacled cutter hung over the port side of the sloop-ship.
A narrow staircase led down into the hull where the spirits and

other contraband lay. The Gemini was very small and could not afford to employ a master of arms. Therefore, in case of scuffles with the local militias or, more likely, the magistrate's soldiers, there was a cabinet within the captain's cabin stuffed to the brim with pistols, dirks, powder, shot, sailor's axes and other weapons.

I was first placed on capstan duty under the tyrannical eye, for he had but one, of Angus "Brimstone" McBride. The story went that he had been marooned off the coast of Hispaniola and had never bothered to signal any Spanish ships for fear of being hung from a yardarm. So he hid there, his raven tufts of hair glistening with sweat from the Caribbean sun, until a gull plucked up enough courage to come and peck one of his steel blue eyes. And so when Captain C. peeled his stinking carcass from the boiling rock and "nursed" the hellish Scot back to health, old Brimstone sworn loyalty to the old man.

To my young inexperienced back, it seemed as though the anchor weighed at least 1000 stone, though I know this is an exaggeration's. My plight was worsened when the black-locked Scotsman was stumbling drunk nearly every morning. At first I would try to mutter my Psalms and Commandments, but the blustering Gael would bark and slur, "GIVE US A SHANTY, WHARF RATS!"

Ye bonnie bunch o' maidens, ho!

Come down, ye bonnie maidens, Come down

There's much a flask o' gin tae go.

Come down, ye bonnie maidens, come down!"

At first, the sinful tunes stung all that was left of my conscience almost as much as McBride's nine-tails did whenever I would drop to my knees from exhaustion. But as the last of my convictions eroded away, I began to love the Scotsman's shanties, and sang them with gusto.

And so my unrighteous, angry melody rang a thunderous din inside my spirit until that fateful day when it reached a terrifying crescendo.

I found one friend who softened the blow of my soul's demise: my sea-brother Parthak. He was the dark skinned African galley slave, and among all the coal-hearted rogues on board the Gemini, he had a heart as bright and stalwart as a diamond in the mines of Solomon. He had been on board ship for years and possessed very good English. He would bring us capstan boys are barley grool at midday. He must have taken a liking to me for he would occasionally stuff bits of salt pork into my bowl, having properly concealed it within the mush. I am glad today that he saw what he did in me, for I would have surely met my death falling underneath the capstan and Brimstone's forked "tongue' if Parthak had not come to my aid. Every time he would hand me the bowl, he would whisper in my ear, "Take heart, brother. Rise up before they take away your name."
That bit of courage imparted through those words is what drove me to persevere through the pain and the even worse hell that was to come a short while later.

At this time, I had been serving as a cabin boy for almost two years. One day, when we were in the open sea well between Kent and Calais, a violent scuffling sound came from the Clagger's cabin. Benjamin Dale, a scrawny boy originally from the marshes had been serving as the old man's "valet", a job the rest of us dreaded as it entailed serving as his personal whipping stand. At the end of the scuffle came the rasp of steel and a bloodcurdling scream. The old man emerged from his cabin, still a bit drunk and carrying poor young Dale's limp form. Tossing the corpse unceremoniously over the starboard bow, old man Clagger staggered over to brimstone and slurred, "Mr. McBride, I shall no longer require that bilge rat Dale's service. Which other one of these seal turds can you recommend to serve as a good, strong valet?"

From my years at the capstan, my arms as well as the muscles in my legs had begun to bulge, so that in build I resembled a slightly shorter Captain Clagger. And so the big Scotsman's single eye alighted its gaze on me.

"The Cornish one would be able to carry your pistols for you and can tote a crate of madeira. What thinks you, Captain?"
"Excellent thought, me ol' Brimstone! Come along, rat tooth." He seized my arm in a vice-tight grip and dragged me off to that third circle of hell: his cabin.

Stave 2 The Blook

To my God, family, readers and subscribers. For my new bundle of joy, Connor Baby #3! Can't wait to meet you!~Uncle Bubby

In this "Best of" collection, Marshal Myers shares the best posts from his now retired sworddreamer blog. The blog ran from May 2010 to May 2013 and can still be viewed in its entirety at sworddreamer.wordpress.com.

Power Ballad

Posted on March 30, 2011 by sworddreamer

I thought I'd share a story that is the only vaguely scifi story I've ever written. Enjoy!

Power Ballad

Dedicated with Love and Prayers to Jamie George, Andrew Littlefield and the Staff at the George Center for Music Therapy. You inspire me!

Michelle awoke to a familiar high-pitched beeping. She looked at the clock. 6 AM. She groaned. Both she and Gabrielle had taken up the human habit of sleeping, much to the chagrin of their boss, who was code-named Big Daddy.

In their natural form, Michelle and Gabrielle looked human, though human eyes were not designed to look upon beings of their kind. They were extraterrestrials, of a sort. Big Daddy had given them bodies resembling attractive human young women in their early twenties. They sometimes wished to see their home in sector Caelum 3, but they knew their missions across the galaxies were of high importance.

Michelle knew well the sound that had awakened her. It was Big Daddy's mission camera, which he used to communicate with the agents of Lux across the galaxies. "Wh-what did I miss?" a slightly groggy, singsong voice asked.

Michelle turned to see Gabrielle walking slowly toward the communication monitor, rubbing sleep from her eyes. Both Gabrielle and Michelle were about the same height in their human form. Michelle had very dark straight hair, a light complexion and blue eyes. Gabrielle had wavy dirty blond hair and coffee brown eyes.

"Good morning, sleepy head. You haven't missed anything. I haven't answered the call yet."

Michelle walked over to the communication monitor and pushed the Accept button. The screen buzzed and soon showed Big Daddy in his human form. "Good morning, agents!" He said jovially. "Sleeping late again?"

"When you have human bodies, you have to eat and sleep like a human." Gabrielle laughed.

"I have a new mission for you, a very important mission. The dark force is trying to take over another planet. This planet, Tirian, is very much like the original planet. Same atmosphere, flora, fauna and human population. The dark master arrived a few years ago under the guise of mega-businessmen Alistair Roth of the Asteroth Corporation, a company that promises utopia in exchange for leadership. They have already set up a metropolitan, almost completely totalitarian state. Our enemy's technology developers are working on a mind control system that will completely enslave the planet. It will be launched in a few hours. Through some of Special Agent Mike's string pulling under my orders, the savant special-education school in the capital city is in need of new team music teachers.

"That's where you come in. I'm sending you to pose as special ed music teachers. Many of these students already have a special connection with me and will sing from example. You must teach them some of these songs from the original planet. I will give you glasses to see what I am doing while they're singing."

He pressed a button and two old leather-bound books appeared in front of them. He pressed another button and two female business suits replaced their bath robes. Picking up the books, they used their special, Caelum 3 hypervision to memorize the power ballads.

"Now I'm going to transport you from the station to Tirian. It will be very dangerous, but the power ballads will help protect you. I will be with you, as always. After this mission, you can return to Caelum 3 for sabbatical. Go with my blessing."

There was a beam of light from the space station as the two agents of Lux shot towards their destination.

Alistair Roth sat at his mahogany desk in his office on the highest floor of Asteroth's metropolitan office building. Everything was going according to plan. Soon the planet would be entirely in his grip, and there was nothing that pesky Big Daddy could do about it. He grinned wickedly. His assistant, Mr. Jann, entered the room.

"Is everything ready?"

"Yes, sir. All the mind boxes, which they foolishly think are radios and other news devices, are hooked up to your main computer. All you have to do is send your brain waves through the network, and everyone on this planet will be slaves to your will."

"Excellent, " Mr. Roth laughed. "It's only a matter of time, Big Daddy. Only a matter of time."

Michelle and Gabrielle materialized around the corner from the special ed music school. Like every building in the capital city of Tirian, it was guarded by a police squad armed with flamethrowers. They wore their communication devices on their helmets.

"If we don't do everything just right, it could be curtains for our human bodies." Gabrielle said telepathically.

"Just follow my lead," Michelle responded, likewise inaudibly.

The lead officer pointed his flamethrower at Michelle. "What are you doing here?" he demanded. "These are business and school hours. Regulation does not permit civilians to be on the streets at this time.

"We are the new music teachers for this school."
"Oh, yeah," he snarled, "prove it. Sing us a little ditty."

"Very well," she said, mentally selecting a simple song from the book and praying that they did not have their communication devices on.

"As I went down in the river to pray

Studying about that good old way

And who shall wear the starry crown,

Good Lord, show me the way.

Oh sinners, let's go down

Let's go down, don't you wanna come down?

Oh sinners, let's go down,

Down in the river to pray."

The officer lowered his flamethrower. "I'm sorry, ma'am," he said, a tear coming to his eye. "Please, go on in."

Gabrielle and Michelle walked past the troop of policemen into the school. They were greeted by a proper looking man in a business suit. "Hello, ladies. I've been expecting you. I am Mr. Naumann, the interim teacher. I will go introduce you to your class."

They entered a brightly painted room with about twenty kids seated in wheelchairs and standing in walkers. There was a piano, as well as a table with a violin and a xylophone.

"These kids," Naumann whispered, "may not be able to say much, but they have the voices of angels."

"I'm sure," said Gabrielle, winking.

As she walked by the table, Gabrielle bumped it, sending the ever-present mind box crashing to the floor. Mr. Naumann was speechless.

"Oh don't worry about that. We'll get it cleaned up later. For now, let's start."

"Here is the list of recommended songs." Naumann stammered, still quite flustered.

The two women scanned the titles. "A-S-T-Asteroth", "Mr. Alistair's Good City", "Hooray for Mr. Roth". Yep. All enemy propaganda.

"Hi everyone!" Gabrielle said in a loud cheerful voice. "I think we'll start with something different today. Ms. Michelle is going to help me on the violin."
Michelle picked up the violin and started to play a tune originally conceived by a human on the original planet named Bach.

At the proper time, Gabrielle started to sing:

"Jesu, joy of man's desiring,
Holy wisdom, love most bright;
Drawn by Thee, our souls aspiring
Soar to uncreated light.
Word of God, our flesh that fashioned,
With the fire of life impassioned,

Striving still to truth unknown,
Soaring, dying round Thy throne.

"Through the way where hope is guiding,
Hark, what peaceful music rings;
Where the flock, in Thee confiding,
Drink of joy from deathless springs.
Theirs is beauty's fairest pleasure;
Theirs is wisdom's holiest treasure.
Thou dost ever lead Thine own
In the love of joys unknown."

Gabrielle motioned for the kids to join in, and their singing was almost as beautiful as the singing on Caelum 3.

Alastair Roth was in his office with Mr. Jann. His computer was hooked up for the takeover. And his fingers tingled with excitement. All he had to was press the enter key and he would send his brain waves through the mind boxes across the planet. They would be slaves to his will. Just as his finger was about to touch the key the computer shorted out, and began to glow. Quickly becoming very frustrated, he growled, "Jann, why is this happening? You said everything would work perfectly."

Mr. Jann hurriedly pressed some buttons on his GPS. "The interference is coming from the special ed school. Wavelengths are coming out from there that are so strong that they are destroying the communication capability of the mind boxes. This could take years to repair. The people will get angry and Asteroth Inc. will be finished."

"There could only be one explanation," Alistair huffed. "Agents of the Lux."

While the kids were singing, the two special agents put on their glasses and saw that the singing voices of the children were becoming currents of powerful Light that were destroying Asteroth's deceitful grip on the planet. They had accomplished their mission.

When the children were finished singing the hymn, Michelle and Gabrielle looked back to see that Mr. Naumann was crying. "That was beautiful. Please teach them more of those songs."

"I think you are more cut out for this work than we are," Gabrielle said smiling. She gave him the hymnal, and another book, saying, "Read to them from this book. It's called the Word."

They then left for the place where they would port home to Caelum 3. As they were just about to port, they heard a gruff voice shouting at them. It was Alastair Roth. "You may have won this time, Angelorum, but it's not the end. I will be back."

"But soon it will be the end, Hassatan," the cherubim said together. "In the end, fire and sulfur is reserved for you and yours."

The Enemy cried out in rage and was gone. Gabrielle looked at her companion and said, "Come on, Michal, let's go home."

There was a flash of light in the sky above Tirian as two cherubim traveled home to the Third Heaven.

Prince William's Bride

Posted on <u>April 11, 2011</u> by <u>sworddreamer</u>

Here is another fairytale I wrote for Miriam. It is a parable of sorts.

Prince William's Bride

Once upon a time, in the faraway kingdom of Winsbury, there lived a handsome knightly Prince named William. William was brave and bold, often riding his horse into battle against ogres and other nasty monsters. Though it was true that William's life was exciting, he was lonely. One night, he dreamed of a maiden in a dark, dank tower in a land surrounded by shadow. It was apparent from the dream that the poor girl didn't even know she was in a kingdom of shadow. She was not beautiful by Winsbury standards, but to William, she was the most beautiful woman in the world. William went to Liam, the king's wizard to see if he could interpret the dream. After sitting a long time, blowing smoke rings from his pipe, Liam said, "The girl in your dream is the Princess of the Shadowlands. It is a dark evil place to the South, which, since the great war, has been cut off from Winsbury."

William went to his father, King Allen, and said, "I am going to take a donkey and ride down to the Shadowlands to woo its Princess. I will put on the disguise of a beggar of the Shadowlands."

He put on poor ragged clothes and journeyed to the tower where the Princess Mariana, for that was her name, lived. He entered the tower as a servant and started to become friends with her. Then he told her who he truly was. He asked her to marry him and she said yes. Before William and Mariana could marry, she had to become a woman of Winsbury. So in the dead of night, he took her to the North and baptized her in the crystal pool outside his father's Castle. Then they were married with much celebration. Taking her back to her dark tower, he said, "I will leave you here for a while. But I will be back soon to conquer the Shadowlands so we can be together forever." So he left to ready his army for invasion. The years passed, and every morning at sunrise, Mariana would look to the north for a sign of his coming. Her father, King Dowder, would tell her that he had forgotten her, or sometimes tell her that her husband was merely a dream. Then, just as she started to believe that he would never come, he burst out of the horizon on a white horse, dressed in gleaming armor. He reclaim the Shadowlands for his father, and they were made beautiful again. He took her to Winsbury Castle where they celebrated the victory with a great feast. Then, and only then, could it be said that they lived happily ever after.

The Sword, Lady and Light

Now that my third book is published I wanted to share this essay I wrote shortly after finishing Light Bringer. It chronicles my personal journey so far in my adventure writing for God's glory.

The Sword, the Lady and the Light

Me at a local bookstore with my first 2 books

I have wanted for a long time to lay down in writing the history of how my novels came to be. Up until October of 2008, I had been writing useless pulp fiction. Even though Jeff Dun sent me numerous e-mails encouraging me in my writing and encouraging me to write for the Lord, I didn't listen. But then in September of 2008, I had spinal fusion surgery and had to spend over two weeks recovering. During the last portion of this time I ODed on Lord of the Rings. One day while watching my best friend play a videogame I resolved that I would write something epic, not just the old blood and thunder. For the next few days, I outlined the basic plot of Sword Dreamer and sent it to Jeff. Jeff was overjoyed and sent me his work phone number in case I needed to call him during the day. Good news for me, bad news for Mariana McLaurin the receptionist.

I rushed through the plot of Sword Dreamer and finished it in nine days. It still was unlike anything else I'd ever written. I was the first person I know of to create black elves. I did this partially so that if I became famous one day, anti-Christian authors like Philip Pullman could not accuse me of being racist. Sword Dreamer was at that time 15,000 words. But Jeff told me that to be picked up by a traditional publisher my manuscript would have to be at least three times that size. At first I thought I wouldn't be able to do it. But keeping myself on a steady diet of Lord of the Rings, and other such movies and Youtube videos, I expanded it out to 45k. Jeff sent it out to 12 publishers in early February, while I still kept expanding it slightly.

My niece, Miriam Connor, was born in January of 2009. I wanted to write a story for her. Also, my mom and I had been reading the book Jeff gave us, Jonathan Strange and Mr. Norrell. This late Georgian fairy tale was extremely well-written and one day after reading it, I began to think of what it would be like if a forest suddenly started growing in an old library. That was the beginning of Lady of Naofatir. When it had firmly cemented itself in my mind, it was a romance loose allegory of the bride of Christ. In creating Naofatir and its inhabitants, the Tuatha na Naofatir, I drew on my knowledge of Celtic mythology, mostly Irish, and the beautiful forests that I had seen in movies such as The Chronicles of Narnia. I had to do a lot of historical research for the Victorian part of the book and because of that I expanded my knowledge of British history. For the part in Naofatir, I drew on the Celtic mindset of the cyclical battle between good and evil, but showed how Christ broke the cycle with His death and resurrection. Mariana served as a test audience for the book, and as the model for the cover, for which I am very grateful.

I finished Naofatir on April 23, 2009. After that I had one or two false starts in books that I didn't really have my heart in. And so I did not write a novel for almost 7 months. During that time, Jeff created Electric Moon Publishing because no traditional publisher would take Sword Dreamer.

Late in 2009, I began to watch the ABC show Legend of the Seeker, which is based off of Terry Goodkind's Sword of Truth novels. After watching a few episodes, I began to want to create my own wizard, my own Gandalf, my own Zeddicus Zul'Zorander. And so one night while pacing up and down the hall, I envisioned a city, separated from the rest of the world by a magical boundary (now where did that come from? He he he) in a state of constant starless night where a holy order of mage-priests fights the forces of darkness. This was the beginning of Light Bringer. I envisioned it as a short story but my dad urged me to make it into a novel. And I did. But I did it in a very special way. Jeff had sent me Stephen King's On Writing, and I read there that he does not plot out his stories, preferring to discover the ending as he writes it. I had an idea for a beginning and an end but I prayed that God would give me the ideas to flesh out the story. At times I began to get very discouraged, thinking that I would never finish the book. The theme song for this book, as I find a worship song to be the theme song for every book I write, was Chris Tomlin's "God of this City". I reflected that if greater things were still to be done in the city of Silvardrassil, greater things were still to be done in my writing.

I have written three novels but I know that it is not the end. I plan to keep writing for the Lord's glory until I die or He returns.

PS Due to financial constraints, it was over a year between my finishing Light Bringer and it being published.

Desert Poem

Posted on May 2, 2011 by sworddreamer

Here is a poem mirroring the boredom and self-doubt I felt when I didn't finish a book for almost a year. Every time I thought about giving up on *Light Bringer,* I would hear Chris Tomlin singing in my head about how greater things are still to be done. That was God's way of telling me that my service to him through writing wasn't over. *Light Bringer* was truly a milestone for me. I learned not to give up and bathed in the waters of divine creativity once more. I hope you enjoy the poem!

In the Desert

Long have I sojourned in the desert of Bor

Trying to find the city Greytor

Where the river runs wide through a valley unseen

Bringing New Life to the hillocks of green.

Long have I been away from all kin and kith.

Sometimes I believe the city a myth.

Oft times I thought I saw her jeweled spires.

But those were but heat waves of fleeting desires.

Many days since I ran out of supplies.

The fiery glare dances before my eyes.

My sword trails to earth. My mail clings like mesh.

The scorpions gather to feast on my flesh.

But, looking up with bloodshot eyes, I see

A heaven lit pathway straight before me.

With my last ounce of strength, I stumble on

Until my feet from scorching sand are gone.

I come to the Valley with its shining towers

Where the All-seeing One refreshes my powers.

Before on my journey I continue,

I stop and bathe in the river anew.

Centaur Story

Posted on <u>May 9, 2011</u> by <u>sworddreamer</u>

This story takes place in Haverland, the setting of two short poems I've previously posted. I wanted to do something with centaurs, in the vein of the star-gazing warriors of Narnia. Galen Steelstorm can't compare with Roonwit or Glenstorm, but I like him. Hopefully you will too!

Galen's Breakfast

Last night, Galen Steelstorm had gotten positively no sleep whatsoever. And if you think your grandmum or granddad is cranky or in some cases hungry after getting up from a sleepless night, you have yet to see said crankiness from a centaur. If any of you lads or lasses have been fortunate enough to be at the Ascot, and even more fortunate to have a tour of the stables, you know that all horses scratch themselves by rolling around in the hay. But you see, a half-man half-horse has no way of reaching his flanks with his human arms. Furthermore, if he tried to roll around, as a horse would, he would only receive a massive pain in his back. Furthermore, Quinner, the night owl had been a little too familiar with the elderberry bush near his tree, and was singing to the maid in the moon all night.

Thus it was that when Sir Steelstorm awoke that morning, he was very cranky, as I have explained. And there is only thing that can slake a centaur's hunger when he is cranky. "Fried goblin!" Galen rumbled.

(It may be proper for me to pause here and explain why someone like our hungry hero would eat another talking creature. Centaurs are one of the many races of the noble alliance that the Emperor in the Sky commanded to kill the servants of the Dark Lord and never make peace with that Evil One's followers. So, as stomach-turning as it may sound, He is pleased when a centaur eats a goblin.)

Galen strapped on his breastplate and put on his antlered helmet over his dark flowing locks, slung his hunting sword over his shoulder and thundered down through the Elven wood. It just so happened that that golden-haired righter of wrongs, the leather-wearing, fedora-topped Elven highwayman Matthias Mercy-Giver was along the Elven path that day. "Good Morrow, Friend Galen," he said, almost bouncing up like a harroo, for he was very giddy this particular morning. "Thou hast a wrathful look about thee. Art thou well?"

"Look," the centaur growled, half-whinnying with hunger. "I don't care much for your highwayman jargon. The truth of the matter is, if I don't set fried goblin between my teeth within the hour, my tail hairs will catch on fire because of my rage. Do you understand?"

The elf nodded, saying, "Ah, a quest! Yorts and away!" He drew his broadsword and thundered out through the underbrush. They were at this time very near to the Elven dancing lawn where the wood elves held counsel. They happened to meet a portly harroo, whose gnome face and hairy kangaroo legs were stained with grease, from the mutton leg on which he was gorging himself.

"Hearken, brother harroo. Knowest thou where we can find a goblin?"

"*Gob, gob!* Lord Killthrift is meeting with Ragwart the goblin general, alone on the dancing lawn. He's giving away free food!"

The breakfast-questing duo thundered away before the gluttonous harroo had a chance to mention that Killthrift was negotiating a peace treaty with the goblin. So you can just imagine the shocked look on the Elven Lord's face when a well armed centaur and an Elven rogue burst onto the dancing lawn and carried off startled Ragwart amidst a shower of goblinish curses.

Back at Galen's Meadow, after the centaur had eaten his fill, Lord Killthrift came with an escort of knights. "A fine mess you've gotten me into, centaur," he cried, boiling with rage. "Warchief Droolin has declared open war."

"It is written in the Scriptures of this land," Galen replied, "that the Emperor in the Sky forbids treaties with the creatures created by the Dark Lord. Maybe the Emperor used my hunger for your benefit. Besides, who knows what terrible things would happen to Haverland if a cranky centaur like me hadn't eaten his breakfast." After the centaur said this, everyone, even Lord Killthrift, had a good, hearty laugh.

The Elven Knight

Posted on June 2, 2011 by sworddreamer

Here is a song about an elf knight who has adventures in Haverland.

Sir Marzimor

Sir Marzimor was an elven knight

A-too-ra-lae- dee-dong dilly

He took sword and shield and went out to fight

A-too-ra-lae- dee-dong dilly

He climbed upon a hill of shale

All clad in a coat of mail.

Too-rae-hae-a-too-rae-hae-a-too-dee-dong-dilly.

A dragon from his sleep awoke

A-too-ra-lae- dee-dong dilly

He bellowed forth both fire and smoke

A-too-ra-lae- dee-dong dilly

A swishy Swash went the sword

The dragon charged the elven lord.

Too-rae-hae-a-too-rae-hae-a-too-dee-dong-dilly.

The Knight's blade pierced the dragon's hide

A-too-ra-lae- dee-dong dilly

A-snicker-snack, the dragon died.

A-too-ra-lae- dee-dong dilly

He wrenched free his mighty brand

The bravest knight in Haverland

Too-rae-hae-a-too-rae-hae-a-too-dee-dong-dilly.

Knight in Shining Armor Story

Posted on June 7, 2011 by sworddreamer

For a long time, I've wanted to do a story with knights in shining armor, who live according to the five knightly Virtues: Chastity, generosity, fidelity, prowess and honor. I hope you enjoy it!

Sir Peter and the Troll

Once upon a time, about two score years before the Everfrost Quest, the Township of Veylandin in southeastern Pallanon had a young lord with long raven hair named Peter, Peter von Wulfbain to be exact. Before Peter's father,

Galway, had died, he had spoken an oracle over his son. "Our ancestor, Ulfius, slew a great-wolf in the Everfrost War, but I foresee, my son, that you will have an even greater victory."

At the time of this story, Peter was about eighteen years of age. Ever since he was old enough to ride out, he loved the five virtues of chivalry: faithfulness, honesty, courtesy, generosity, and prowess. Though he was very practiced in the first four, he longed to prove his prowess on the battlefield, his courage and bravery for the Lord God.

One day, in Midsummer, when the evenings were especially hot, there came a great troll to the walls of Veylandin. He cried out in a loud voice. "I shall do, by meat and crue, what the great-wolf failed to do. By my mace, and my small brain, I shall slay puny Wulfbain."

This continued day and night, until Sir Peter was very bothered. Finally he went to young dwarven smith Dunnir and said to the ebon-skinned dwarf, "I need you to make me a sword, with a very broad and sharp blade, so sharp that it can pierce this wicked brother to the heart." Dunnir invited his friend from Roldburg Castle, the wiry bald human alchemist Francois de Conlois, to come help with the philosophy of forging the blade. Surely his powders and tinctures could avail much.

The two men worked long and hard at the forge; Dunnir beating with his hammer, François coating it with powders and tinctures, the properties of which only an alchemist could understand. And all the while, the troll spewed forth his tirade. At last the blade was finished. To test it, young Peter went up to one of the anvils and struck it lightly. It was such a good blade, that it cleaved the entire anvil in two from top to bottom. Peter was pleased. He named the blade Ettin-Bane.

He made his peace with God and went out to do battle with the troll the next day. He was clad in a hauberk and red cape. The bearing upon the silver field of his shield was of a golden lion rampart with a black great-wolf under its back paw. He wore a forward sloping great helm divided with a visor upon his head. When he came to the place of battle, he cried out in a loud voice, "With the host of heaven as my witnesses, I shall send you to the fiery caves below."

The troll merely laughed at him and began to rain down blows with his mace. Even with his alchemically reinforced blade, Peter had trouble parrying the mad strokes, and he found that with the troll's great strength, he could not counterstrike. But then he remembered that in battle, a knight of God must invoke the holy power of God when fighting creatures of darkness. He began to declare in a clarion voice, "A Knight is a warrior of light and truth, the power of God is manifest in his heart, he speaks forth the truth of God's holy books. He is faithful to the cause to which God has called him. He is not overcome by evil but overcomes evil with the goodness of God. Lord, to you be the glory of the victory."

He cut the troll across the chest in a great sweeping blow, and the cut sparkled with holy light. Then the troll fell to the ground with a great crash. Peter had proved his prowess.

News of Sir Peter's victory spread. So great was his fame that King Jaerython came on a royal visit to Veylandin and awarded Sir Peter with a gold chain to wear around his neck and silver spurs to put on his feet. Sir Galway's prophecy came true. His son had had a greater victory than even his sainted ancestor.

And oh, Dunnir and François' skills came to be quite in demand. But little did they know that Peter's sword was not their masterpiece, not by a long stretch. They would one day forge a masterpiece that would be remembered through all the ages of Pallanon. But that is another story.

Eat your hearts out, Coriakin and Gandalf!

Posted on June 15, 2011 by sworddreamer

I decided that Haverland needed its own magician, like Coriakin from Narnia's *Voyage of the Dawn Treader* or maybe even Gandalf the Gray, as he appears in J.R.R. Tolkien's *The Hobbit* children's book of Middle-Earth fame. Enjoy!

Mage of Haverland

Hi-ho, Mister Gramarien, the portly star magician.

He came from far beyond the stars

While the elf-prince was wishing.

His robe is burgundy a-printed with some stars of gold,

Though his head is like a monk's

He doesn't look that old.

Upon his long dark beard

Is not one silver hair.

He lives in Castle Dafty Pud

With his dancing bear.

He gives much wisely council

To Elven Lord Killthrift.

Magister Gramarien, the Emperor's great gift.

Garden of Life Poem

Posted on June 21, 2011 by sworddreamer

I thought I'd share a free verse poem that I wrote. No, this isn't about the Gardens of Life from the original Shannara trilogy by fantasy author Terry Brooks.

The Eden He Built

He shall build a cathedral of the forest for my dwelling

A tree of Life growing in its midst that was once the Tree of Suffering

I shall eat of its fruit and drink of its wine

I shall feast at His table

I shall dwell in this Garden of Life

'Til it bursts forth from His soul like a rushing river

And envelopes the World in its Light forever.

Elvish Bushido

Posted on June 28, 2011 by sworddreamer

If any of you have read *Sword Dreamer*, you have read about Almiras the Warrior, Surgessar's father, the greatest swordsman in the *Sword Dreamer* universe, a sort of elven Miyamoto Musashi. I decided to put down in his own words maxims on the art and philosophy of the sword.

Proverbs of Almiras the Warrior

Wise sayings of Almiras the Warrior, passed down to his son, Surgessar, on the art of swordsmanship and the way of the sword

The true value of a sword is not in its sharpness or quickness, but in that which it defends.

Just as mastery of only one weapon is folly, so too is peace of body without peace of mind and spirit. Yield all three to the King That Is, for these eternal circles of being are ever linked.

We clad our torsos in mail, not our souls.

As a sword is an extension of a swordsman's arm, likewise are his actions extensions of his heart.

Though we are elves, we are not immune to the wiles of the Dark Enemy. A faithless warrior is no different than the Frékan (Vólderíns).

There are two dragons, my son, at war in the soul of every man, dwarf, and elf. The first dragon is love and tranquility, all that is good. The other is hatred and strife, bent on destruction. Choose well which one you feed.

Most Humans merely respect the King That Is. A true swordsman relies on him.

If you are forced to foreswear marriage and the love of women, do not, my son, foreswear the love of the King That Is and the path to which he has called you.

The true battle is in the heart and the mind. Those who find victory on those battlefields, though they are slain, shall rise victorious over all.

Not all are able to wield a sword of steel, but the swordsmanship of the heart is an art open to all.

To find out more about Almiras, go to this link
http://www.amazon.com/Sword-Dreamer-Marshal-Myers/dp/1453638229/ref=sr_1_1?ie=UTF8&s=books&qid=1309266748&sr=1-1

The Dwarf King's Daughter

Posted on July 5, 2011 by sworddreamer

Here is a Haverland story that, among other things, answers the the question, albeit in a different universe, What Thorin Oakenshield's daughter was doing while he was fighting goblins in *The Hobbit*. That said, I doubt if Thorin had a daughter or will have one in Peter Jackson's the Hobbit movies, the first of which will be released in theater s on December 19, 2012. Can't wait!

The Dwarf King's Daughter

Once upon a time in Haverland, the dwarf king went off on a campaign against
the goblins. He had a pretty little daughter named Nuna. Nuna always thought of
herself as a good little girl (or dwarfling, if you will), but in all truth,
Nuna was very nasty. It got even worse after her father went away to war. Her

mother the Queen and all her nursemaids tried and tried to manage her, but it
did no good. One day, when her mother and nurse maid were dressing her, they
accidentally scratched her. Nuna screamed and said, "I'll hate you forever and
always. I'm a big girl, do you hear? And when I am Queen, I'll have you thrown
in the dungeon."

She ran out of the hall of stone and out through the wood until she was very lost. She did not know how far she had gone. Only that
the woods were dark and cold. Then she saw a silvery white light and slowly
walked toward it. Strangely, the light wasn't coming from a moon or star. It
came from a great white house, before which a pale, beautiful, very tall lady was
standing. She was as tall as an elf (which, for a dwarf girl, is very tall).
Her hair was the color of thistledown. Another strange thing was that she
looked very young, but very old in her eyes.

She smiled and said, "Welcome! I am Lady Nuna. It was I that gave you your name. I see you believe that you no longer need yourmother, so I am going to take care of you. Come in." She fairly glided into her house as if she was walking on air. She fed the little girl Nuna from a babybottle, which the dwarf child thought was very silly indeed. Yet it was the sweetest thing she had ever tasted. The girl thought the lady would take her to
a stately bed such as she slept in at the castle. But instead she took her to a
gigantic crib and laid her inside. When the morning came, and the Lady was
preparing breakfast, the dwarf girl tried to escape. But she had not gone ten

paces before a craving for the milk of the White Lady led her back. As the days
wore on, the craving weakened, until at last the Lady kissed the princess'
forehead, and said, "You are ready to go home now. "

The girl Nuna found that she really did miss her
mother the Queen. But all the same she said to the beautiful White Lady, "But I
will miss you. You taught me to be a little girl again." The Lady kissed the
little girl again, and said, "Don't worry. I always have and always will be
with you."

So it was that the princess learned to be a little
girl again. She went home and apologized to nursey and mummy. Strangely, mummy
and nursey did not act as if she had been away long. And when she told them of
the White Lady in the wood, they said she had made up the whole story. But she
never forgot Lady Nuna, and how she had taken care of little Nuna. Everything
was happy and even happier when daddy the king came home. And Nuna grew,
respected her mummy and daddy out of love, with the faith of a child, as the beautiful
Lady in the wood had taught her.

Song of the Morning Star

Posted on July 12, 2011 by sworddreamer

Ever since studying J.R.R. Tolkien's *Tale of Earindil the Mariner*, I have been interested in the Morning Star, which is seen as a Bringer of the Light, Bringer of a new day in many premodern cultures. Ergo, I have written an in inspirational poem focused on the Morning Star, harkening back to the Star that led the Magi to the Christ Child. Enjoy!

The Sun's Mace

You are known by many names
By many warriors and great thanes
Light Bringer of battle grace
You are ever the Sun's Mace.
Aruvandil, Aruvandil
Your gracious spike we see and feel
The paladins that dwell inside the sun
Of their gear you're the greatest one
Rising upon the starry spire
You were made by the Living Fire
Though pagan men know not your Master
You show deliv'rance from disaster.
On seeing you, Patrick would say,
"I bind unto myself today."
O Herald of that, by which men say,
"I shall start anew today."
Holy weapon, the Sky Knight's grace
You are the sun's,
And the Son's Mace.

The Highwayman Poem

Posted on July 22, 2011 by sworddreamer

It's a pleasant coincidence that yesterday was my parents' anniversary and my newest Haverland poems ends with a betrothal. This poem is about Matthias Mercy-Giver, who for me is the archetypal highwayman. He has the Elizabethan speech and garb of Solomon Kane, the courage and honor of Reepicheep, the loyalty of Alfred Knoyes' Highwayman, and the courtesy of Sir Gawain, and, as always, a knack for famous last words, like Inigo Montoya of *The Princess Bride*, or Errol Flynn. Let me tell you of his latest adventure.

Highwayman's Quest

Matthias, he rode out one night.

In his mind was this:

To slay the cruel Goblin Knight, Jarumbo Cockeltrice.

He had captured Goldaglen, the daughter of Killthrift,

Offered the elf king a reward,

Her hand as a gift.

He came to the knight's dark bastion,

Took out his grapple hook,

The tower, it was all a'quiet,

'Twas no one there to look

It swished up, a-swishy swash,

Hooked onto a merlon

He needed not the foreign words,

So he just climbed on

He climbed in through a high window,

Saw her tied with steel thread.

He breathed a deep sigh of relief,

That she was not dead

Jarumbo rumbled, "I see you!

You think you're so wise,

I will have you for my stew!

You shall not take my prize!"

Cried Matthias, "Out on ye,

O slave of the Dark One!

The One giveth strength to my steel.

I'm a true silvan son."

Matthias' blades and goblin axe

Gave lots of feints and attacks.

The elf's broadsword, in and out,

Flying gracefully,

Slashed Jarumbo a dire blow

Slicing through the knee.

The goblin knight fell, clutching his knee,

Amazed at the disaster

This time no mercy, Matthias

Sent him to his master.

"Mercy for all, except servants

Of the Enemy.

Therefore, I have showed not

My mercy to thee."

So saying, the highwayman

Stopped and cleaned his brand.

Untying Goldaglen's bonds,

He knelt and kissed her hand.

On Christian Fantasy

By Marshal Myers

I am a long-time reader and fan of epic fantasy, both Christian and secular, and have come to realize the differences between the two. In Christian fantasy, we see an etching of the true story, the great story that the true immortal storyteller is weaving, albeit through a glass darkly, for these sub-created tales, at their best, are merely reflections of the First Author's creativity, and the First Author is matchless.

In Christian fantasy we see the towers of Cair Paravel, the blessed realms of Valinor and Aslan's country, and unlike the tales of Arthur, in these baptized stories, we actually follow our King to His homeland. In Christian fantasy are brave Paladin Kings who are courageous and true. Sir Peter Wolfsbane was a Knight of the Most Noble Order of the Lion, the sons of Elrond bastions of courage against the forces of the Dark Lord. Sir Lancelot du Lac was a rapist, an adulterer and an insurrectionist. King Elendil was a faithful leader, beloved of the One. Arthur committed incest that led to his downfall and the downfall of his "heavenly" kingdom. Eomer was humble and loyal. Beowulf was a prideful hothead who only cared about his own renown.

Reepicheep sailed for Aslan's country, and was willing to lay down his life of adventure for the greatest prize and the greatest adventure. Bran sailed aimlessly after a woman that had caught his lustful eye. Caspian brought peace between two warring factions. Cuchulainn inflamed an already bitter rivalry that led to even more deaths. Aragorn and Beren waited for the proper time to wed their loves. Sigurd fathered a child with Brynhild and then left her for Gudrun. Gandalf the Grey is an angelic spirit sent by a higher power. Merlin is the son of a demon.

There is something about Christian fantasy that draws us further up and further in and always leaves us with the happily ever after. Many secular mythologies and fantasies lack even a satisfying dénouement. The curse upon the Volsungs continues even in the second generation. But in Christian fantasy the Shire is reborn, and though he cries many tears, Sam knows as he watches Frodo leave the Shire, that he and his many children will someday be reunited with Mr. Frodo in a land that the Enemy cannot touch. Even though Lucy is afraid of being sent away, Aslan assures her that she will never have to leave again back to her lackluster world of sorrow and pain.

Christian fantasy has the only true happily ever afters. As I said before, these are shadows of the true happily ever after that will come sooner than we think. The greatest Paladin King will return leading his glorious army, and the greatest happily ever after will come true. Our fantasy shall become reality.

Riding on the Wings of Dragon

Posted on August 3, 2011 by sworddreamer

I thought I'd share the essay I wrote for the "I Speak Dragon" contest for users of Nuance Dragon speech-to-text products. Above is a video I made coinciding with the theme of the essay. Enjoy!

Riding on the Wings of Dragon

There has always been a courageous warrior inside of me. When I was a little
boy, my greatest desire was to ride off into battle like High King Peter of
Narnia, to slay giants and goblins; to be a hero. But I had two big problems.
First problem: this is the real world, not Narnia. Second problem: I have
cerebral palsy and have used a wheelchair for mobility all my life. When I was
young, how I longed to take karate and play superheroes with my friends. But,

alas! I found that I could only be a knight and a hero in my imagination.

But now, all my daydreaming and star-wishing has found a place to soar. I have
begun a career as a novelist. I want to give the world stories of heroes who
are courageous and true, just as I desire to be. Before I had Dragon Naturally
Speaking, I was forced to write by typing with one finger, which is very
tedious. But then the chivalrous would-be knight found a kindly Dragon on which
to ride. About a year after learning to speak Dragon, I was inspired to write
my first novel.

My Dragon has taken me on journeys beyond the confines of my wheelchair to distant lands of high adventure. Dragon is simple for physically challenged people to use and has allowed me to begin to fly into the world of my novels riding on the back of a Dragon that breathes forth an endless jet of fiery prose. I hope to continue this soaring adventure for years to come. I have written and published three novels and have been told by other physically challenged individuals that I have inspired them to reach for their true potential.

Dragon, partnered with my imagination, allows me to enjoy the adventures I would not
otherwise encounter. I can be a knight riding out to slay a giant or rescue a
damsel; I can be a Viking that sails adventurous seas on a dragon longship; I
can be a samurai in search of three wishes from the luck dragon and have many
more epic adventures that I can't yet begin to count. Thanks to my Dragon, I am
able to transform into the courageous hero that has always been triumphant in

my heart and imagination. I look forward to many more adventures riding the
winds of valor on the wings of Dragon.

Marshal Myers

<u>Song of the Heartland</u>

Posted on <u>August 10, 2011</u> by <u>sworddreamer</u>

This poem came to me after listening to Dougie Maclean's "Singing Land". Enjoy!

Song of the Heartland

I shall sing of the land of His soul

Where the golden thunders roll

I shall sing from the dawn through the noon

Of the high jew'led mountain do I croon.

I see crystal-winged birds flying the silv'ry sky

To bask in the glory of the King on high.

I shall cast down my staff and leave my sword

To dwell always in the heartland of the Lord.

Paladin Song

I don't really play WoW or D&D but my favorite class is the Paladin. This sums up the essentials, spiritually speaking, of a good Paladin.

Paladin

A paladin is a warrior of Light

From the arm of the Lord does he draw his might

His heart more powerful than his sword

A holy weapon in the hand of the Lord

An empty vessel though his shoulders be broad,

A humble, poor fellow servant of God.

To read more about the paladins I have created in my fantasy novels and short stories, visit www.marshalmyers.com

Diary of a Mad Elf Prince

Posted on August 15, 2011 by sworddreamer

Here is another Haverland story that I hope will provide some comic relief. Prince Kennedor told me he hopes you don't find this as annoying as the diary of a certain Eustace Scrubb who was very queezy on a ship that if memory serves is called the *Dawn Treader*. Anyhow, he's always talking about this ridiculous world called Narnia. Well folks are always havering in Haverand. Special thanks to Prince Kenny of the

Elven Wood for allowing me to publish this diary entry. Enjoy!

From the Diary of Elven Prince Kennedor "Kenny", son of Killthrift, Elf Prince of Haverland

50th day of Gramarye Time

Today I went to Prof. Gramarien's at Castle Dafty Pud for my weekly lesson in practical gramarye and whatever else my troll body of a teacher deemed worthy. (Papa, if you find this diary entry, please don't misinterpret this. I am quite fond of Mr. MG, it is just that every visit to his Castle is an adventure in itself, such as would test the mettle of even Sir Marzimour.) Today for my lunch, I brought a haunch of white stag steak. Polybus the dancing bear smelled it as I was coming through the barbican and toppled me over as though we were playing a game of the dwarvish football. All that Mr. "Haggisy" Magister said when he came down to see about the noise was "Wull, I seem to have forgotten to feed Old Polybus this morning."

Unfortunately for me, the plump prestidigitator had been teaching levitation to a bunch of haroos the night before and had forgotten to cancel the spell of levitation in his library and when he did, my chair, which is the long-legged stool of petrified oak, came crashing down on my foot, which caused me to jump up and down, "singing" in a high-pitched voice like a water siren. Then Mr. G spent a long time trying to light his pipe. When he had finally completed this irrelevant task, we finally got around to talking

about magic, but instead of finally teaching me to shoot fire out of my hands,

as he has falsely promised on many occasions, he made me try once again to

summon a book from the shelves and back again, sort of a leather and paper

mumble-the-peg. All Mr. Magister did when I almost broke my nose as the spine

flew toward it, was chuckle and admonish me to be more careful. As if I could

be more careful without being a star mage of the first order like the laughing

coot. Then the Great Knock made me stare through his scrying mirror to watch

the endless dancing of the stars. As if I care that Gungadell is in the House

of Naravis. Both fortunately and unfortunately for me was, the bumbling wizard

tried to make up for my nose by adding fae tears as a dressing for my lunch,

which only made me queezy and need to cut the lesson short. He offered to lend

Polybus to take me home but I summoned Galen Steelstorm the centaur warrior

instead. Once I was back in the Elven Wood, I was very friendly with the privy

bucket because of fae tear reflux. As I sit here with my quill and parchment, I

look forward to the day when I can finally shoot fire out of my hands and all

my dilly-dallying with Mr. MG finally pays off.

Kennedor, son of Killthrift

The Sage of Time

Posted on August 17, 2011 by sworddreamer

Here's a nice poem with Hylian overtones that came to me today. I hope you enjoy it!

The Sage of Time

What wisdom have you, sage of time,

Words pouring forth in endless Rhyme?

Does not the temple of thy Master

Hold the brands of time long lost?

With your hands quell each disaster

From doors countless heroes accost.

Lead me to the blade of my hope,

Marked by Tri-Force One-Bound-Three

Held by stone and not by rope.

That I might much better serve Thee

The Knights of the Order of the Sun

Posted on August 29, 2011 by sworddreamer

CS Lewis said that the best thing about Narnia was that it combined talking animals and knights in armor. Apparently, he was just as passionate about the archetype of the knight in shining armor as I am. I decided that Haverland needed its own League of Heroes, a League of Legends like the knights of the round table of Camelot, or the red branch knights or Fenians of Irish Lore. Come sing with me the Anthem of the Knights of the Order of the Sun, the elf paladins of the Elven Wood.

Anthem of the Knights of the Order of the Sun

Recorded by Barlenath Burso, Minstrel of the Elven Wood

Sing with the Knights of the Order of the Sun

Ding dong ring dong dilly oh!

Swinging our blades, we fight as one

Ding dong ring dong dilly oh.

Led by Marzimour, the son of Greongail

Ding a dring dong dilly oh!

The Holy Light gives sheen to our mail

Ding a dring dong dilly oh!

For the Emperor ever do we fight

Ding dong ring dong dilly oh.

The bane of shadows, disciples of the Light

Ding dong ring dong dilly oh.

Dingdoh ding dong dilly

Ding dong dilly!

Be Near, O God, Be Near

Posted on September 3, 2011 by sworddreamer

It came to me today that nearness to God is the point of the whole gospel. I have been worrying about money, the future and my career, but
today, after a long time of emotional unrest, I came to realize how deeply God
loves me. For a long time, I've seen him as this awesome, strange force that may
be pleased with me and may not. I served him out of fear and apple
polishing. But then I realized that yes, he is awesome, almighty and
all-powerful, but he's also humble, kind and loving. I want him to wrap his arms
around me and drift off to sleep in his gentle embrace and sweet melody.

Penny's World: A Blog within a Blog

Today, I kind of wanted to go outside my comfort zone and do something different. I just made up a fictional character with a fictional blog, and pepper it with some obscure mythology references. I apologize if I get stuff wrong, factually or emotionally.

Penny's World

For Nathaniel Snow

Bio: Hello! My name is Penny Galifanakis. I am 19. I live in Ithaca, Alabama. For those of you who are wondering, yes, my full name

is Penelope Athena Galifinakis. Ha ha, laugh it up! I'm Greek, as you can see.
You will also see that I have not uploaded a profile pic. I will explain in a
later post. Hope you enjoy my blog!

June 19, 2001

Today is the ten-year anniversary of Otis Athenton's asking me to marry him. I know, we were only like nine, and for all I know, to
him, I still had cooties.   That was the
same day that my mom became professor of ancient studies at Troyes University.
I had always planned to go there, but that was before THAT happened. Anyhow,
instead of giving me a cereal box ring, he gave me a brass bracelet, that had
cost him eight weeks allowance. It looked sort of Greek. Then he totally threw
his friends' opinions to the wind and gave me a little smooch on the lips. I'll
never quite forget that, but then I guess you always remember a first kiss. If
only that relationship could've lasted, but fate decided otherwise. Oh well,
all that for another blog post, or a trip to my therapist. You know which kind
because now I need both. Tootles!

June 27, 2001

LOL! I was going through some of our old photo albums with mom today and I found a picture of me when I was a baby just
learning to crawl. Silly, my favorite toy clown, was just out of reach so I
crawled out of my crib to get him. I still couldn't reach him and got my foot

caught under the crib. I started to cry not because I was hurt, but because I
still couldn't get Silly. No pun intended.

Mom, being the panicky British lady she is, came in
and shouted "Alex!" (That's my dad) "She's
caught between Silly and her crib, she is!"

Mom picked me up and put me back in bed, because I
couldn't walk very well by myself yet. It's amazing to me that 18 years later
we're back to that scenario again. Until another day, friends.

July 10, 2001

Uncle Paul came over for dinner last night. I never
will get quite used to his eye patch. He
lost it about a year before my incident, so he had some
empathy with me when I
was in the hospital. He is a doctor, a podiatrist actually. It's kind of hard
to Do that with one eye, but he does a fantastic job. When I was in second
grade I had a great time reading his business card "Paul E. Phemos, podiatrist"
. We had Greek lamb last night. Uncle Paul made it. Yum!

Comment: Telly Mahckus on "August 10, 2011"

Hey, Penny! I love your blog! I've been reading it for the past 10 years! Happy
late 29th birthday, BTW! I like the pictures of your knitting projects! You
sound like a neat person! My question is: why are there no pictures of you on
your blog? I'd love to see what you look like.

Response to Telly Mahckus:

Hi, Telly. Thanks for your interest in my blog. I'm
about to tell you something that I haven't told any of my
readers. The reason
why I only blog about the past and don't post a profile
picture is that I don't
want anybody to see me the way I am now. You see, 11 years
ago this past May, I
was in a terrible car accident on the way home from
graduation. Luckily Otis
wasn't in the car with me. It paralyzed me from the waist
down and I'm in a
wheelchair.   Otis left me to go to
school at Troyes University. He wouldn't even come see me
in the hospital. In
college, he dated both my best friends, Kaley Ipso and Sierra
Sae. For many
years I was hurt and heartbroken deep down inside. This blog
was sort of my
catharsis, you could say. It all changed about two months
ago, when I went to
an evangelical church, (my family has never been big
churchgoers). The pastor's
sermon was on true love, and how Jesus is the only true
lover, better than any
boyfriend or husband, who will never leave us when the
going gets tough. For
years now, (20 years, if you count from the time he first
"proposed" to
me), I've been waiting for Otis, much like the Penelope from
The Odyssey (there's my Greek geekiness
coming out, LOL.) The pastor's sermon made me think, why
was I waiting for my "Odysseus"
when he would never come and I could have the most
faithful lover in the
universe? I surrendered my life to
Christ. My heart cried *Kyrie eleison,*
Kriste eleison (Lord have mercy, Christ have mercy). I and even my
parents
have seen a great change in my attitude. God's working on

them. Your comment
confirmed something I've been feeling for a while now. I
should use my blog to
write about my new joy, and pour joy into the lives of others,
not just pine
after what has been and what now can never be. I'll upload a
profile pic soon!

Thanks for the encouragement, I really appreciate
it. This is Penelope "Penny" Athena Galifanakis, wheelchair
cruising Queen of
Ithaca, Alabama, signing out. Peace out, my friend, and God
bless!

Paladin's Destiny: Fall from Grace

For a long time, I've wanted to write a story, a parable of
sorts, that would show in a fairy tale sense, the beginning of
the epic battle between light and darkness in which we find
ourselves. This is what finally came from that desire. Enjoy!

The Breaking of Wittandrassil: Paladin Rising

"Tell me again ancient one, why do we need the Knights of
the order of Tree?" The Speaker who posed this question was
a young man, scarce eighteen. His name was Torith Donan,
the youngest initiate in the Order and he had been born long
after the war with the demons.

"Ah, young sir," chuckled old Galeth, twenty-ninth Sage of
the Warding Staff, as he stroked his long white beard and
leaned upon the sacred artifact. "That is a tale as old as the
Valley of Crystal itself. Long ago, when the balance of magic
was unstable and the earth belched forth fire and spume, the
demons rose from their unholy halls and wrought arcane

destruction upon the Valley of Crystal. My ancestor, Aronoth, beseeched the High One, and He entrusted my ancestor with the Warding Staff, and with the power of the staff my forefather conjured forth twelve magic swords, holy brand's blessed by the high one to banish and vanquish demons. Aronoth selected twelve men, of pure heart, to fight the demons. Together with the enchantments of my forebear they drove the demons back to the pits from which they came. The High One stretched forth His hand and sealed them away. Planting a mighty tree Wittandrassil to bind them with its holy magic so that they may never rise to destroy the Valley of Crystal ever again. The power of the tree is harnessed through the wittenstone, the holy gem at the root of the tree. Let us pray that it never becomes dislodged, for if it does, the demons will break free of their bonds. But now let us go back to the village and eat."

Being the youngest member of the order, Torith was given the duty of watching Galeth's granddaughter, Annandaila. At first, he thought this duty merely one of a glorified nanny but slowly a change came over him. As he saw her dancing in her white silk and gossamer dresses before the great white tree, his heart began to melt and a new strange feeling came over him. One day as they sat before the white tree, Annandaila, who was quite naïve to the magical workings of the Valley, looked down and said, "Torith, there is a white jewel stuck in the roots of the tree. Give me your dagger and I will pry it out. It will make a fine brooch."

"Annan, you mustn't!"
But the girl did not listen. She snatched up Torith's dagger, flew over to the white tree, and began to carve out the wittenstone. The moment it was in her hand there was a great rending and crashing as the white tree Wittandrassil split asunder. Annandaila fell with a scream into the fiery void. The demons rushed forth from the fiery void like a black, crimson tide. Lava belched forth from the earth, turning the lush vegetation of the Valley into ash and cinders.

The warning horn baled the call to battle. Paladins in shining mail and plate armor rushed forth, swinging flashing broadswords pouring forth holy light. Even with the skill and faith of these holy warriors, the demons pressed on, bathing the Valley in darkness and flame. Their desecration was complete. The battle had been like a fog enshrouded dream for Torith. But he did, unknowingly, strike a blow for the cause of righteousness. One of the twelve primary paladins, Gildras, wielder of the holy sword Faea, had fallen back, scarred to the heart by a demon claw. Feebly lifting holy blade and offering it to Torrith he whispered, "The old order is dead. A new paladin must rise. Today you become that Paladin. You are our last hope." Then he died. As Torith was staring speechless at the blade,a demon pounced upon him, knocking him on his back. His instant reaction was to hold the sword in front of him. The holy brand pierced the demon to the heart, the blade glowing with a white fire as it touched the tainted blood. Then the demon was banished back to the fiery void.

After the battle, the demons escaped out of the Valley, to wreak their destruction on the outside world. There was only one other survivor of the battle, Galeth the Sage of the warding staff. His face was grim and as cold as a statue's as he walked toward Torith over the torn earth.

"You have lost your innocence, boy. This is your last day in this paradise, for this paradise is no more." Handing the young man the wittenstone, the old Sage said "The gem is drained of its potency, as is my staff. You are all that is left of the order of the tree. You must gather all the lost vestiges of the holy magic back into the stone so that my staff may have power again and Wittandrassil might be replanted, but first you must rescue Annandaila, for she is held prisoner in the void. This is your destiny, and though you did not choose it, you have been chosen for this sacred task. Go. And may the High One be with you."

At first, Torith Donan thought he might weep, for his sadness was deep and overwhelming. Yet he gritted his teeth and marched off into the distance, hoping to find his destiny and his redemption.

The Lute Man

I heard the original Billy Joel song in a movie yesterday, and, being the fantasy fan that Iam, thought it would be funny to transport it to the Warcraft universe. Enjoy!

The Lute Man

It's nine o'clock on a Sterrinday.

Regular crowd's kinda dead.

There's a Tauren warrior sitting next to me,

Munching down on some health-givin' bread.

He says, "Son, can you play me a melody,

Even though this bread's kinda stale?

But it's fierce and it's sweet,

And I knew complete

When I wore a younger cow's mail."

Sing us a song, you're the lute man.

Sing us a song tonight.

And when we're in the mood for an instance song,

You got us feeling all right."

Keldron the barkeep, he's a friend of mine.

He gives me my mead for free.

He's quick with a jibe,

And he'll light up your pipe,

But there's some place that he'd rather be.

He says, "Kael, I believe this is killing me!"

And the smile goes away from his face.

"I'm just sure that I could be a Paladin.

If I could get out of this place."

Sing us a song you're the lute man.

Sing us a song tonight.

And when we're in the mood for an instance song,

You got us feeling all right.

And Silvanus is practicin' politics,

As her undead rogues pull up a chair.

It's too bad that they only wear leather,

But it's better than fighting bone-bare.

Mankirk is an orc warrior lonely guy,

Who can't seem to find his lost wife.

And he's talking to Gryder,

Who tames the wind riders,

And probably will all his life.

And my lute, it sounds like a carnival,

And the atmosphere smells like malt beer.

And the undead that slouch,

They put gold in my pouch,

And say, "Elf, what are you doing here?"

Sing us a song, you're the lute man.

Sing us a song tonight.

And when we're in the mood for an instance song,

You got us feeling all right.

Grumpy Old Dungeonmaster? I think not!

Posted on September 29, 2011 by sworddreamer

I remember a conversation I had with a friend who knew a little bit more about tabletop RPGs than I did. I asked if there was anything that a Dungeonmaster couldn't do, like kill all the player characters for no reason, and my friend said no. The Dungeonmaster can do whatever he wants. When I was younger, I thought of God as a sort of cosmic Dungeonmaster, ready to turn the forces nature against me if I didn't do everything right. But then I came to realize the truth of this quote by theologian AW Tozer.

"The whole outlook of mankind might be changed if we could all believe that we dwell under a friendly sky and that the God of heaven, though exalted in power and majesty, is eager to be friends with us."

That said I must be careful not to go to the opposite end of the spectrum. God is just. As portrayed beautifully by CS Lewis throughout The Chronicles of Narnia, like Aslan, God is both wonderful and terrible. But, contrary to what William of Occam claimed, God cannot change the standards of right and wrong, or his mercy and justice. They are part of his character.

Though I may continue to play RPGs, I will never again think of God as the Grumpy Old Dungeonmaster.

Nothing New Under the Sun

When I started writing fiction, I was constantly worrying about the legal implications of taking ideas and elements from other works. Slowly I realized the truth of Tolkien's belief that only God is capable of independent creation. We are only capable of subcreation, or in other words, "plagiarizing God" and others who have created before us. Below is a poem I wrote on the subject, along with a segment from the video series "Everything's A Remix", a documentary on the pervading practice of copying facets from other works. This segment comments on creative plagiarism in the entertaintment industry.

"Nothing new in the world,"

The king says.

Nothing new indeed!

Everything a retold story.

Never new stitchings weaved.

There are wondrous things to see,

And fine worlds to explore.

But you can never, ever be

Where no one's been before.

Only sub-creation

That and nothing more

The only New Creation

Is by the Creator.

Sword Dreamer Anniversary Poem

Posted on October 13, 2011 by sworddreamer

This Saturday October 15th is the 3rd anniversary of the
Creation of Sword Dreamer. I will have been writing
professionally for 3 years. My work is heavily influenced by
Tolkien, and up until a few years ago I thought the
Silmarillion was a very sad book. Main reason was that the
Dark Lord Morgoth is never completely defeated within the
work. But then I discovered the glorious end of the Middle

Earth canon. Therefore, I thought I would offer a simlar glimpse of the end of the Sword Dreamer universe. Enjoy!

Fiann Fiannad

There shall come the day

When the Ever-King

Shall fight the final battle

'Gainst the hoards of the Darkling*.

That day, all of the Children of Gildéador

Shall join the fight to cleanse the Earth

Now and evermore.

All those who have thus pledged fealty to Him,

Shall join in the resinging of the Being Hymn.

It shall remake Éalindé

Growing ever stronger.

Halifar shall be with his son,

Wéostan with his father.

*The Dark Enemy

God through the Glass of the Wardrobe

Posted on October 18, 2011 by sworddreamer

I was listening to a sermon by Chip Ingram today about the second commandment, and how we make idols out of the pictures and views we have of God and Jesus, because to paraphrase Tozer, it lowers our view of God. I'm writing this post to clarify in my own mind my views on the subject, as relates to my and the Inklings' writings. To make an idol is to make a physical representation of God or a god. Tolkien "cordially disliked allegory". There is no allegory in the Middle Earth writings. Eru Iluvatar is not a symbol or representation of God. He *is* God, *as God would appear in that universe.* By the same token, although allegory abounds in the Narnia series, Lewis did not view them as allegorical but as suppositional, asking and answering the question "who would Jesus be in a world of talking animals?" It is for this reason that I somewhat dislike my novels being dubbed as allegories, though I am not thoroughly opposed to using allegory perse. My works may be seen as parables of a sort but not all parables are allegories. Echu is not a symbol of Jesus. Echu is Jesus, as Jesus would appear in that universe. This is why in The Voyage of the Dawn Treader, Aslan says that in Lucy's world he is known "by a different Name." This is not idolatry or allegory, but supposition.

A Rhyme for the Season

October through December is my favorite time of year. As it gets colder, people start thinking about the church-based holidays (although with an original pagan background,) which were Christianized and popularized by church fathers such as Nikolaus of Myra. But as commercialism has overshadowed the spiritual value of these holidays, I thought I'd write something to turn my thoughts back to the time-honored spiritual value of these holidays to Christians. Enjoy!

A Rhyme for the Season

Health to you, my noble lords

Health to you, my ladies

A wassail-o, merry-o

To all the lads and babies

Bring you in the harvest feast

Before you slay the Yule bird

Give coin to the leper,

To wield St. Martin's sword.

Bring in the tree of Boniface

As harvest feast's put out.

For the approach of the Christ's Mass

Let us give a great shout

A Psalm

Posted on October 26, 2011 by sworddreamer

I BIND UNTO MYSELF THE SAME SPIRIT THAT
DESCENDED UPON MY LORD

I CALL UPON THE NAME THAT IS A WELLSPRING
OF POWER,
TO BE A CONDUIT OF THE SAME POWER
THAT RAISED THE DEAD, EVEN MY LORD
HIMSELF,
ABIDE IN ME AND FLOOD ME WITH YOUR HOLY
WATERS,
LIKE AN AVALANCHE FROM YOUR HOLY
MOUNTAINS
Called forth by the praises of your people
Always and ever, forever to be. Amen

Celtic Christian Poem

Posted on October 28, 2011

A week or so ago my parents and I were watching a Catholic
TV broadcast where the priest was talking about Christ as the
Conqueror, conquering the power of death through the cross.
I found Father Barron's premise to be very biblical, and I
love to think of Jesus as a conquering warrior king, riding in
on a white horse to save the kingdom. I think this
pseudonym poem I wrote gives voice to that view. Enjoy!

Sister Emer's Song

I shall sing of my paladin

My knight in gleaming mail,

Far greater than Fionn

Far Greater than Mael

He charges on a white horse

For to save all ye

But first was greatly bloodied all for me.

He is great and good

His sword's a bloodied rood, he stood

Pierced both through his hands through his feet

-Sister Emer of Kildare

Hanging out with the church fathers and monks

Posted on November 2, 2011 by sworddreamer

Hi all! I have basically been aditing a class on church history with my friend and care-giver. This is my first journal entry and deals with the positives and negatives of the church fathers and monasticisms.. This is *just* my opinion. I DO NOT WISH TO OFFEND ANYONE. I want this to be a pleasant blog all readers can enjoy. Blessings!

Today I studied the church fathers of late antiquity and how they relate to the spiritual worldview of their time, and afterwards, of the

Middle Ages. Although some of these men may have been misguided in some of

their teachings, their contributions to the church, and by extension, Western

though should not be discarded. For example John Chrysostom, although he

included passages in his writings, that taste somewhat of early anti-Semitism, he

still was arguably the greatest preacher of late antiquity. In much the same

way, St. Augustine of Hippo formulated the thesis of salvation that is still

widely used today. And yet, likely because of his earlier raucous lifestyle, he

taught that all sexual contact was spiritually wrong, but more importantly, he

helped formulate the view of purgatory that was extorted by the church for over

1000 years. I wonder if, much as I did when I was younger, he found mere

repentance inadequate to alleviate his guilt. That being said, his God-orchestrated

view of both church and secular history is to Christian historians and was

never before used by secular historians such as Herodotus and Pliny the Elder.

The last chapter dealt with the development of Roman Catholic liturgy and tradition. To find out more my views about the adoption of

other holidays into the church calendar, see my previous post.

I also read about the beginnings of monastic life thanks to men such as St. Anthony. Although these men often had misguided modes of repentance

and soul-searched overly much, their major contribution to Western society,
which proved invaluable, was the preservation of the Bible, so that when the
time came right, it could be translated into the common language. Although
physically disabled people like myself died out pretty fast in the Middle Ages,
I still see these monasteries as places that provided havens for people that
were not necessarily healthy enough to survive in the blood and steel world of the Middle
Ages.

Although it is not nearly as important as preserving the Bible, being a
fantasy author, I have much for which to thank the monasteries, because even in
their heyday, they elicited a mysterious view of the holy man of the church, as
one with abstruse wisdom, endowed with special powers by God. This has been
somewhat misinterpreted by modern fantasy novels and other products, such as
the cleric or priest class in fantasy role-playing games such as Dungeons &
Dragons or World of Warcraft. Although this is understandable, I think it would
behoove the makers of these games to realize that, some of the clerics that
provided the inspiration for these "holy magic users", were more in touch with
the true God than the make-believe characters created by the entertainment
companies.

Star Song

Posted on November 8, 2011 by sworddreamer

My pastor has started a series of sermons on worship songs, and this reminded me that the whole of Creation is a song, a celestial hymn to God. Job 38:7 talks about how the stars were the first of all creation to sing praises to God. Genesis 1 is written in Hebrew verse, as if God sang the universe into existence. I have written a poem voicing my fascination with the song of creation, and whatthe old hymn writers called the music of the spheres. Enjoy!

Star-Song

Sing a song with the stars

Join in their heavenly dance

The planets hum in silver bars

Wayward souls to entrance,

Does not the shepherd lad upon earthen hill

Sing with the angels, sky-dwelling still

Dance tall trees, West wind blow.

Sing all things both high and low.

Sing with one voice, glorious

For the Leader of the Chorus

Harvest and Yule Poem

Posted on November 12, 2011 by sworddreamer

This is my favorite time of year, not only because I started writing professionally during this season, but because not only of the feeling of anticipation of Christ's birth but of the festive feelings of the turning of the year, and the anticipation of the new one to come, that was brought to America from the Old World. Therefore I wrote an Old World poem of harvest and Yule-tide. Enjoy!

Song for Year's Turn

Sing a song for the turn of leaves

Though David's Day be past, wear the leek,

Fill my glass with cordial,

Through auburn fields ride,

Cease not to be merry,

"Til there comes the Christmas-tide

A Letter From Father Christmas

Posted on November 26, 2011 by sworddreamer

Early last year, after a joyous Christmas with my niece, her first year to believe in Santa, I decided to follow in the steps of J.R.R. Tolkien and write her a letter from Father Christmas. I haven't believed in Santa in years. But, in a manner of speaking, I always willl, for I believe that the reason most kids believe in fairy tales is because it's easier for them to have childlike faith. I pray that my heart will always stay soft. So now you see why, figuratively, I'll always believe in Santa Claus. Merry Christmas!

Dear Miriam,

It's your old friend, Father Christmas, here at Christmas Castle in the North Pole. Merry Christmas! Did you like the baby I brought you last year? I'm typing this letter on my magic Nice List typewriter. I am having tea with the Winter Woodsman. I had to turn down the fireplace in the sitting room at Christmas Castle because he was getting too warm, because he is covered from neck to toe in golden-brown fur. The cookie crumbs get stuck in his mangy beard, poor fellow. Oh, ho-ho-ho! Mrs. Claus will have to bake him a new axe handle, for he has gotten hungry and eaten his old one(it's made of gingerbread, you see). He'll go out to cut wood to make our manger scene, because Jesus is why we all are here at Christmas Castle. Later Mrs. Claus and I will go ice skating with Frostina, queen of the snow fairies. She has sparkling silver hair and wears a ball gown of pale blue snow-worm silk. She says if you remember to thank God for the great gift of Jesus, she may send you a magic poem next year. Mrs. Claus and the elves send their love.

Jesus is born!

Father Christmas, Esq. AKA Santa Claus

Another Letter from Father Christmas

Posted on <u>December 6, 2011</u> by <u>sworddreamer</u>

Here is the second letter to Miriam from Father Christmas. The world of Christmas Castle is expanded a little.

Enjoy!

Dear Miriam,

Ho-Ho-Ho! It's your old friend, Father Christmas, here at Christmas Castle! Yesterday, I took the sleigh across Blue Crystal Lake to Queen Frostina's Castle. She gave me the poem she wrote for you as a reward for remembering that Jesus is the reason for Christmas:

> He came from far beyond the stars
>
> From past Jupiter and past Mars
>
> He is with you, he'll not depart,
>
> For He lives inside your heart.

The poem, as you may have guessed, is about Jesus.

Frostina and her ladies in waiting danced a ballet for Mrs. Claus and me, with lots of pretty pirouettes and arabesques. In the middle of it, however, the Winter Woodsman and his best chum, Braydob the white snow satyr, got carried away with their game of snowball hockey, and burst through the door, sending the snowball whizzing through the throne room and into the fireplace. Needless to say, it put out the fire. Frostina was quite flustered. The Winter Woodsman howled his apologies and Braydob put his curly–q horns in his hands and snorted for shame. But I suspect they'll all forget this mess by Christmas Day!

Ho-Ho-Ho!

Christ is King!

Merry Christmas!

Father Christmas, AKA Santa Claus

Christmas Haiku

Posted on <u>December 23, 2011</u> by <u>sworddreamer</u>

Hello! Sorry I haven't blogged in a while, but I must say, this year has been the year of the book, insofar as reading goes. Currently I'm working on *Heaven's Net Is Wide,* the prequel to the Tales of the Otori series by Lian Hearn, an interweaving of Japanese mythology and history. I'm interested in feudal Japan, particularly the era of the Jesuits from 1554-1614, when there were Christian samurai. In keeping with the spirit of the season, I have written a sort of "haiku" about the birth of Christ from the perspective of a converted samurai. Enjoy Merry Christmas! Domo!

The Angels Above, The Onis Beneath.

Sing a song with the retainers of God,

Heaven's net is narrow,

Sing for the babe Iesu

The message of whom the Orange Robes brought us.

Heaven's ladder coming down

Warriors of Heaven descending

Born of an earth girl, who has known no man,

The foul keepers of the old ways said that Izinami

Had married Izinagi,

And thus the gods were born

But it is not true.

Iesu is the only Godling

Lift your swords to defend his Name

Victory over the onis below

Ride with the angels above

Iesu saburu! Hai!

Quotes From the Book

Posted on January 1, 2012 by sworddreamer

Hi all! Happy New Year! I thought I'd start off the new year with a look back at things I've learned from my characters. In my opinion, to a well-connected author, his characters are his friends. He hurts when they hurt. Interesting side note: William Goldman burst into tears while writing Westley's death scene in *The Princess Bride*. I myself got a little misty-eyed while writing Balladin's speech at the end of *Light*

Bringer. So I thought I'd kick the year off with thought-provoking quotes from my characters. These aren't actual quotes from the books, just quotes I invented and can imagine them saying. Enjoy!

The true worth of a blade is not in the quality of its forging but in the quality of its wielder's soul. -Almiras the Warrior

One who gazes at the stars should seek instead to gazes at the blackness of his own soul or seek the face of the One who set the stars upon their heavenly courses. -Surgessar

The measure of a leader of a nation is not avoiding going to war but in never giving his enemies cause to attack. -King Rothgaric

Let it be said of us that we were not merely creatures of habit but peoples who influenced both people and creatures toward good habits. -M. Gramarien

A paladin without faith is like a hilt with no blade. –Balladin of Silvardrassil

Prince Kenny: Show me the tome that is the most powerful of all.
Prof. Gramarien: Here it is. *The Tome of Holy Wisdom.* All my powers and wisdom are meaningless without it. Listen well to its Song. Hide it in your heart. Then you shall truly be empowered.

The greatest battle is fought not on the battlefield but in the heart of the warrior. -Almiras the Warrior

Blood of Wolf, Blood of God

Posted on January 14, 2012 by sworddreamer

The other day I wrote a horror story that was sort of a mashup between Edgar Allen Poe's Gothic Horror, Frank Peretti's spiritual warfare books and Stephenie Meyer's Twilight Saga. There is nothing that condones the dark powers in this story. Enjoy!

Blood of Wolf, Blood of God

Brenda Wulf woke up in a sweat in her hotel room in rural Saxony. She was staying in the village of Schwarzburg, about fifty miles from Dresden. She had thought that the big dog that had bitten her on her hiking trip the previous day had not been rabid. Dr. Kruger, the village doctor, had even given her an anti-rabies inoculation as a precaution. But that had not stopped the dreams. The dreams. They chilled her blood, and yet awoke in her subconscious mind a barbaric, insatiable desire for it. Her dreams that night had been as red as blood. In them, it was as if she wore night vision goggles that could read the heat signature of animals and humans. She could see the iron-rich liquid coursing through their veins like currents of electricity from an electrical outlet, and seeing it gave her a renewed, almost inhuman energy that screamed through her mind a dark, indecipherable code, as the canting of a demonic mass. Then, the words came to her for the first time. *Das blut. What? German? She barely spoke it. Why in the world was she thinking in that language? It meant something like "the blood". Blood. Blood. Das blut. Adrenaline coursed through her brain and down into her arms causing them to bulge. She compulsively licked her top teeth, which were becoming more and more jagged. She was overpowered with an insatiable thirst for blood. Das blut. She must taste blood, or else die in mortal agony.* Hair began to sprout on her arms in the back of her neck. Those two devil words hammered themselves into her skull with a vengeance. *DAS BLUT.*

Completely slave to the thirst for blood, she tore out of the window of her hotel room. She was no longer Brenda, but a demoniac she-wolf of the night. All humanity was gone, ripped away by the blood of the wolves of hell. She bounded through the forest, paws tearing the earth, now able to physically see the scents of blood wafting through the air. But then she saw something, something bright and terrible. It was a great light, burning with a Holy Fire. A beam shot out from the great light, and bore into her now darkened soul. In a loud voice it proclaimed forth words of power that caused the she-werewolf to cower in trembling fear. "En Nomine et Sanguinis Cristorurm, vete, demonio!"

A dark mist wrenched out of the tortured woman and she was once again Brenda Wulf. She saw that where the great light had been, there stood a man in the garb of a priest. "You are free, daughter. The blood of our Lord Jesus Christ, and the Power therein, has saved you from this demonic dominance. I charge you to never tell this to anyone, but I am a member of a secret ecumenical Christian organization, which specializes in exorcisms of this sort. Bear in mind that it was not I who freed you but the Lord Jesus. Some of these things which you call fairytales and myths are but shades of truth of powers both good and evil, some of heaven, some of hell. Rejoice now, daughter, for the blood of the God of heaven has saved you from the blood of the wolf of hell." For the first time in her life, Brenda Wulf bowed her head to pray.

A Fairy Tale for Mama

Posted on January 20, 2012 by sworddreamer

February marks the the ten-year anniversary of my mom discovering her osteo sarcoma bone cancer in her femur. It was a long hard road, but the Lord walked the road with us. Even after her amputation, I knew that God would one day give her a new leg, a real one. On that day I'll stand up out of this wheelchair for the last time. Being a lover and creator of fairy tales, I wrote a fairy tale poem about her experiences and the blessed hope we share together. It's sort of like a Brother's Grimm fairytale. Enjoy!

The Old Queen and the Great Wizard

There was a wise and noble queen

Very old but fair to see

She wore a crown of rhyme and meter

There was no one fairer, sweeter

Then darkness befell her kingdom

Then a small manling did come

And with a rusty woodsman's blade

The little man cut off her leg

Said she, "Take it for your food.

For the Great Wizard is good,

Though I have a leg of wood."

She dwelt for years with kith and kin

But never did walk straight again

One night she lay in the sleep dome

And the great wizard took her home.

In the wizard's castle white,

She dwelled forever in delight

He conjured for her a leg good

So up straight she finally stood.

Wisdom of the Highborn

Posted on February 1, 2012 by sworddreamer

I was listening to Tolkien related songs the other day, and the thought came to me that, as the wisdm of the men of Tolkien's Middle Earth is nothing compared to the wisdom of his elves, so too our wisdom is foolishness compared to God's everlasting wisdom. I wrote this poem on the subject. Enjoy!

Wisdom of the Highborn

Am I but an outcast of Kells,

Wand'ring the realms of earthen hells?

Can we, but scions of the middle realm

Climb the ladder to see your helm?

Can all the wisdom of elves and men

Pierce your truth like dragon skin?

For all the wisdom we possess

Is worth not even one caress

When compared to Truth that we

Shall someday soon receive from Thee,

When we come to dwell heavenly.

Fairy Tales Poem

Posted on <u>February 1, 2012</u> by <u>sworddreamer</u>

Fairy Tales

We've always heard those charming tales

Of fairy kings and nightingales.

Of tiny ships with milk-white sails,

Blown to sea by gentle gales.

And yet, we sit and ask ourselves:

What's this to do with Something else?

The basic message to receive

Is simply this: Just to believe.

The Glory of Love

Posted on February 14, 2012 by sworddreamer

Everyone wants a prince, a pure knight in shining armor…

But, let's face it, ladies. There is only one Man, Lover and Prince REALLY like that. His name is Jesus. He will never let you down. I'm going to be transparent. I just turned 23, have only been on one date, and have never actually kissed a girl. (audience gasps!) But even though this wheelchair has its ups and downs, I am constantly romanced and captivated by the great Lover of Souls. Happy Valentines Day!

PS To read my novel *Lady of Naofatir,* a portayal of Christ as the grreatest lover of souls visit my my website at http://www.marshalmyers.com

Brothers in Arms

Posted on February 23, 2012 by sworddreamer

Several weeks ago, a good friend of mine who I introduced to Dragon Naturally Speaking software for writing wrote me a poem about how my writing and testimonial about Dragon inspired him to become a writer as well. This got me thinking about how my caregivers, friends, and I, as long as they are followers of Christ, are brothers in arms epic warriors and knights of righteousness, on the battlefield of the spiritual plane, though we don't fight like paladins in World of Warcraft or other such games. Our campaigns are much grander than that. As Tron said (paraphrased) in Tron: Legacy, I will always fight alongside you. My Brothers in Arms, I SALUTE YOU!

The Song of Creation

Posted on March 7, 2012 by sworddreamer

I wanted to share something that I learned from the writings of Madeleine L'Engle, J.R.R. Tolkien and C.S. Lewis. I truly believe that all of creation, in its original intent is a Glorious Song, a Divine Symphony for the glory of God. I've written somewhat of an epic parable about it. Hopefully it will bless you.

It has been many years since the Great Song began, when the Father of All first sang forth the Mighty Symphony. And throughout all the eons that have followed, never was heard so great a Song, or so beautiful a Singer. His Voice brought Light into the Void and dispelled the power of the Dark One. And though the Dark One has long sought to forge his own music and pervert the Great Music begun by the Father of All, this he can never do, for the Great Music brings Creation and all things holy and beautiful, and though, through the wiles of the dark one, the Lesser Ones, into whom the King has breathed Life and spirit have long been beguiled and unknowingly aided Darkness, still, through the sacrifice of the one true Avatar, we may again learn to lift our voices to sing our part in the Great Song of Creation

RPG Rap

Posted on March 12, 2012 by sworddreamer

Even though I don't listen to much rap, it is a type of poetry and I enjoy watching videos of internet comedians singing all diffirent styles of music. Being the fantasy fan I am, I decided to write a rap, an homage to the classic tropes of the fantasy rpg genre. I'm not trying to make any moral or social statements. This is simply for enjoyment. Hope you enjoy as well!

RPG Rap

I just ran a raid down in the Sunwell

And my neighbor she thinks I summon demons from hell

But I'm too busy slaying dragons and such

I've got so much gold, my guild guys never go Dutch.

On my real nose, you can see a big zit

But my crystalline axe does 80 damage per hit

I'm a Christian kid, Never been to seminary

But I got a benediction from the Scarlet Monastery

I'm really nice to you if you're a noob,

You can watch my walkthroughs posted onto Youtube

As you've probably guessed, I've got no girlfriend.

But I can turn into an eagle and then sail on the wind.

'Til another song on another day

And oh, I never sell no items on ebay

'Cause if I did my account would be gone

And I wouldn't be here a-singin' this song

St. Patrick's Day

Posted on March 16, 2012 by sworddreamer

I bind unto myself today the strong name of the trinity
By invocation of the same, the three in one and one in three
I bind unto myself also, by power of faith, Christ's incarnation,
His baptism in the Jordan River, his death on cross for my salvation.
St. Patrick's Breastplate
Tomorrow is not about leprechanus or wearing green, it's about a man who felt obliged to answer the call of the Holy Spirit.

I have written a similar hymn or "Lorica" that I hope you enjoy.

Lorica

I arise today.
Give me clean hands
That I might accomplish the work
You have prepared for me.
Give me clean lips
That I might speak Your praises
Give me renewed eyes that I might
Look upon Your beauty.
Give me a renewed mind that I might
Meditate upon Your precepts.
I arise today.

To read about my Irish romance novel, in which the story of St. Paddy is mentioned, go to http://www.marshalmyers.com

Gladness on the Tree

Posted on April 3, 2012 by sworddreamer

Thank you for the inspiration G.K. Chesterton. A poem for Easter and Resurrection. He paid my debt.

Gladness on the Tree

The sky was darkened and the stars did not show dim,
And upon a cross there hung a figure trim.
In His eyes the pain could see.
But, as He hung on the Suffering Tree,
He thought of you and of me,
He thought of all 'twould come to Him.

Song of Eirik

Posted on April 9, 2012 by sworddreamer

Over the weekend I wrote a poem that was, in a way, my own rephrasing of the Song of Solomon. It is set in the world of my third novel, *Light Bringer,* and shows the love of Eirik, the newly-baptized king of the Giants, for his queen, Astrid. "Svara" is a pagan priestess, a "Berserk" is a warrior with the mind of a bear, a seax is a dagger and Vulfenman is the Giants' or "Juntings'" word for the bryttevulf humanoid wolfmen. To read more about *Light Bringer* visit my website http://www.marshalmyers.com Enjoy!

Song of Eirik

King (Kyning) Eirik's Song for Queen Astrid, which he sang at their second wedding after his conversion

She is my song, my poem, my endless kenning.

My life's love, my honor-binding.

In the gold of her hair there is no dross,

Her eyes like orbs, bucklers bathed in sea-foam

Though sword and spear may pierce me,

And Vulfenman's fang scratch my flesh

There is nothing that soothes and assuages my wounds

Like her kiss and caress.

There is a bond no Svara can break

That which no Berserk can unmake

By tooth, paw or axe.

Upon my hearth where the fire burns red

Does she light the fire of my heart

And I gather her head against my chest

To feel the beating that only she can know.

Though she bears my sons and heirs in pain

And carries them next to her heart in grief and pain.

Neither the passage of grey-wanderer time

Nor the scars wrought by sword and Seax

Can scrape away one mark, of the great beauty

The Radiant King enthroned in silver halls,

The Father of All,

Has lavishly bestowed

Like the riches of a Dragon hoard

Like a ring-giver king's hoard

Upon my Golden lover

All the ballads of the Highland men of the South

Cannot praise enough the beauty of

My jewel of the mountains

My flower of the valleys and dells

To which no battle glory, no gleaming sword

No fine mail or beautiful trinket will ever compare.

I shall ever love my Golden Junting maid

Through whom the line of my house is and ever shall be
reckoned

To whom I bind my life's-soul.

We Are The Seven

Posted on April 20, 2012 by sworddreamer

For a long time, I have been interested in angels and the interaction between heaven and earth. I wrote this to experiment with and experience the mind of an angel, as impossible as that is in reality. I see the junctions between Gods world and our world as the times when the miraculos occors. I have wanted to be an angel before, but I would want to serve God willingly rather than being forced to do so. But I digress. I am human and do not understand much of heavenly matters. Enjoy!

We Are The Seven

"It is nearly time," Avrael said to Lamathrath leaning in close, this time not making use of telepathy. "The paths of the universes shall soon collide, though mayhap not soon in the reckoning of the children of Terram. Indeed, if it were soon by their counting we would no longer need the Items the Master has entrusted to us."

"Right you are, my friend," Lamathrath replied. "There are some who eagerly await the remaking of Terram. Though, as far as we are concerned, we, who are barred from the choice of the Destroyer would not hesitate to destroy this world and all worlds with it, if the master ordered us to do so."

"I am given the knowledge of many things," said Avrael, in the steadfast and commanding tone of his race. "And yet, with all my knowledge, I lack understanding of one thing. "Why, if the young children of Terram think so often of a base version of our origin, why they would not worship of their own free will the Heir of the Master, who alone reveals the truth of this place. The children of Terram are very adept at all matters cerebral, but the matter of the heart is another tale."

"And yet even this great tale will come to an end," mused Lamathrath telepathically. "And we shall play a part in its ending. For, along with our five brothers, we are the Seven, entrusted with the seven seals, the judgment of heaven. Let us pray that everyone will come to the Light of the Lord, the God of the universes, so that they will not have to face his wrath poured out through us. Indeed, if I had a will as the humans have, I would like to know the message that I have spoken so often by the will of the Master, that it is his undying boundless love that should draw them in, and in this drawing his wrath, though it will come, has no place. For the greatest thing that remains at the end of all worlds is love, and only the humans may know it in full. Such is the way of things." The Angels ceased their nonverbal musings and once again sang forth the praises of their God.

Who put the lobster in the lobster tail pot helmet?

Posted on <u>May 14, 2012</u> by <u>sworddreamer</u>

For England and for Cromwell

I was in the UK for the past 2 to 3 weeks and while there I experienced more history than I have my entire life. One of my favorite excursions while in the UK was going to Conwy (pronounced Conway) Castle in Wales, one of the best-preserved Plantagenet castles in Wales with the most well-preserved medieval walls in Britain. The castle was built around 1283 by Edward I after he had defeated and killed Llewellyn the Last, the last independent King of Wales. Many of the castles in Wales, to which English common folk migrated were built to keep the Welsh from uprising. Even more pleasing to me than getting to see a real life Castle and touch its walls was that it had a sword and armor shop called the Knight Shop, part of a small chain of weapon shops in the UK. You can visit their website at http://www.theknightshop.com I loved perusing the weapons and armor and decided to buy a Capeline, more commonly known as a lobster tail pot helmet, probably named so because of the metal plates that slope down protecting the back of the neck. The capeline saw in the early to mid-17th-century. In England it was particularly years during the English Civil War, by the parliamentary Puritan roundheads. The cavalry units often wore it along with ordinary clothes, a breastplate, (which was still handy for protecting the torso against early musket balls , leather gauntlets and a cavalry rapier. The lobster tail pot helmet also saw widely use in Poland, by the still heavily armored hussar cavalry, who would make their mark on European history in 1683 when, led by King Jan Sobieski, they rescued Vienna from the Ottoman Turks. What also interests me about the lobster pot is that it was the later of two main styles of helmets to be used by the Europeans in colonial America, the former being the morion of Conquistador fame. The armed guards wore them during the Salem witch trials of 1692. But leaving its darker history behind, I feel that wearing it I have the faith of an early Puritan praising my God from whom all blessings flow. And though I was not born to fight in the Glorious Revolution of 1688, I fight with my brothers and sisters in Christ in the glorious revolution of love.

Prince Charming and King David: Striking Parallels

Posted on May 23, 2012 by sworddreamer

I was thinking about ABC'S **Once Upon a Time** last weekend and I found these similarites with the story of David in scripture.

1. Prince James's name means "usurper" and his doppleganger's name is David. David usurped the throne from the unrighteous Saul much as James usurped the throne from George.

2. David and James were shepherds who became warriors and kings. Their reigns were times of prosperity that ended relatively not long after their deaths.

3. Saul arranged for David to marry Michal, and George arranged for James (who had saved his kingdom, like the historical David saved Saul's) to marry Midas' daughter.

4. Neither Michal nor Catherine were able to have children because of their husbands' righteous hearts

5. Saul used magic against David by consulting the witch of Endor. George and Regina, whether directly or indirectly, use magic against Snow White and Charming.

I find that, speaking in archetype and referencing Revelation 20 and 21, both Prince Charming (Jesus) and King David will return to reign over us in our Happily Ever After. Even so, come swiftly, Lord Jesus.

An English Magnate's Pocket Book

Posted on May 31, 2012 by sworddreamer

Tatton House Library

Having recently returned from the UK I've been thinking about exchange rates and other such things. When I visited

Tatton Park and the Tatton House manor, I was blown away by how, to borrow the collloquialism, loaded the Edgerton Family was. If Naofatir ever gets optioned for a movie, I want the Eldwoan Manor scenes to be filmed at Tatton House. I didn't decide on the particulars when I was writing Naofatir, but have decided that Lawrence Eldwoan made 7000 pounds a year after entering into the coal business in the late 1820s. But you know what, it didn't give Miriam true joy. Only Echu could do that, and I have to constantly remind myself that only the True Prince can give true joy. Based on inflation and exchange rate, I found the average value in 2010 of £7000 from 1830 is $720000.00. The range of values is from $464000.00 to $951000.00.   The average value in 2010 of £7000 from 1830 is $738000.00. The range of values is from $535000.00 to $1290000.00.

Money, money, money. It never will make me happy. That's why I try, oftentimes unsuccessfully, to live my life according to Proverbs 30:7. Just enough is enough for me.

To find out more about *Lady of Naofatir* go to http://www.marshalmyers.com

What did the Elfin Knight look like?

Posted on June 13, 2012 by sworddreamer

My breastplate and lobster tail pot helmet

One of my favorite songs by British traditional folk singer Kate Rusby is "The Elfin Knight." Whenever I hear a song with historical references, I like to look it up. I discovered that Rusby's modern rephrasing of this song is related in theme to the song *Scarborough Fair* and that both are about winsome lovers who set impossible tasks for the people who want to marry them. The song The Elfin Knight originates in the early 1600s and is of Scottish origin. While I was in England I purchased my lobster tail pot helmet, which sparked an interest in the 17th century and the English Civil War.

One thing that cannot be gleaned simply by watching Richard Harris in *Cromwell*, is the reason for the Scottish battles taking place shortly before the Short Parliament. King Charles Stuart, King of both England and Scotland, had been trying to impose Anglican church government on the Scottish church, which in the Anglicised Lowlands was largely Presbyterian and in the Highlands largely Catholic. The Scots being the feisty Celts I've always loved, didn't like this and between 1639 and 1640 there were two wars known as the Bishops' Wars where large amounts of English soldiers fought Scottish armies under the command of Scottish general Alexander Leslie. The Scots were eventually defeated, as usual. The governmental turmoil produced by the wars eventually led to the English Civil War. Even though typically the Scottish soldiers had inferior weapons and armor to the English, their commanders, as did the English, probably wore lobster pot tail helmets and steel breastplates and carried 17th century rapiers, somewhat similar to the armor and rapier shown in the picture. I was looking at a medieval illumination the other day of the four Horsemen of the Apocalypse. It was from the 13th-century and they had high medieval armor and weapons. Therefore, as with the stories of Arthur and *The Canterbury Tales*, it is a constant factor that when retelling stories we will imagine the knight or the hero with modern anachronisms. Therefore, I think it is safe to say that the Elfin Knight looked at that time a bit like a roundhead or cavalier. Now if you will excuse me, this elfin Knight needs to go on top of the hill to blow his horn (no pun intended).

The Song of Creation

Posted on July 3, 2012 by sworddreamer

The Song of Creation

The song of Creation fills my heart.

The Song of Creation fills my heart

I sing for the Conductor of the Art

The Song of Creation fills my Heart.

The song of Creation fills my soul

The Song of Creation fills my soul

It fills me to the brim and makes me whole

The Song of Creation fills my Soul

The Song of Creation fills my life

The Song of Creation fills my life

It burns away all the pain and strife

The Song of Creation fills my life.

The Song of Creation fills my heart.

The Song of Creation fills my heart

I sing for the Conductor of the Art

The Song of Creation fills my heart.

Sing now with all created things

Sing now with all created things

With ants that crawl the ground and birds with wings.

Sing now with all created things.

Hallelujah from my heart

Hallelujah from my heart.

Ever I shall sing how great Thou art.

Hallelujah from my heart.

The Lie After the Copyright Notice

Posted on July 6, 2012 by sworddreamer

I don't read these writers anymore, but H.P. Lovecraft said that the most interesting thing about Robert E. Howard's fiction was that Howard himself was in every one of his stories. It struck me today that I'm in each of my stories. Leofric dreamed of being a warrior, flew into a rage at his mom and dad, dealt with self-doubt, indecision and post-facto guilt, Macha experienced long bouts of depression, Miriam sought true love in vain, Rothgaric didn't want to have authority, Balladin developed a sleep-depriving and recurring obsession, Sigryn desired for the Power of God to move in her life, etc. ad infinitum. Any resemblance to actual persons is purely coincidental. No way, man!

Summer of the Super Saiyan

Posted on August 2, 2012 by sworddreamer

Camp Infinity gives out superlatives to all campers. This year, mine was the Dragonball Z-themed super saiyan award for going over 9000!!!!!! (Being the best I could be) Thanks, guys!

Hi, all. Sorry I haven't posted in a while. I just got back from a week at Camp Twin Lakes, http://www.camptwinlakes.org/ , a disability and long-term illness campground. Families of Children Under Stress partners with Twin Lakes to host Camp Infinity, a camp for disabled teens and young adults. The camp offers the normal activties any summer camp has, but these activities are tailored to meet the specific needs of the campers. These activities include swimming in an accessible pool, climbing rock wall, miniature golf, zip-lining, gym time etc. All cabins are accessible and feature wheelchair accessible toilets and showers. FOCUS, http://www.focus-ga.org/ , helps to provide volunteering professional medical staff for all health and disability concerns. I am am now 23 and have attended Camp Infinity since its creation in 2007, and looking back at these varied snapshots of my life, can see my steady yet shaky transition from adolescence to adulthood. And I owe much of my maturing to my friends at Camp Infinity. I love you guys and look forward to building more cherished memories for years to come.

Dragon Riders of Heaven

Posted on August 13, 2012 by sworddreamer

NOTE: This is a work of fiction that has been forming in my brain a long time. It should NOT be taken as truth, biblically or scientifically.

Dragon Riders of Heaven

The colors swam before my eyes, splashing and playing brilliantly colors of blue topaz brown carnelian, ruby red and many others that even the sons of Tubal-Cain would not have been able to identify. Then I saw a magnificent figure standing before me. He looked somewhat like the many giants that strode the land, though he posed a more awe-inspiring figure. His skin was as bright as burnished bronze, his hair and beard like snow fire, and his clothes radiant as lightning.

"Sir," I stammered. "How did I come to be here? Where am I?"

"Dear Yesshica," he intoned in a voice mighty as the wind of the desert. "I am Lamathrath, one of the appointed to the end of days, as well as your guardian. I was there when you came from the womb and walked with you all your life, though you could not see me, for seraphim rarely take on physical bodies as opposed to the nephilim. Daughter of Noah, daughter of Seth, you have done well. You have preached your last sermon. Look back. The sons of Tubal-Cain ambushed you, as you now cannot remember. You are in the physical body dead. But now comes the greatest adventure. You are to join the riders of heaven. You have heard and no doubt seen some of the beasts that used to dwell with your forefather Adam in the Garden of Paradise. We have every type of animal in the lands of heaven that has ever walked beard and many of the seraphim have chosen to ride on the backs of these creatures when we wore with the enemy. Oh, and by the by, do not worry about your father Noah. He shall finish the boat and take many of the baby creatures with him into it. After the flood the time of giant man and animals will soon be over. But I am forgetting myself. Come let us pick out your Steed."

He led me into a great menagerie filled with all sorts of great dragons and beasts. Stopping before the first cage, he indicated a winged Dragon with a semi-conical, semi-triangular head and a sharp beak. "The learned men of another age call this by a name that I believe begins with ptera. After the deluge they shall migrate to the islands to the West of Ararat. Your brother Japeth will have a son named Javan who will be the father of a race of philosophers and sailors who dwell independently of one another in a sea called the Aegean. Several generations from now, a great swordsman and mariner by the name of Jason shall drive them from the Javanite Lands. They shall call them harpies and furies."

He led me to another cage. Pointing to a Dragon with a great spiked back, he said this is ac stegosaurus. Your father Noah will take some of these and similar breeds with him as companion animals on his journey to the far east. Many years later, when these beasts are very rare, the Noahites of Cathay and Nippon shall see them as signs of good fortune, as opposed to the sons of Japheth in Europa and Scania, who will hunt them to become heroes."

Next he took me to a great pool were a long necked Dragon swimming in great circles stirring up the water. "This," said Lamathrath, will be called several thousand years from now a plesiosaur. Many of them will dwell in the Sarum islands, where the sons of Gomer, the Celtae, shall come to dwell."

He came to a great two legged Dragon whose breath was very hot and smelled of what the alchemists of the present age, (I was coming into my angelic knowledge) deem to be chlorine and methane gas. "The breath of the Dragon called "King T" might be able to stun or even kill a man. This shall be the most common Dragon known near the end of time. Great warriors of the Japhethites in Scania and northern Europa named Siegfried and Beowulf so again great renowned in the legends of their people for slaying them.

"These are the only dragons allowed to novice riders. Someday you may be able to ride a behemoth, or brave the seas on the back of the Leviathan. It is rather silly, but theories concerning dragons shall spring up in the last days of Earth that will cause many people to doubt our God. But our only concern right now is to ride them to war."
I selected what the Greeks called a harpy and Lamathrath gave me a sword, buckler, and bow. I made the decision none too soon. For the horn of Michael blared across the heavens and we, the Dragon riders of heaven, rode to war.

Journey back to Naofatir

This is Thomas Ananias Hunter Goldwhite, Scottish banking magnate, philanthropist and orator who recently purchased

Eldwoan Manor after the mysterious disappearance of heiress Miriam O'Connor. He plans to donate the mansion along with its extensive library to his new educational organisation, the Miriam O'Connor Memorial Mythical Society. 8 February, 1838

Lucretia Susan Jerevendre

15 Baker Street

London, England, United Kingdom of Great Britain and Ireland

My Dear Bride,

I do not write you with levity, as I did earlier this month, for the strangest thing has happened, the like of which I have never seen in my twenty-five years of practice of law. I wrote to you briefly of the oddly nostalgic adventure I experienced while escorting Ms. Miriam O'Connor to Eldwoan Manor at Berwick upon Tweed. It came as a shock of the highest degree to discover that less than two months after coming to reside at her new estate, the young Ms. O'Connor has disappeared. She had taken to reading alone for hours in the library of the manor, which given her aforementioned character and disposition does not surprise me in the least. But it just so happened one day, only several weeks ago, that Ms. McCurdy, the ridiculously jovial maid of whom I have spoken to you often, brought Ms. O'Connor's midmorning tea to find that she had vanished. After a thorough search of the library premises, the only thing that she could find of Ms. O'Connor was a torn piece of her frock and a spot of battered blood on the floor just below the loft. She even cajoled the most uncongenial Mr. Clivers into ascending the stairs to the loft to search for her beloved mistress. I have always been suspicious of that one, (Mr. Clivers, I mean to say) and he immediately sent for me, and once I arrived just three days past, he insisted that Miriam O'Connor was most certainly dead, and contrived some blasted boulderdash, (pardon the expletive) that all of the Eldwoan estate should past to him. There was a rather raucous display between Maryellen McCurdy and Clivers on this point, with many words and cognomens that would make your face redden, I have no doubt. I was in no mood to act as arbitrator over this, and immediately left the premises to have a shandy at the Blue-Eyed Crow. While I was there who should enter the establishment than the distinguished Thomas Ananias Hunter Goldwhite. This entrepreneur banking magnate is said by some to be even wealthier than the late Nathan Rothschild, and is said to be the richest man residing in Scotland. Not knowing who he was at the time, and wanting a bit of a drinking companion, I, you could either say wisely or foolishly, poured out my woes to the man and he said that he mayhap could help me.

We searched through my papers concerning Mr. Eldwoan and discovered that should no heirs have been appointed, the estate would pass to the highest bidder.

We set up an auction, of which he was in attendance, and Mr. Goldwhite proceeded to win the auction, purchasing the manor for a little in excess of £50,000. No doubt with his meager salary, Clivers could not afford that. (I believe I last saw him drinking himself into a stupor at the Blue-Eyed Crow, muttering expletives concerning Mr. Goldwhite under his breath.) I questioned Mr. Goldwhite as to whether he intended to settle down at Eldwoan Manor and he said he did not, but had been so moved by the story of Ms. O'Connor and her childlike faith that he would set up the mansion to be somewhat of a conservatory for those who loved fairytales. He has been in connection with two gentlemen with such interests by the names of Ronaldson and Stokesey, to whom he has given permission to act as executive officers of the conservatory. It shall be called the Miriam O'Connor Memorial Mythic Society. They have laid plans to have the building open to students and the public by the end of next year. I shall miss Miriam O'Connor, and regret that you shall never have the opportunity to meet her. Wherever she is, I pray that God gives her soul rest.

Yours affectionately,

Peter Digory Jerevendre

"My Lord, husband and lover," said Rhiannon, coyly running her hand through Echu's golden-green locks. "There is but one thing that vexes me on this our hundredth wedding anniversary."

"And what is that, my love?" said the King of the Tuatha, caressing her lightly.

"Macha and Balor's son Niall is of age to become a warrior. The cycle has come full circle. The next generation has grown. The Dorchadas shall soon rise again. And yet I have been unable to conceive our child."

The Golden King chuckled, and said, "Do not worry my love. I have vanquished the Dorchadas forever. It shall never arise again. There is no need for the Child of Promise." "But, my heart, will I ever leave you? Surely if I came strangely to this world, strangely I can go back."

"That shall never be so," Echu affirmed in a gentle yet solemn tone. "For you see, when Crethwyr came to this world from your world, his body had already died. This is the only way folk of your world may permanently come here. Do not be afraid my love, but in your world you are now dead. Do not think of things that were, think only of the things that are, and the things yet to be. For even if you did pass again into your world, I would still be there with you, for there I am known by a different Name." The Golden King of the Tuatha na Naofatir embraced his wife, and as they lay in their wedding bower, which they had sung for one another, they heard the undending song of the forest, and it was good.

I Choose Joy!

Posted on October 17, 2012 by sworddreamer

I'm FINALLY back with a long-overdo blog. A lot has happened since I last blogged. The Lord has worked a great change in me. Let's look back to see how it happened, my brother in law and I are very involved in biblical dream interpretation. While visiting early this summer, I had a dream that I was playing a table-top role-playing game with my best friend and I was game master. The game master controls what happens in the story line of the game. But every time I would start telling the story, something would interrupt me. My brother in law told me it meant I had the potential in the Holy Spirit to write my own destiny, but something inside me was stopping me. I later discovered it was my focusing on my capricious feelings. Slowly, I began a purge. I gave control of my finances to my dad. I stopped pining after wealth and literary success. In short, I made it my personal prayer that God would take away everything that was preventing me from enjoying everyday life. I was able to finish the novel that had taken me over 2 years to write due to imagined financial worries and misguided aspirations. I finally realized that ephemeral happiness is a feeling, but the everlasting Spiritual fruit of joy is a choice. To misquote Joshua, "As for me and my house, we will choose joy."

Writing my own Destiny

Posted on October 23, 2012 by sworddreamer

I have been doing GREAT. I have really taken up this "What we think we are we become" way of writing my own destiny. What I really want though, in a manner of speaking is for what I write to be real.

I now quote the essay a friend wrote about me to share my mantra on living my life.

Marshal Myers has taught me so much about Cerebral Palsy, he has let me work with him through his treatment and he has let me in on a glimpse of his everyday life. I asked him if he would change his life if he could and to my surprise he responded, "If I may speak freely, I believe that God will get more glory from me living my life and showing people how happy I can be despite my disability than if I were healed."

It's just hard to believe sometimes in the great adventure to come if some of the impossible ones you read about ie fighting dragons and armies of goblins will never happen, but now that I think about it if they were real, would they still seem like adventures? I'm just musing to myself now.

Epic Fantasy Psalm

Posted on November 14, 2012 by sworddreamer

Forgive me, O High King of Heaven's home,
For sowing strife among thine own
For though I possess the wisdom of Elvendom
And know hidden paths of dwarven stones,
Both underdark and overlight
Though I have feasted in the Halls of Light
With him who wields the hammer of the stars,
It is all for naught and melts with the wyrm's breath
And my wounds conjure the balor-demon of hate.
Wash me in the silver white waters of the Avalonian Lake
Free me from the hellish drake;
That I may dwell in your will for all my days.

Thomas Goldwhite

Posted on November 27, 2012 by sworddreamer

The Autobiography of Thomas Goldwhite

I was born in the now-abandoned village of Glenbreogan in the Highlands of Scotland on July 24, the Year of our Lord 1807. Though no one who knows my current status would believe me, I am of fairly poor origins. The Goldwhites had been gunsmiths since the Bishop Wars with Charles II and made guns to outfit the regiments of Alexander Leslie. Business was small but steady. My mother, Catriona, taught me to speak the Gaelic language alongside English and did her utmost, with great success, to instill in me a love of my mother tongue.

As many will remember, when I was born, the British Empire was at war with Napoleon. It came as a great surprise to my father, Angus, that an emissary from London came to visit my father one day requesting a large contract of guns to be supplied until the end of the war. However it was not until the end of the war in '15 that my father received the contract for his guns to become standard issue for the entire Scottish Regiment. I never knew that he was then worth several million pounds until one day when I was about eight years of age, he came into our house and handed me a £100 note. He promptly announced that we were moving to Edinburgh and that I would receive the life and the education that he had always wanted for me to have.

Little did he know that this would make me as wild as my Pictish ancestors. I took on the habit of engaging in prizefighting and wagering, much to his financial and spiritual chagrin (we are originally of Covenanter stock).

He would take my disheveled, bruised, and most often slightly intoxicated form into the drawing room and rail on in his thick brogue about how money was not eternal and could not always save me but that if I let go of my wild passions and lusts for wealth I would be free to write my own destiny "By the Pouer o' Criost in ye."

Och, but his admonitions fell on deaf ears. I was at this time about 21 years of age. But then two events occurred that would reshape my destiny forever. First, I met Shona MacBradislee.

She was a highland lass with a thicker brogue than even my father, a small yet beautiful woman with curly golden locks and blue eyes like the North Sea after a storm. She and I were kindred spirits with the exception of the fact that I had a lust for money and material possessions. After the proper courtship I decided I would be fairly daft if I did not propose. She had many friends who were of Methodist stock and she said that she would have to prayerfully consider it with much time "in the spirit." I kenned not then what that meant. My mother invited her to go on holiday with us back into the Highlands during the winter of 1829. Then on one horrible yet wonderful night she told me that she had accepted my proposal, but would need to walk with me alone to discuss our future so we struck on up into the Highlands alone. I still remember the conversation we had on that chilled winter night.

The moon was full so we could see each other perfectly. She was as beautiful as the Queen of Faerie, but something troubled her, as I could plainly see.

"Thomas, I love ye 'tis true but there is one thing in ye, a broad shock that I canne abide even a wee bit."
"What be that, bonnie?"

"I ken ye were born into poverty but ye've had riches long enough to know that you dunne really need them. All a man needs is to know the Lairt Jesus and to make him known. You dunne deign give your porters or servants much more than mere farthings for their efforts and ye always pass by disheveled beggars in the streets without even givin' them a kind word. You dunne give any money to the church annual always whittle down the price on everything. How will I know if you really care for me or if you care about for money and shall see me only as a toy. You must root out that evil seed of avarice from your heart, Thomas Goldwhite, else I can never love ye as my husband."

I would have replied to defend myself but just as I open my often speak there was a blinding flash of lightning a torrential highland rain began to pour down upon us. I tried to shield her as best I could but could not find the path back under my feet. She began to cough and wheeze. I was no physician but I knew the signs of pneumonia when I saw them. I found a small hillside cave, frigid but dry, and let her into it. Laying here down on the cold cavern floor I endeavored to warm her. She began to fade fast despite my efforts and I waited and prayed for daybreak. In that moment I began for the first time in years to pray. I prayed and prayed that God would hear me and extend my bonnie loves life. I began to pray in Gaelic "Athair ar Neamh," I prayed. "Do not judge her for my unrighteousness. I make this solemn vow that I shall give until I can give no more not only of my wealth but of my life, my love and my honor. It is all yours. It is all yours, for I am but an ant and have nothing save what I have by your consent. Hear me, O God I pray."

There is nothing I can say save it was a miracle that my beloved Shona made it through the night. It happened that a goatherd from one of the farms nearby was walking past the Hill. I hailed him but it would seem to a bystander that I was a madman assaulting him I was so desperate. When he had recovered from the shock of seeing me, I enlisted his help in taking Shona back to the house we were renting for our holiday. As a first act of goodwill I gave the lad a cheque for £1500 which caused him to nearly faint dead away. My family send for the local physician and to my great relief Dr. Carlisle said that my beloved Shona would live. While I was still waiting for her to regain consciousness I went to my father and explained everything. You would not imagine the relief friend plainly on his face when I told him of my new mission in life. I could read in his face that he was at last proud of me.

Shortly after she recovered, Shona and I married. It only really occurred to me later that Shona is the Gaelic word for happy of joyful. When I finally let go of my desire for wealth and pomp, I had true joy.

Currently, I am the leading banking entrepreneur and investor in Scotland. However I do not say this out of pride for the Lord makes all men for a purpose, be they rich or poor. I have always given half of my income, to the church and charitable organizations. I am worth in excess of £100,000,000. However, I envy the poor man his anonymity. My children, Angus, Murron, Mairead and Donald are my true treasures. I have recently been honored with the rank of knight. But as I said before, God makes men what they are, not the Queen. I shall always be a true son of Scotland but I hope to be an even truer son of God.

Sir Thomas Goldwhite, 1842

A Christmas Confession

Posted on <u>December 18, 2012</u> by <u>sworddreamer</u>

I believed in Santa until I was 13. There, I said it. And I find, a decade later, that having believed in this fairy tale helped me believe in The True Fairytale, of Prince Charming Jesus coming to earth to save us, for although apologetics exists, when it all boils down to it you must believe the message of our Savior in your heart, for as He said, "Blessed are those who do not see yet believe."

Merry Christmas to all, and to all a good night!

Happy Birthday, Master of Middle Earth

Posted on <u>January 3, 2013</u> by <u>sworddreamer</u>

Today, 121 years ago, John Ronald Reuel Tolkien, the creator of the Middle Earth legendarium, was born. He began working on what would become The Silmarillion in 1917 at the age of 25, while recovering from World War I trench fever. A master in the study of linguistics, he wanted to create the most beautiful in the world, but needed a world for that language to inhabit. This is one of the reasons he labored so meticulously to create Middle Earth.

Finally, as actor Richard Armitage of The Hobbit film fame said, Tolkien preferred not to categorize his books as fantasy because in Tolkien, something that imitators such as myself lack in our works, is an awe-inspiring sense that yes, the reader believes that what he is reading actually happened. But I must say, as Stephen King voiced excellently in writing, we imitators are trying to bring Frodo and Sam back from the Grey Havens, because Professor Tolkien is no longer here to do it for us. Happy Birthday, Professor. Namarie!

Models of "Character"

Posted on January 24, 2013

These are my models of behavior, both real and fictional
Self-confidence: Merida NicDunbrogh and Gotz von Berlinchingen
Conviction: Huma Dragonbane, William Wallace and Thomas Marshall
Loyalty: Kaz the Minotaur, Drizzt Do'Urden
Piety and Humility: Cadderly Bonaduce
Willingness to change heart: Vander the Firbolg
Re-Evaluating motives: Drizzt Do'Urden and Thomas Marshal
Innocent love and heart: Princesses Zelda and Lily
Steadfastness: Samwise Gamgee
Selfless leadership: Aragorn Elessar
Generosity: Thomas Goldwhite and Lord Cedric of Gelden Hall
Writing my own destiny: Thomas Goldwhite, Merida and most importantly the Holy Spirit
Self-Sacrifice: Above all else, Jesus Christ

Vaering Song

Posted on February 2, 2013 by sworddreamer

Vaering Song

We were born with sword and axe in hand
For men of the North are we
We stand with men of Pallanon,

Lest the Helheim hounds break free
By elven bow or dwarvish rune
Are our great swords made
The true God sends a holy kiss
To ev'ry silvered blade
We have abandoned daemon gods
For the one God first
Like the Spirit o'er the whale's home
Our souls now uncursed
We shall serve those of King Jaer
Clad in mail and fur of bear
We shall serve him to the last
Yea, ev'ry man and thane
We shall stand with the rider's nine,
'Til comes the winter's bane.

PS Happy Groundhog Day for Americans or Candlemas for my European readers!

He Restoreth My Soul

Posted on February 12, 2013 by sworddreamer

Everyone, even if they have a passing knowledge of the Bible, have heard at least parts of Psalm 23. I have never fully understood the verse that reads "He restoreth my soul" until today. I have been struggling emotionally. Every Christian at least in America has heard preaching on the mind, will and emotions. My aunt's pastor calls them the thinker, chooser and feeler. Another thing not often articulated is that the soul and the spirit, although used interchangeably, are two distinct terms. The soul is the seat of deep emotions, and as the epic rock band Dream Theater sings, "The Spirit carries on" after death. So when the Lord restores our souls, he restores, emotional balance, and that's the promise I hold onto, even in the dark night of my soul.

The Greatest DPS

Posted on February 26, 2013 by sworddreamer

Well met, fellow roleplayers. I call your attention to one of the worst fantasy movies of the past decade. Namely, 2005"s direct to DVD Dungeons and Dragons: Wrath of the Dragon God. For the sake of the Oscars, I don't recommend watching it, but the story is that the vengeful sorcerer Damodar is trying to summon the titular dragon god to wreak vengeance on the kingdom of Izmir. The general of Izmir takes a band of adventurers to defeat Damodar. In the climax of the movie, the general's wife discovers that the only thing that can defeat the dragon god is faith. I started thinking about the movie in my Scripture reading today. I always like to think of myself as a paladin, and the paladin's greatest weapon is his faith, and not faith in a fictitious deity in an RPG. Faith in the True God. It is interesting to me how Satan is both likened to a Dragon in scripture and called the "god of this world". And so, like the fellowship from Izmir, I shall over overcome the dragon god by the blood of the Lamb and the word of my testimony. Take a moment today and read Hebrews 11 before you log onto the server or sit down with your 20-sided dice. Farewell, adventurers!

Good Times wth Weapons

Posted on March 8, 2013 by sworddreamer

It all started in Chinatown in Washington DC in midsummer of 2003. I was 14. We were passing through and happened to pass by a store called the Kung Fu Gift Shop. I happened to see a sword in the window that I believe now was a tai chi jian of some sort. I casually remarked to dad that I would like to have a sword like that. Dad took me to go pick out a sword during a break in the activities the next day. He bought a $25 sword that was light enough for me to swing. In the months and years that followed, I collected and collected and spent hours a day looking up different weapons and armor. At first I scooped up every sword or cheap weapon I could find. As I learned more and more, I began to shop more wisely. Yesterday, I received my hundredth item. Dad has said my bedroom looks like a museum. In the heart of every boy is a desire to in some way take up arms and banish the forces of darkness to the pits from whence they crawled. And if my collection and gathered knowledge helps other men do that, they have accomplished their purpose. Here's to the next ten years!

Author's Reflection

Posted on March 19, 2013 by sworddreamer

As I write the destinies of my characters, I write my own as well. Writing for me is a miracle, a way for God to bring the miracle of peace to my soul. As my brother told me once told me, I can write my own destiny by the power of the Spirit, and my writing vocation is an integral part. The more I write, the more God teaches me. Like the Pevensie children in Aslan's Country, my adventures are just beginning.

I am a Time Lord

Posted on March 21, 2013 by sworddreamer

Here's one for the Dr. Who/Star Wars fans. I have been frustrated lately with how blase my life is. But then I realized that I am a time lord and a space lord. I can go anywhere in this or any universe and do anything. I have wielded every conceivable type of weapon, ridden pegasi, defeated demons, danced with fairies, kissed princesses and elf maids, conquered kingdoms, become the wealthiest man in the world, led troops in battle, slain more foes than I can count and much, much more. I can truly say when I die that I've led many full lives. Most people live only one. PARENTS: Read to your kids. Kids: Write your own destinies in your stories.

The Lbrary of Lamathrath

Posted on April 13, 2013 by sworddreamer

A few years ago, I posted an article commenting on how all human creativity is to some extent derivative (ie Terry Brooks with the *Sword of Shannara* etc.). However, there is a point when such derivations become less obvious. Side Comment:

Such is the case with the third Mithgar novel, *Dragondoom*. At these times artists, while still in a similar vein to their predecessors, develop their own specific style, niche or "voice", if you will. While my high school writing was heavily influenced to the point of direct copying by Robert E. Howard, after my graduation and medical situation, I remembered my first love, Tolkien's Middle Earth writing's. I went on writing my first three books, each of them set in a different universe, and those who have read them can detect the influence of Middle Earth and Narnia.

It took me two and a half years to complete my fourth novel, during which time I read reams of Dungeons & Dragons, Warcraft, and other such fiction. All of this culminated in the creation of my multiverse and fourth novel. Just like in the popular scifi show *Fringe,* there are an infinite, ever expanding number of universes. The Trinity is known and worshiped in all settings but by different name. (This isn't Unitarianism. It's the same logic used by CS Lewis in Narnia.) Jesus will come and sacrificially save every world at different times. At the end of all time, God will open up the pathways to all universes to his servants, the faithful in all worlds. Just like in my fourth novel the Chronicler of these other worlds existing at a nexus between them is the inter-dimensional angelic scribe Lamathrath, who observes and records the history of the worlds. His creation had a lot of influences: Dragonlance's Astinus, with his scholarliness and immortality; Fringe's Observer September with his good will and foresight; and the apostle Paul with his faithfulness and Godly spirituality. So, one could say that, all my books are in the Library of Lamathrath and he wrote them. He is the glue that connects my work. I am grateful to God for all the adventures I've had writing, but also grateful to Lamathrath. He helped me find my own voice.

A Tale for May Day

May 1, 2013

Hello, all! Some of you may have read my most recent book, *Tome of the Paladins* and journeyed with me to the land of Pallanon. Today in the spirit of May Day, I am posting a story set in Pallanon, the Alf-anon Plains specifically.

NOTE: The Alf-anon elves are a psuedo-Gaelic culture. As such, this tale contains many Gaelic and Scots terms and phrases.

Dance 'Em Tae Dee

Sit down, me child. And I'll weave ye a tale of the days of Auld Lang Syne. Now, in the early days of our clan, the clan MacBraegan, there was a mighty chieftain named Ardenn. He was as big as the great-wolves he fought, and he had fought many in his day for he was reared during the time of the Tain Cuana. No one could wield sword and axe like him. Often he would wade into the midst of the Wolf demons, twirling his huge bearded axe as if it were a little more than a willow wand. "That's rrright, ye sniveling jackal jobbies, back to Helheim with ye, for I'm a raven-haired son of clan Braegan!" And he would return to his wife, the redhaired Maire, and her loving arms. "Aye, mo chroi," chided the Queen. "I fear ye're becomin' far too battle-bodied an' battle-minded for the likes o' me. Maybe sommat will soften your heart someday."

She knew not the wisdom with which she spoke. For within a year the Queen took a child to womb. And fortunately, as is quite rare, both mother and babe were healthy. The child was a beautiful lass, whom they named Shona, which, as ye well know, means "joy". In features, heart and demeanor, she resembled her mother, with long fiery red hair captivating eyes. Yet it was her passion to follow after her father's ilk, to learn of blade craft and riding. But the one thing that pleased the Queen about her bairn was her legs, or that is to say, the way she used them. She put a new fiery spin to all the jigs and reels. Often on the days of the Elven Festival she would dance long after the moon disappeared from the sky. As she began to grow older, and blossoming into the flower of her youth, both parents knew that God had blessed them with the future clan leader, their proud heir. Until the day everything changed.

One winter's night Ardenn decided to take Shona a'riding. So he saddled her pony and his great highland horse. When they were about 12 miles agone from the rath, they were by a rocky crag, when the chieftain heard a mysterious howl. There had not been a great-wolf sighted in those lands for nearly a 12-month. Ardenn did not want to alarm his daughter. Nevertheless, he shifted one massive hand to rest on the hilt of his claymore.

A hellish snarling sound grew in the distance and the chieftain was about to spur his horse to gallop back to the rath, but then, out of the heather-shrouded shadows, loomed two devilish eyes. The Helheim canine seemed to materialize out of the midnight mist. Ardenn could fill the demon breath as hot as forge fire. The great-wolf's maw frothed a viscous yellow as the pit-spume ran trickling down its fangs. Ardenn could feel little Shona trembling, and he croon softly in the tongue the Highlands to assuage her fear. "Bring yair worst, ye cu o' hell!" the elven giant spat, brandishing his hunting spear. He knew not the irony of his challenge, for the great-wolf pounced, knocking both riders to the ground. Before the Elven chieftain could recover, he heard a sound that nearly wrenched his heart from his breast, screams of anguished pain in a voice he knew all too well. The demon dog had Shona by the leg and was thrashing her around like a rag doll.

I m-must strike the devil in the hairt, Ardenn thought, his mind ablaze with wrath and grief. He prayed a silent prayer of invocation, took careful aim and let the shaft fly. The weapon sailed through the air and the night sky was rent with another cry of pain, this one demonic and raging. The Wolf dropped the poor lassie to the ground and fell over dead. The chieftain rushed to his daughter's side and cradled her in his arms. Though the poor girl had passed out cold from shock she was still shivering, a terrible sign. If the poison from the great-wolf's fangs reached her heart, that would be the terrible end. And her leg was already scarred and mutilated beyond repair. Many tears blint Ardenn's eye as he made a torch from the heather and reached for his axe.

Shona NicBraegan lay in a dreamless sleep for three weeks after her father carried her home. The shock of the Wolf attack had nearly been too great. Her mother sat constantly by her bedside changing the dressing on the stump and dampening her feverish head with cool cloths.

"Oh, me lassie. God, *Aithar ar Neamh,* give me back my bairn. And YOU, oh enemy of God, ye canne take my daughter, she is spirit of my spirit, bone of my bone and flesh of my flesh. The Laird brought her to this life from my womb, and you willne have her." Then mysteriously she began to pray in wosen magical speech, which no one knows save the Spirit of God.

And so, God heard the prayer of Queen Maire's heart. The young elfess lived. But the proud hopes that big Ardenn had held, dreams of a strong clan chieftainess, were gone. So too it seemed were Shona's days of merrymaking in the dance. But that did not stop her, for she tried with all the rhiastrad and strength she could muster. The first time she tried to dance upon the wooden leg her father had made, she fell flat on her pudennum. Her father shook his head and said "It be but a lost cause, mo gaol, I know how much it meant to you, but you'll just end up skelpin' yerself." And yet she tried long after her father had gone to bed every night.

It was about that time that Ardenn and some other chieftains formed a massive army to go fight the foul folk near the forest of Trillven to the South. Ardenn decided to take every able-bodied warrior on the campaign, as there had been no sign of the foul folk on the plains for some time. Little did he know that Agaldrog, a general of the half trolls was circumventing the outlying villages of Clan Braegan, to strike at the heart of McBraegan lands.

One night, long after her father and the men had gone, Shona, just come into full womanhood, was sleeping on her bed of black bear fur. In her dreams she saw Braegan Proudbanner, founder of clan MacBraegan. A great knot-worked axe was in his hand, the symbol of the clan, and he was a clothed in a tartan-marked brigandine, the metal shining like fire.

"Tack this axe child. Foul folk be comin'." You are the only one what's fit tae fight."

"But I canne fight. I've only got one leg."

"Take the axe. Take it and you shall dance again. Take it, and dance 'em tae dee. God is with ye."
Young Shona bolted up in bed, full of the Spirit of God. She put on the socket of her leg, took up her crutch and ran to the armory. She removed the great axe of Braegan Proudbanner from its hallowed place on the wall of the armory, shoved it into the wooden socket, and rushed out of the fortress eager for battle and even more eager to dance. She met a full cohort of foul folk, most of them half trolls, on the plane before the rath. Many of the foul folk were stupidly astonished at the appearance of an elf girl with an axe for a leg. "Let's have some sport with you before we eatses you!" hissed one as he rushed her, war club upraised. But then she twirled in place as in a Highland dance and the gnarly head fell to the ground. At first the other trollish warriors did not know what to think (as is most often the case with their kind). Then they decided to attack en masse.

For them it was a mistake but for Shona it was craic and glory. She twirled and kicked in a graceful yet furious dance of death. The Highland bagpipes, chanters, bodhrans, and lutes were playing warrior ballads in her head and through her dance for the glory of God flowed the favor of God and high above Pallanon God was pleased. Finally though, she seemed to meet her match for Agaldrog at last waded into the fight. But through the whirring of their steel, the very voice of God seemed to drive into Agaldrog's ears, echoing the voice of Queen Maire and her declaration years ago. "You canne have my daughter!" At last with a cry of "Smishe nic clan Braegannach." (Alfanonian elvish: I am a daughter of clan Braegan!) Shona, daughter of Ardenn, whirled one last time and the ax blade clove the half-troll general's head from his shoulders. She stood there for several minutes, surveying her work but not comprehending what she had done as the Highland battle fury faded from her eyes.

Only then did she turn and see her father, the leaders of the other clans and their armies, staring at her. For a moment the huge elf chieftain could not speak and his mouth hung open in shock. But then he dismounted from his horse and ran toward her. Holding her face in his massive hands he said, choking on the words. "You are the bravest, most beautiful, most glorious elfling I or any other chieftain of the Alf-anon Plains have ever sired. Do know what you've done, girl? You saved the whole clan. Bless you, lassie!"
He turned to his fellow chieftains, and raised his daughter's hand in his. "Now hear me. This is Shona Nic Braegan, my daughter. Bone of my bone, flesh of my flesh, spirit of my spirit. If any jobbied man among thinks a young woman with one leg canne be clan chieftain, he will have to answer to me or to me daughter, Shona Bladefoot. I proclaim her as my heir. May she lead the clan well when I have come to the time to meet my God face to face. What say ye to that?" Everyone in the assembly cheered. And that is how a one-legged, fiery-tressed elf girl named Shona became the greatest hero to come from the line of clan Braegan.

Welcome to the Future

Posted on May 29, 2013 by sworddreamer

I look back on this 4+ year journey of writing and reflect on all I have learned. If you've read my last few posts, you know that God has worked a great change in me. I now no longer care how many books I sell nor how much money I make. Occasionally my publishing ventures caused strife in my family. Therefore my last book is my last book to be published. BUT, don't jump to conclusions. My adventures in writing for the Lord are far from over. I have long desired to write in and manage a shared universe, admiring, admiring franchises such as Star Wars, Warcraft and Dragonlance. With the invention of the inter dimensional angelic scribe Lamathrath (as mentioned in a previous post), comes the Library of Lamathrath Blog at http://www.lamathrath.net. The blog will have stories that anyone can read. These stories will be set in and serve to expand the five worlds depicted in my novels. The first author to join me in this exciting adventure is my long-time friend and fellow cerebral palsy overcomer Josh Cusick. Together we will not let our limitations stand in our way and make an indelible mark in the world of fantasy literature that we hope will bless and encourage many people. Huzzah!

The following is the only available critique of Myers' work, an interview conducted by academian Gage Clark.

Overcoming All Odds: Interview with Marshal Myers

It is very difficult for an aspiring author to make a name for himself or herself in this evolving world. There are many obstacles that stand in the way of success as an author, including economical distress, lack of demand, and judgement of peers. These obstacles, however, pale in comparison to those faced by Marshal Myers. Marshal, the author of multiple fantasy novels, with titles including Sword Dreamer and Tome of the Paladins, was born with cerebral palsy. Cerebral palsy is a movement disorder that affects posture, muscle tone, and mobility. Marshal has taken his disorder with stride, never letting it get in the way of what he wants to accomplish. In our interview, his disorder was of course discussed, but it was not the focal point of my questions. I wanted to learn how Marshal was able to become successful as an author and a person, not simply as a man suffering from cerebral palsy. Guided and supported by his caring family, Marshal achieved with great success his dreams of becoming a published author with a literary style and imagination reminiscent of C.S. Lewis and J.R.R. Tolkien. In my interview with him, Marshal explained his writing process, how he began his journey to becoming an author, and much more. It his with great pleasure that I had the opportunity to interview this great man.

My first question was the only topic regarding cerebral palsy. I asked Marshal if he drew any inspiration from his disorder when writing his books. His answer did not surprise me, as I have known Marshal for many years, and I have read his books. He explained to me that he intentionally created certain characters in his novels with attributes similar to him and his disorder. For example, in Sword Dreamer, the protagonist Leofric "is unable to achieve his dream of being a warrior, as destiny has chosen a different path for him." As a child, Marshal "longed to take karate and play superheroes with [his] friends," but his disorder prevented him from taking part. Another example is mention in Lady of Naofatir. Miriam, the protagonist, longs to find love, but circumstances have prevented her from doing so. She finds the love of God, as does Marshal. It was interesting to get an in-depth look on the characters and how they reflect the author and his surroundings. For my second question I simply asked Marshal at what age he began writing. He told me that his writing began at age thirteen, when he would jot down short stories. His writing then shifted to a more experienced aspect at age sixteen, "when [he] began writing with one finger everyday. These stories were the forerunners of what would be published later on down the road. It was not until Marshal turned eighteen that his books began to take on a discernible form . At this point in his life, he acquired speech software for his computer that was able to put down the full force of his imagination into a novel.

I next asked Marshal if he could ask a question to his source of inspiration, J.R.R. Tolkien, what it would be. His answer surprised me. He would want to ask Tolkien "what the best way would be to incorporate fantasy aspects such as magic and mythology into writing so as not to offend anyone." There are certain religious groups that take offense to fantasy novels, calling them things like witchcraft. Marshal writes for a Christian audience, and he would want to know the best way to incorporate the fantastical elements that Tolkien writes with and use them without offending his primary audience.

The following question was standard. I asked Marshal what the most difficult part of getting a book published. He told me that the hardest part for him was the "economic downfall that was making it almost impossible to find a publisher." Luckily, Marshal is friends with a man who became his first publisher, and who put him on the road to self-publishing. It is nearly impossible for a self-published author to gain any credibility for his or her works, but Marshal has proven that even self-publishers can make a difference in the writing community. I then asked Marshal a difficult question that related to the previous question. I wondered if he believes that he has accomplished all that he has wanted to. His response was simple: "Absolutely." According to Marshal, the hardest part about actually writing a book his "finding your own voice." He says that anyone can write something and call it a story, but it takes a true author to find his or her own personal voice with which to write. My next question was a bit more personal. I asked Marshal what was the best or most positive feedback that he had received from his novels. He told me that the best thing he heard was from a woman at his church who told him that her son would not read anything but his books, and after finishing them, the son started to read more and more often. Marshal believes that the best thing an author can achieve is to inspire people to simply read or write.

My final question to Marshal was the most informative. I asked him what it felt like to be published for the first time. He told me that it was hard to explain his feelings at the time of his first published work, which was an article in his high school literary magazine. He told me that being published was not his main goal of his writing, but he was extremely pleased when it happened. He wanted to write them at first for himself, as a way to express his imagination in a more conceivable way. Marshal feels that being published is "one of [his] greatest accomplishments."

My interview with Marshal Myers was a highly informative and enjoyable experience. It was truly a pleasurable experience to get to know the reasoning and inspiration behind all of his stories. I have known Marshal for many years, and this was the first time I was able to truly appreciate the hard work and dedication it takes for him to write and publish his works. It is my hope that everyone would take the time to read his stories. I believe that Marshal is one of the most talented fantasy authors of his generation, and I cannot wait to read his next novel.

Also by Marshal Myers

visit www.marshalmyers.com

Sword Dreamer

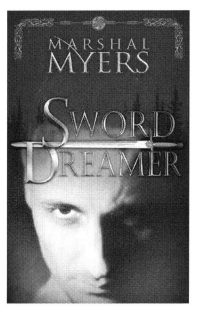

Young Léofric is troubled with strange visions of battle he does not understand. But when two warriors – an elf and a man – arrive to lead him away to war, Léofric learns that he is the Sword Dreamer, the legendary seer whose visions of pending battles are vital for brining an end to the civil war that rages Irminsul.

Now he must train for his role, use his visions to aid the Kind's Army, and defeat the vengeful and power-hungry Gollmorn and his evil army. But can Léofric's burgeioning skills help stop the war and defeat Gollmorn, or will the towering Silver City of Auraheim fall under the shadow of a madman's tyranny? More importantly, will Léofric finally learn who he is and find his place with the True King, the almighty King That Is?

Lady of Naofatir

Miriam O'Connor is a young Victorian Irish school teacher with an avaricious love for reading and mythology. She is overjoyed when she inherits a mansion in northern England filled with a treasure trove of mythological texts. What she truly desires, however, is to find a man like those in the old stories, who will love her truly and defend her honor.

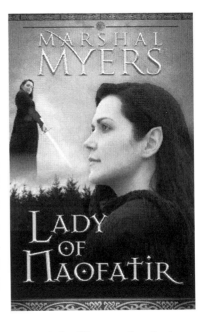

One day while reading in the attic of the library, she finds an old book filled with cryptic writing. When she opens it, it whisks her off to the beautiful golden green country of Naofatir, where the fairylike inhabitants are caught in a battle against their terrible Enemy, the Dorchadas. There, she meets the great prince of Naofatir, and comes to discover how she can play a part in helping him save the beautiful land from destruction.

Light Bringer

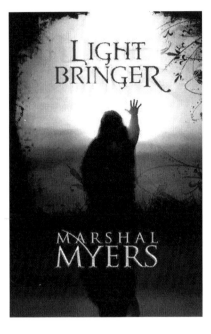

For centuries, the city of Silvardrassil has been cut off from the rest of the world and thrust into a state of eternal, starless night because of the folly of Fehar, who opened a connection between the city and the realm of the Shadow King.

The Legion of Silvardrassil has fought the forces of the Enemy with the magical aid of the Light Bringers, a holy order of mage-priests whom the Radiant King has endowed with the power to bend the elements. The people of the city are slowly dying, but prophecy foretells that the last and greatest Light Bringer is coming.

Paladins

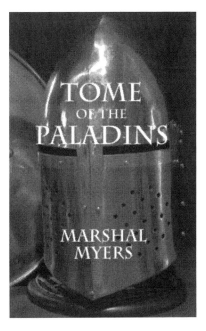

Embark with three different bands of heroes on three different quests, discover how the Creator of all things is worshipped in every world he has created, whether by elves dwarves or men. Witness how these ordinary men become bastions of light and champions of all things pure. Discover in this tome what it means to be a paragon of virtue; what it means to be a Paladin.

24524679R00167

Made in the USA
Columbia, SC
24 August 2018